TAKEN

SINNERS OF BOSTON #2

VANESSA WALTZ

VANESSA WALTZ

ABOUT THE BOOK

I stole my trophy wife

Her father killed my brother, so I took Carmela hostage.

I didn't know how to execute my revenge, but when the innocent little honey attempts to bargain for her father's life, I devise the perfect plan.

I won't just take my revenge.

I'll savor it.

She's desperate to save her father.

Her offer: One night. No strings.

My counter-offer: The rest of my life, no strings, but plenty of rope.

I need a mother for my two kids. A wife to warm my bed. A lover to break.

That's Carmela.

I thought my only battle would be between us...in the bedroom....but marrying her incited a war I never saw coming.

If I don't win...I lose everything.

I lose her.

Author's note: Taken is a single dad, standalone dark mafia romance. This is book #2 of Sinners of Boston series. However, these books can be read in any order.

This Beauty and the Beast-inspired dark and titillating romance is not for the faint of heart, but if you like over-the-top alpha heroes, troubled heroines, and impossibly evil villains, you'll love this book. Deals with sensitive subjects some might find triggering

ONE
CARMELA

I MIGHT BE dead in a few hours.

I'd committed no crime in the eyes of the law, but in the menacing gaze of Michael Costa, I'd done the unforgivable. I crashed his daughter's birthday party.

One didn't enter the home of a notorious gangster without an invitation, especially if you were among his enemies, but the doorman neglected to check my name as I arrived, wearing couture and a big smile. After a quick search of my clutch, he waved me forward.

The gift shifted in my hands, curly ribbon sprawling across the unicorn wrapping. I'd gotten the girl an Easy-Bake Oven. Growing up, it was my favorite toy. Hopefully, the seven-year-old had an interest in cooking. Poor kid desperately needed fun after what had happened to her mother.

The wrought-iron gate of the Tudor-style manor, which hung over the street like a gargoyle, swung open easily as I pushed it with a finger. Two front-facing gables overlooking leaded windows glared at the road. A dense English garden surrounded the inner courtyard, where a few people mingled, clutching their Cristal. Plants wove across each other in waves of lavender cosmos and pink foxgloves. Unkempt rose bushes snarled the fence. A meandering stone path led to a fountain with a granite table and bench. It was charming and beautiful —much like its owner.

Dappled sunlight broke over my head as I strolled under a Japanese maple and headed to the foyer. My nerves jangled every alarm bell as I crossed the threshold, as if I were signing my death warrant.

How the hell would I walk out?

Dad was counting on me. I'd worry about that later.

I wandered into the mansion. Talk and laughter filled the dreary space with the illusion of warmth. Most of the attendees were face-saving assholes—Costa soldiers and their wives, sucking at the power teat. I drifted among a coterie of rosé drinkers under the beamed ceiling. The chandelier glowed soft and effervescent, casting everyone in a dreamlike hue. Gold was the theme of this party.

Shining plates and forks adorned every surface of Michael's home, which seemed to protest all the glitz. Some homes oozed comfort from the color or the arrangement of the furniture, but this was cold and masculine. Steel, cool brown, and dark blues dominated the décor. Everything from Restoration Hardware furnished the rooms—so not my style. I couldn't imagine living in such an intimidating place.

Where was Michael?

He wasn't smoking with the men outside. I didn't spot him in the kitchen, where his mother coaxed guests with appetizers. I lingered by the bathrooms, but he never came out. I lacked the bravery to climb the stairs. That could get me into even more trouble.

My fingers dug into the wrapping paper as I pushed my present onto a console table. I slipped the envelope with the card over the box, hoping her father believed the well wishes for his daughter. I headed in the direction of the corridor leading to other areas, colliding with a ball of energy.

A boy tumbled backward.

"Oops!" I caught his arm and righted him. "Are you okay?"

A navy vest covered his tiny chest, and he wore matching slacks over black tennis shoes. The small child tottered forward, his round eyes locked on mine. A wide grin split his cherub face, which was a dead ringer to the man for whom I searched.

Good Lord, I'd almost bowled over Michael's son.

"Matteo, you've gotten big." I kneeled as he smoothed his messy curls. "Look at your outfit. You're so handsome."

"Pick me up, Carmela!"

My heart melted. "You remember my name."

"Pick me up."

I shouldn't have, but I couldn't resist the little fingers beckoning me. I hiked him onto my hip.

"Better?"

Matteo nodded, beaming. "I like your hair. It's pretty."

"Thank you."

He lifted a thick strand, balling it in his chubby fist. Then he whipped me like a horse. He broke into hysterical giggles when I jogged in a circle. His happiness made me smile.

How could something so pure and innocent come from Michael?

I needed to find him.

I adjusted my hold on Matteo as I scanned the guests, searching for the man of the house. "Where's your daddy?"

"*Here.*"

His voice was smoke rolling over whiskey. A man's hand palmed my naked back and slid upward, anchoring on my shoulder. He squeezed, his grip punishing. Then his body pressed into me.

Shit.

My gaze tore from the bubbly four-year-old to a man with a lean build, wearing a midnight suit over a fitted white T-shirt. Michael was a demi-god sculpted by loving hands, starting from his long lashes to his full lips and dimpled chin. Warm brown waves cropped short at his neck framed a rakishly handsome face. The Michael I'd known was rarely without a smirk—but the one who stood next to me now pulsed with hostile energy.

Probably because I held his child.

"Matteo, *gentle.*" Michael's fingers clasped over his son's, which still grasped my hair. "Be nice. Don't pull."

"But I like it!"

"I know you do, pal." Amusement and fierce pride rumbled through his words. "You do this to every pretty girl who walks in here. You are utterly shameless. So much like your old man."

Michael's touch vanished, and then he brushed my stomach as he shifted Matteo from my arms. As he did so, he beamed with a warmth that seemed to rearrange air molecules.

He kissed his son. "Stop chasing girls and go play."

"Will you play with me?"

"Yes, honey. Later. I love you."

"I love me, too!"

Laughing, Michael handed him to a nanny. "Keep him busy."

Pain stabbed my gut as I drank in Michael's tenderness for his son and the love between them. A sickening wave of jealousy slammed into me. It was the wrong time and place, but the reminder that I lacked that missing piece sucked all the joy from my heart. A sallow-faced woman took Matteo as he waved to his father.

Once Matteo disappeared, Michael's radiance dulled to a depressing black.

"Carmela. We should catch up somewhere private."

"Sure."

His tone was light, but the grip circling my wrist was vise-like. He dragged me from the party and guided me toward a door. When it opened, I hesitated. A darkened bedroom waited.

The gentle push became a shove.

I stumbled forward. A chill rode my spine at the click of the lock sliding.

Michael grabbed me before I turned, his hand snaking into my hair while the other yanked me against his chest. The sting reminded me who this man was—a ruthless gangster.

"What the *fuck* are you doing here? How did you get in?"

Fighting him would've made things worse, so I allowed him to bare my throat. Michael's hooded eyes blazed with emotion. He seemed deeply unnerved.

"I brought a gift and walked in."

"You're at my house, *uninvited*, holding my kid. What were you planning to do? Walk out with him?"

His suspicion wrenched my insides.

"Of course not. I'm not here to hurt anyone."

"*Bullshit.*"

"I'm just here to talk."

"Not in the mood for a chat, Carmela. Especially with you."

"What did *I* do?"

"You're related to your father. That's enough." Michael relaxed, transferring his grasp to my neck as he pushed me against the wall. "What were you doing with my son?"

I swallowed hard, ignoring the jolt his touch gave me. "I was looking for you, and he asked me to pick him up, so I did. That's all. I swear."

"What was your plan?"

This was blowing up in my face.

"Michael, you weren't answering my calls. Then I remembered this party. I figured it was worth a shot."

"You thought you'd ambush me at my daughter's birthday?"

"*Yes.*"

His expression full of deep mistrust, Michael seized my purse and rifled through its contents, only finding my wallet and keys. I didn't even bring a phone. I'd wanted zero opportunities to call for help.

"You were crazy to come here."

"I don't have anything to lose."

"That's what *you* think." He zipped the clutch and tapped my shoulder, menace radiating from his body.

"Michael, what happened to us?"

Michael tossed my bag onto the bed and dropped the aggression, his smile tugging into that playful slant I recognized. "Don't sound so wounded, Carmela. I'll get the wrong idea."

"I have to fix this. Tell me what to do."

"There's nothing you can do." He glanced at my cleavage and must've been satisfied because he dragged his eyes up with a grin. "You get props for dressing the part, but it's time for your sweet ass to leave."

"*No.*"

"Go while I allow it."

I didn't budge. "No."

"May I remind you what I can do to you and your whole family?"

My stomach churned. "I'm here on behalf of them."

"You mean most of them?"

Michael's taunt lifted the hairs on my arm.

I'm too late to save my dad.

The pounding music from outside faded.

"Michael, no. Please tell me he's still alive."

"I have no clue what you're talking about."

"Oh, come on! You know why I'm here. Tell me what you want, and I'll give it to you. Money?"

"Look at this fucking place. I don't need your money."

What else did I have? "We have properties in Italy."

"No."

"I could introduce you to the mayor. I'll hand over the title of my dad's mansion. You could burn it, put it in your will, *sell it.*"

"What good is that house to me?"

"Michael, tell me what you want!"

"Watching you guess is making my night." Michael lapped up my desperation with a greedy smile.

My mouth went dry.

This was part of his mind game. He'd make me believe I had a shot, and then he'd throw me out. If all the material possessions wouldn't sway him, what did I have to trade? There had to be something I could do.

Matteo's beaming grin flashed through my head.

His kids.

"I can help you. Think about your children—how much they could use a woman in their lives. They lost their mother a year ago. It can't be easy, raising them by yourself. I'll keep the house in order."

"You want to be the *help*?"

"Michael, you have everything but me."

He raised a brow. "You sure about that?"

His knuckles grazed my neck, lingering where my pulse was the strongest. He could do whatever he wanted. Nobody would cry for help if he strangled me—or dragged me to the bed—which, under his feverish gaze, seemed far more likely.

The air between us heated into a sauna I was desperate to escape.

"Do you want me or not?"

"There isn't a man in the free world who doesn't. But your dad killed someone I love. So I'm killing him."

"Take me instead."

"Excuse me?"

"*Take me.* Do what you want with me." My stomach tensed as the scent of leather filled my nose, bringing with it painful images.

Michael made a sound at the back of his throat. A pleased rumble that paired perfectly with his teasing smirk. "Tempting, but no. Fucking you won't take the sting out of my murdered brother."

"One night. No strings."

"The rest of my life, no strings, but plenty of rope." His smile was a dark promise. "I don't need a fuck doll. No. You'll be my wife."

He took a step away as I absorbed that bombshell. The shockwave blasted through my pretense of calm because being tied to him was my worst nightmare. Lying underneath Michael as he used me was much more preferable to marrying him.

"You're joking."

"I'm not."

It was well-known that Michael loved to play with his food before he ate it. I opened my mouth to demand that he stop screwing around, but not a hint of mischief glimmered in Michael's gaze.

"I don't believe this."

"You laid it out for me. I have two kids who miss their mom. They need a strong, confident woman with a good head on her shoulders. That's you, Carmela. Aside from the poor judgment you showed by trespassing."

"You'd rather me be their replacement mom?"

"I want your soul, to own you and taste your kiss when I give you an orgasm. I'd love to rip off that dress, fuck you with your heels still strapped on, make you kneel, and teach you to submit. God, the things I'll do to you." He backed me against the wall, his expression ravenous. "I've waited for you to notice me the way I've noticed you."

Oh, I had.

Before this mess with my father, Michael Costa was a stable fixture, a happy-go-lucky devil, always ready with a playful quip. I'd watched him break down my moody brother-in-law. After my sister's baby was born, he was among the first to visit. The occasions Michael and I had bumped into each other stuck in my memory because he expressed his interest in me without a drop of shyness. Exchanges with him were heavy on innuendo. Once, he'd steadied my balance with a hand on my back, and I'd thought about how amazing it felt all week. Despite that—and the fact that my loneliness gnawed at me every night—I stayed the hell away from Michael.

I *couldn't*.

I'd expected him to demand sex for my father's life, or an exchange that'd cement my position as *hostage*—not *partner*.

"You're a status symbol, vengeance, and a trophy wife rolled into one pretty package. I want you off the market and wearing my ring."

Gangsters made terrible boyfriends and even worse husbands. Been there and all that. I couldn't jump into something permanent with another Nick, a man who broke my heart and almost shattered me.

It would destroy me. "I'll do *anything* else."

A bestial grin carved into his face. "You could allow me to kill Ignacio."

I can't believe this. "If I agree, then what?"

"We get married." He smoothed his lapels, running his fingers over the silk. "And I'll release Ignacio."

"Just like that?"

"*Just like that.* But he is cut from your life. The details can wait, but I'm not compromising. You know what your dad did. This is his *only* way out. Marry me—or he's dead."

I'd torch the world for my father. He was the only man I trusted. He'd kicked in doors of men who'd wronged me. He'd always been an unwavering force, and now he was *helpless.* Dad needed me.

Was I going to let him down?

No.

"Okay."

"I didn't catch that. What did you say?"

Dread pitted my stomach. He was toying with me, and it was just the beginning.

"I'll marry you."

TWO

MICHAEL

FAMILY WAS EVERYTHING.

I loved nothing like I did my babies, but it was an obsessive love. It brought out the worst in me. Like when I beat up a shopkeeper for slapping my daughter's hand. I left him on the sidewalk with mangled limbs and shattered pride, wailing at witnesses for help. Nobody had assisted him because, in my neighborhood, everybody knew me and what I represented.

I had one rule.

Don't fuck with my kids.

Those who threatened my son and daughter died painful deaths. They were my legacy, body, soul. Anybody who risked their safety bought a ticket to the morgue, or more likely, a grave around the Quabbin Reservoir.

Which prompted me to the front gates of my mansion to stare down the world's biggest moron. The security guard I'd hired stood at an impressive height of six-foot-four and came well-recommended by his peers. He'd served in Afghanistan and graduated from a top-tier executive protection school, and he'd allowed a stranger to enter my home.

Bryan was built like an ox, but the steroids must've deteriorated his brain. His square jaw ticked as I approached him with a photo of Carmela on my phone.

"Recognize this woman?"

He gaped at the picture I took after locking her up. "Yeah...I think. She walked in about thirty minutes ago."

"Did she give you a blowjob?"

His brows furrowed. "No."

"Were you distracted by her tits?"

His nostrils flared, and a ripple of rage went through me. He had no right to be angry, the dumbass. "I don't understand the question."

"Why the fuck did you let in someone who wasn't on the guest list?"

A spasm of panic twitched his face. "She was carrying a gift."

"Anything could've been inside."

"Mr. Costa, I'd never put your family at risk. She had nothing on her."

"You have *one* fucking job—check their names."

I wouldn't use that agency again. If he was that guileless, I had zero faith in the rest of their employees.

"I'm sorry, Mr. Costa. It'll never happen again."

"Damn straight. You're fired." I shoved him onto the sidewalk, glowering. "Get out of here before I do something I regret."

I snagged a money clip and tossed his hourly rate into the air. I watched him scramble after the cash as it scattered with the wind. He was lucky Carmela was the honey I'd lusted after for months.

I could've killed her for bulldozing my boundaries and touching my kid. The fact that she'd strolled through my security without a hitch strangled me, but I knew Carmela. I'd seen her at Christmas parties, and she'd babysat my children with her sister, Mia. She'd never hurt a child.

She was tall and fuck-hot, with long espresso-brown hair streaked with caramel highlights. Carmela was Gal Gadot with curves, a stunning woman who'd been the discussion of many drunken card games at Sunset Tavern. Her hourglass figure was a magnet for male attention, which she usually ignored. Half of Boston's underworld had a crush on the leggy Italian goddess with a mouth. Alessio, her former fiancé, had called her difficult. She shot down guys with the delicacy of a flying brick. She was a tough girl.

God, I loved them.

Specifically, I loved bringing them to their knees.

Thinking of her trapped in my bedroom worked me into a frenzy. Once inside, I grabbed a cocktail from the open bar, pressing the chilled glass to my throbbing pulse. I cooled down, and then I rejoined the room awash in wrapping paper. My daughter lay on the rug. The coffee table was pushed aside to make way for the mountain of gifts. Matteo hovered near his sister, bawling.

I knelt beside my son and kissed Matteo's temple. "Are you okay?"

Matteo pouted. "No."

"What's the matter?"

The four-year-old looked at the packages waiting to be opened and burst into fresh tears. "What about *me*?"

I squeezed his chin. "Buddy, you're killing me. It's your *sister's* birthday."

He pointed at the boxes. "But I want one, too!"

Mariette tackled a present wrapped in gold. "Ooh!"

I dragged him over my lap. "You cry every time someone else has a party."

He turned into my chest and sobbed. I rubbed his back, shaking with barely audible laughter. Then I heaved a sigh, fished a small package from my pocket, and pressed it into Matteo's hands.

"Here you go, honey."

Matteo's sobbing quieted. He disengaged and wrestled the truck from the packaging. Two years ago, I held a party for my daughter with nothing for Matteo—what a disaster. He'd been inconsolable. Since then, I never threw a birthday without a gift for the other kid.

I tugged on Mariette's pigtails. "What did you get?"

"Easy-Bake Oven!" Mariette scratched through paper, revealing a giant, pink plastic toy. "It makes cakes! *Wow*."

"That's awesome. Who's it from?"

She peeled an envelope from the box and took out the card, frowning. *"Dear Mariette, As you grow, make sure you dream big. Smile, live, laugh, and have fun! Happy seventh birthday. Love, Carmela.* Who is Carmela?"

I took the card. "She's... Daddy's girlfriend."

Mariette made a face. "Yuck."

The note was a nice touch.

I smiled, picturing the brunette upstairs, wearing that sheer dress. She'd obviously hoped to seduce me and wrangle an arrangement. She got what she wanted. I'd forced her into an engagement.

What was wrong with me?

I could've lied and banged her, but the image of her holding my son had stopped me. I'd always seen myself with a girl like Carmela.

Life hadn't been kind. I knocked up a stripper. Married said girl, whose instincts for motherhood were nonexistent. When she wasn't threatening to take my children, she cheated, scored drugs, and drove me insane. I tried to fix her—rehab, psychiatrists, therapy—nothing worked. I'd been held hostage for six years. So when she died, aching relief had washed over my bones.

Finally *free.*

The last thing I needed was another shitty marriage.

I had a feeling about Carmela.

A stupid feeling, maybe, but it warmed my body. I ignored such an impulse once, and it almost destroyed me. Fortunately, my head and heart screamed the same advice—*Don't let Carmela go.*

So I wouldn't.

THREE
CARMELA

I did not do well in cages.

Especially those that resembled my worst nightmares.

I stood by the leaded windows as daylight leached from the sky. A ball of anxiety throbbed inside me as night descended on the sleepy suburb. Silhouettes of homes disappeared, melting into pitch-black nothingness. Warmth sapped from my bones as the evening mist dissolved the taillights from the last departing guests.

What would he do when he returned?

Clues presented themselves in the bedroom's strange décor. Bronze rings stuck out from the four-poster bed. A cast-iron lattice comprised the headboard. A hook screwed into the ceiling beam. I opened his walk-in closet. Steel boxes lined the top shelf—were they gun safes? I swept aside the rack of bespoke suits, heart pounding when my fingers touched a bundle of nylon rope. Beside it sat a leather blindfold.

My breathing hitched.

We were so *incompatible*.

I'd never known this side of him. Michael was supposed to be one of the good ones. The gossip surrounding the newly minted consigliere never mentioned the room with sex toys. This bondage crap pushed my boundaries to their limit.

The things I will do to you.

Jesus, he wasn't kidding.

Several uncomfortable minutes passed with a walnut-sized lump lodged in my throat. I pictured Michael fisting my hair, bending me over the mattress. A violent shiver ran down my spine.

Footsteps tapped outside.

Oh shit.

I held my breath as the door creaked. A shadow seemed to melt inside.

The light stroked Michael's silhouette with warm colors, illuminating alluring details—a lean form rippling with muscle, the sharp edges defining his angular cheeks, the elegant slope of his nose, and his hooded eyes—lately, always narrowed.

Calculating.

He'd discarded the jacket. The untucked T-shirt combined with his swagger would've made James Dean proud. His irises were a vibrant shade of amber, and as tempting as whiskey on a chilly evening. Black stubble covered his jaw and chin, chiseling his angular features. Completing the look of perfection were his playful grin and the dimples shaping his face. I absorbed his every detail, as though I'd find a secret in his wrinkles that'd free me.

The urge to flatten my hand against his chest to keep him at bay was overpowering. "It's not too late to change your mind."

"Why would I do that?"

"Because you're a decent man."

"Carmela. Sweetheart." He brushed his knuckles against my frozen cheek. "I was nice to you because I wanted to get laid. You're easy to manipulate, and I've had a lot of practice."

"You're a psychopath."

Michael looked bored with the turn in conversation. "I'll be one hundred percent real with you starting now, except around my children."

"Have you reconsidered?"

Please say yes.

"No. Cold feet?"

"I'm no coward. I just don't like to be locked in a freak show for hours."

"Freak show?"

He followed my gaze to the bronze rings, the ceiling hook, and the walk-in closet filled with rope. He lifted his shoulders.

"I wouldn't tie you up on our first night together."

"I didn't realize you were into ropes. Michael, that is...*intense.*"

Before this, I would've attached a thousand different words to Michael—glib, carefree, lighthearted. Everything I'd associated with him had vanished in private.

I'd been deceived. He was a friend of the family who dropped in on Christmas with his adorable kids. The same man who cooed at my sister's newborn had blackmailed me into an engagement.

This was Michael—unmasked.

He fixed me with a stare that heated my blood. "Intense is how I like it."

"So you're a sadist."

"I'm many things, Carmela."

"*Clearly*. Why do you do it?"

"Having a woman at my mercy makes my cock hard." He was so flippant and *crass*, far from the gentleman who'd kissed my knuckles.

"I'll never look at you the same again."

"But you are looking at me."

As if my attention could've wandered with him in the room. Michael used to be a bright spot in a dark universe.

"I never gave you the time of day for a reason." My throat tightened when his smile grew. "Maybe you should've *taken a hint*."

"That you wanted to be chased?"

"I wasn't interested because I'm not attracted to you."

"That's why you got all dolled up and offered yourself as a sex slave." Michael smiled, and gooseflesh pricked my arms. "Never thought you'd do that. It'll be a great story to tell the grandchildren."

Whoa.

"Michael, you need to dial back your expectations. When I fantasize about sex, it's without leather cuffs." Judging from Michael's walk-in closet, he was the least vanilla guy on the fucking planet. "You'll be happier with someone else."

"I don't care about my happiness." He bulldozed past that alarming statement and adopted a chastising tone. "Shouldn't you have higher priorities than my sex life?"

"It's all I can think of."

He tapped my chin. "Well, get your mind out of the gutter. We have rules to discuss."

"Rules?"

"Yes, hon. Rules. Did you believe I'd let you run amok where my kids live and sleep?"

He still hadn't shown evidence that Dad was alive.

"I have to see my father. You owe me proof."

"Your dad is fine." The glimmer in his eyes disappeared. "I give you my word."

"Is that good for anything?"

"Why would I lie?"

Easy. "Because you enjoy screwing with people."

"I'd rather fuck you than mess with your pretty head."

"You'll never touch me, especially with that bondage shit."

"You're sending mixed signals, Carmela." Michael resisted

when I pushed his chest. "Bringing up my kinks over and *over*."

It was hard not to launch at him with everything I had. "I want to see my father!"

"Not yet."

"Why?"

"Because it's my decision, and I'm saying *no*. When the timing is right, I'll allow a visit."

That dug the rusted nail into my pit of rage. "Is this a sick game? Keep me in suspense about whether my father is alive?"

"You don't want to see Ignacio. Trust me."

So he'd been tortured.

Tears slammed into my eyes as I pictured my dad huddled in a concrete cell, gashes marring the face I loved, and God knows what else.

Hate swirled into a heated frenzy. "Whatever you want out of this marriage—you'll never have my love."

"But you'll love my kids."

I opened my mouth to deny it, but I couldn't form the words. There was plenty of room in my heart for two innocent kids, but absolutely none for Michael. Falling for a man almost killed me once. It dragged me into a pitch-black place, and I emerged with mental scars that still bled.

I'd tolerate Michael.

But love him? Never.

FOUR
MICHAEL

THERE WERE seven stages of grief, but I only felt one.

Rage.

Daniel had an anger management problem. A gangster with attitude. *Go figure.* He wasn't the easiest person to deal with. Growing up, we'd had a love-hate relationship. He slapped me around until I packed on enough muscle to strike back. We used to beat the shit out of each other. Once, he stabbed me in the thigh.

My overwhelmed mother sent him to therapists who made him count to ten and bullshit like that. Daniel never hit pause on his aggression. If a fight broke out, he ended it with a gun. And he won.

This time, he hadn't been so lucky.

All I knew was that an altercation had led to Carmela's father sinking two rounds in my brother's head. Knowing Daniel, he probably asked for it. That didn't mean my mom deserved to watch his corpse sink into the ground.

It was my job to pick up the pieces.

"*Ignacio.* Can you hear me?"

I doubted he heard anything but the ringing.

Ignacio slumped on concrete. Carmela's judgmental gaze seemed to glare through her father's eyes. A patchy beard stained with vomit grew in salt-and-pepper chunks. He still wore his Sunday clothes, although he'd stripped to his tank top. Every day, he'd peeled off another blood-soaked layer, discarding it like a tumor excised from his body.

I took it as a sign of progress that he was weakening his resistance, but after countless *fuck-yous* and *fuck-your-mothers*, I decided Ignacio was nowhere close to a mental breakdown.

Stubborn ass.

My brother had been just as bullheaded, and the comparison twisted a knife in my chest. If I'd taken his complaints seriously, Daniel's dispute with Ignacio would've stayed harmless. My mom and sister wouldn't be wrecked. I wouldn't be struggling to move on in a world without him.

"Fuck you," Ignacio growled. "Fuck your mother and your rotten family. I hope they get cancer in the ass and die, all of them."

He'd said it a thousand times already.

"I'm bored with these exchanges." I stooped and grabbed a fistful of his hair. "You tell me to fuck off. I hit you. And round and round we go. What are you trying to prove?"

Ignacio grimaced and spat, crimson staining the floor. The sixty-something-year-old staggered upright, shrugging off his pain like he had for five days.

Carmela's father was one tough bastard.

"Give me what I want, or I'll introduce you to Vinn."

I pointed out my cousin, but it wasn't necessary. Ignacio's gaze never strayed far from the imposing Costa boss.

Vinn stood in a navy hoodie, rolled to tattooed sleeves, beside the Camaro that needed bodywork. The acting boss before him, Alessio Salvatore, put him in intimidating roles. Vinn was tall and big, with biceps as wide as my neck, and he didn't know how to *not* be frightening. I loved the guy, but he had zero self-restraint. He wielded an axe when he should've used a scalpel.

People were scared of Vinn. They zeroed in on what I overlooked. Instead of deadness, I saw decades of trust. Vinn was the kid with nothing to eat until my mom sent me to school with two lunches. He was a tragic character who attracted women like my sister, who wanted to fix him.

I switched on the stereo, which blasted Metallica's *"Ride the Lightning."* Ignacio groaned and pitched forward. Spittle ran from his mouth in a constant stream, and he screamed in unintelligible syllables.

I increased the volume.

Ignacio clawed his ears. The song reached the halfway mark before I stopped the music. His frame straightened to his towering height.

"When I get out, I'll kill you!"

I grabbed his bound hands and shoved him into the metal chair. "Yeah, yeah. You're welcome to try if you escape."

"I swear to Christ. I will burn everything you love to the ground."

"Naz, I have your daughter."

Ignacio froze. A flicker of panic marbleized his bloodshot gaze. He doubled over, cradling his head, whispering a prayer in a shrill voice I'd never heard before.

Jackpot.

"Carmela came to see me. Beautiful girl. Very sweet. Willing to do anything to save you."

All we'd done was talk.

I leaned back, lost in the memory of that hottie strolling into my house like she owned the place. Many qualities of Carmela appealed to me—smoking-hot body, grab-me-by-the-balls confidence, and her affinity for children.

All reservations about marrying Carmela disappeared when I remembered Ignacio's devotion to his daughters. He'd almost started a war with the Irish after a member had assaulted Mia, his youngest. I wanted to twist the blade, so I'd cut him from Carmela.

I would take his darling jewel away from him forever.

Ignacio lunged with a snarl, snapped by Vinn's hand. *"What did you do to my girl?"*

"Everything. It was a wild night."

"I'll kill you! I'll kill your whole fucking family!"

"Relax, Ignacio. She's no worse for wear." I winked at him, provoking another hoarse scream. "Actually, I'm keeping her."

If someone taunted me about Mariette like this, I would stab their nuts with an ice pick. It turned Ignacio into a frothing beast who leaped at me no matter how often Vinn restrained him.

"*No.* Not my daughter, you son of a bitch!"

"Give me information. Save Carmela." A sharp frustration tugged at my chest as he sat, gnashing his teeth. "Or I'll continue to do whatever I want with her."

Nothing.

Maybe he didn't care.

Ignacio attempted to stand. "I can't say anything!"

"I've had it with your bullshit. Tell me, for Christ's sake. What did my brother do? Why did you shoot him? You're dragging this out, and it's pissing me off! Grow a pair and own what you did."

Vinn pushed him down. "*Michael.* Enough."

I refused to change the subject. "Why did you murder the man protecting you?"

"Michael, stop."

I grasped Ignacio's dislocated shoulder and dug my thumb into the joint.

His shriek pierced my eardrums.

"I said *stop.*" Vinn seized my bicep and jerked his head toward the office. "Let's talk."

I shoved him. "I'm not done."

"You are."

Disobeying a direct order from Vinn wasn't an option, even if he was family. I stood, kicking the chair on its side. None of them had ever really seen me angry. They knew me as the fun-loving guy, the peacemaker—the man everybody chose for a godfather role.

Not anymore.

Everything inside was twisted and black.

FIVE
CARMELA

MICHAEL OFFERED ME A BIG, calloused hand. I did *not* want to touch him, but I had little choice. His fingers clasped mine, ironing me with heat. Then he pulled me outside, and we headed downstairs. As I struggled to match his pace, I took in more of the mansion.

Spending my life in this colorless place seemed like torture enough without Michael prowling its interior. As we passed the kitchen, I glanced at the backyard. An English garden surrounded a full, green lawn. A lonely tree house fashioned from the same wood as the mansion stood in the house's shadow. A blue ball sat in the sandbox, which didn't even have a shovel.

God, it was sad.

The house reflected this family's downward spiral because the cottage he'd lived in months ago didn't have this depressing vibe. Wall-mounted photos glowed with Serena's wide grin—his late wife. She'd died in rehab, chasing the same high that put her there.

I hoped the kids were okay.

Staring at their faces pitted my belly with sadness. What happened to them was so unfair. Matteo had been only three years old. I focused on his cherubic face, and a shock jolted my heart when I glanced at Michael. It was hard to connect the grinning man with the dark presence beside me. Michael turned his menace at the family portrait, communicating more with a stare than he could in words.

"They're only up for the kids' sakes."

In the kitchen, a nanny scattered as though ordered to leave once he was in the room. Michael detached from me to greet his children, who sat at the granite countertop.

He beamed at them and shouted, "Who wants pancakes?"

"*Me!*"

I marveled at his transformation from broody asshole to wholesome daddy. "Morning."

The kids crowed a greeting. I joined Michael near the stove as he mixed pancake batter from scratch and dropped blueberries into smiley faces. "Need help? I can start the bacon or cook some eggs."

"Thanks." Michael cleared his throat, softening. "That sounds great."

I grabbed a package of bacon and a carton of eggs. Michael watched my every move, not even letting me cook scrambled eggs in peace.

Once the food was ready, I set the table, and Michael made everyone's plates. I sat beside Matteo, my head pounding as my fiancé served the kids, and then me. Mariette's judgmental blue gaze pierced me as I sat beside her father, who kissed my cheek. I forced a smile as his face glowed with happiness that didn't meet his eyes.

"Kids, we need to talk. Do you remember Carmela?"

Matteo beamed. "Carmel!"

"*Carmela.*" Michael's baritone softened. "Carmel is a city in California."

"Her name is Caramel," boasted Mariette. "Like candy!"

"No. Car-mel-ah. She's Daddy's fiancée. She's staying with us from now on."

Mariette's blonde head snapped up, her lips forming a pout. "*Why?*"

"Because we're getting married."

"*Why?*"

"Because we love each other so much." Michael teased his fingers across my shoulders and planted the softest kiss on my temple. "And we couldn't wait another second to get engaged."

Mariette darkened. She gave her father the stink-eye, and then her haughty disapproval flicked to me.

Believe me, honey. I'm not thrilled about this either.

The four-year-old, however, glowed. "What about Mommy?"

Michael sobered. "Mommy's dead."

Ouch.

I felt that one in the stomach.

It was awful to hear Michael's matter-of-fact delivery, and even worse to see their confusion. How many times had Matteo asked that question, and how did it feel to give that devastating answer?

Mariette frowned at her plate. "Why can't she come back?"

"She's gone. People who die don't come back."

Matteo shrugged and returned to his scrambled eggs. Mariette flushed beet-red, her forehead creased in a deep scowl.

I braced for the outburst.

"I hate you." Mariette stood, her tiny frame vibrating with a fury that seemed to match her father's. "Why are you marrying her? What about *Mommy*?"

A lump lodged in my throat.

"Mommy's dead, and it's your fault!" Mariette seized her glass and hurled it to the floor. It shattered across the marble in hundreds of pieces, and suddenly I wished I didn't have a heart.

Good God.

A horrible silence filled the air, broken by Michael's hammer-like command. "*Go to your room.*"

Mariette howled as she raced upstairs. Michael stared ahead, his expression vacant of all pain, but it poured over me like molasses.

"Do you mind if I talk to her? Michael?"

He sighed deeply. "Go ahead."

I slid off the stool and climbed the staircase, following the sound of her crying into a room shimmering with gold. She lay in her bed, wrapped in her comforter, and her face streamed with tears.

"I don't like you. Go away."

Ouch. "I just want to talk."

"No. Go away."

"Five minutes, and then I'll leave you alone. Promise."

Mariette rolled over, sniffling.

I sank onto the mattress.

How the hell should I approach this? Was there a manual on how to talk to a seven-year-old about their mother's death?

"I know this must be confusing. I'm a stranger, and all of a sudden, I'm in your home, eating breakfast with you, doing things your mommy used to do. I'm not trying to replace her, honey. She'll always be your mom."

Mariette turned toward me, crying. "I miss her."

"I'm sorry, honey." I wiped the hair clinging to her wet cheeks. "I know you're upset, but so is your dad. He misses your mom, too."

"He doesn't. He *hates* Mommy."

Probably true. "Why would you think that?"

"Daddy hates me."

"Your daddy loves you more than anything in the world." That wasn't a lie, at least. "It's his job to keep you safe and happy."

Mariette fell silent and chewed her lip.

I pulled a random children's book from her nightstand. "Can I read you a story?"

"Okay."

I opened the watercolored pages and read until her lashes fluttered. When her body sagged, I undid her ponytail and smoothed her curls on the pillow. Then I replaced the book and stood. I headed for the door.

Michael was at the threshold.

My pulse galloped ahead at the sight of him blocking my exit. His impassive gaze zeroed in on his sleeping daughter. When it swept over me, his lips parted. Raw emotion pulsed from him, dragging me forward like light spiraling into a black hole.

I felt sorry for him.

I didn't think that was possible.

"Michael, she didn't mean it. She misses her mother, and she's lashing out. She doesn't understand what she's saying."

"You said a lot on my behalf."

I followed him into the hall and closed the door. "What was I supposed to say?"

"The *truth*." His features were twisted in the shadows, his smile bestial. "I never loved her. I hated that junkie, waste-of-space bitch. I'm glad she's gone."

"*Michael.*"

"Don't." Michael turned away, as though he couldn't bear the sight of my pity. "Just leave me alone."

"You need to lighten up. They lost their mom. They need laughter and silliness, not the cold, hard truth."

"Jesus Christ, Carmela. *Go away.*"

"What is your problem?"

He wheeled around. *"They're my kids, not yours!"*

I jumped, my heart wrapped in barbed wire. A plea stuck in my throat as his overwhelming rage blackened the hallway. My back struck the wall, and he loomed over me.

Suddenly, I was yanked to a different time. My senses filled with clove smoke, scarred fingers groping where they had no right, and bright lashes of pain on my thighs—and I could not pull from Nick. In my mind, my ex-boyfriend stood in a leather cut, his fist raised to strike.

"Please, don't. *Please.*"

His burning palm touched my cheek.

"Get the fuck off!" I flinched and smacked him away. *"Don't touch me!"*

"Fine," the horrible voice exploded. "Pick a room and stay there."

I ran down the hall and dove into a study, shaking as I slid the lock. Then I dragged a chair under the handle and hid under the desk. I watched the door and waited for it to tremble.

So I braced myself.

SIX

CARMELA

My dreams were ashes.

Soon, I'd marry a man I hated. I'd sign *Carmela Costa* onto a marriage certificate and bind myself forever to a psychopath.

Starting a family was out of the question. Michael's two kids meant he was unlikely to want more.

I leaned my head back so my tears wouldn't blur the mascara.

I sat in a room in the Boston Cathedral, a magnificent colonial structure from the early nineteenth century restored by my brother-in-law, Alessio. The cost of booking it ran in the tens of thousands, but Michael had spared no expense on this sham wedding.

I'd wanted a small ceremony—Michael insisted on a big affair, instructed me to buy a designer dress, and booked a major act for the reception. It was the party of the year, as far as Boston's underworld was concerned. Everybody would be here, from politicians, CEOs, cops on the Costa payroll, and gangsters from every corner of the Northeast.

A ray of sunlight broke through a cloud, stroking my face with warmth. The golden windows were shut against the dazzling sunshine burning through rolling clouds. So inviting. I could so easily open them and jump into that brilliant blue.

Seven days had passed since Michael took me into his home. I'd arranged the details for this last-minute wedding with the help of a planner Michael hired. I thought it'd be a shit show, but over three hundred guests RSVP'd to attend.

The stylist pinned my ebony mane into a thick updo, the silk flowers with pearls for buds standing out like stars. Janet, a willowy makeup artist, dabbed my wrist with swatches of two identical pink lip glosses and peered at the stripes of color. She unscrewed one and painted my mouth.

The church bells tolled, ringing the half-hour.

Janet sighed, looking everywhere but my eyes. She leaned over and tweezed hair from my brow.

"*Perfect.*" She plucked a Q-tip from the pile and soaked my tears. "The photographers will be in any minute."

I wasn't big on displays of emotion. I hated losing control. I'd never even been drunk, which seemed like a significant accomplishment at twenty-seven years old, but I couldn't look into the mirror without tearing up. This should have been the best day of my life.

A fist hammered the door, punctuating the last echo of the bell, and then Michael's smoky voice boomed through. "It's me. Open."

Someone got the door.

Michael stepped through, the sunlight bleaching his expression into something wholesome. Handsome—picture-perfect with the white boutonniere hanging over his lapel. He'd tamed his mocha hair into a slick wave. He wore a navy tuxedo and had softened his beard to a shadow clinging to his neck. His brown eyes glowed with a swirl of golden amber. A gorgeous smile curved his full mouth, completing the look that'd always cemented him as the Safe Guy.

It was a con.

In private, the temperamental bastard barely spoke. During my seven-day isolation, he'd locked me in the east wing of his mansion and popped in only to discuss wedding details, ignoring me so thoroughly it was hard to accept he wanted this marriage.

Michael took in my dress with an appreciative nod. He stopped an inch away, blocking the bright rays. "Everybody out."

Nobody argued with a Costa.

The workers filtered from the room, making so little noise it was as though they passed through the wood. Michael's knuckles grazed my chin. He touched me with the familiarity of a lover.

Before this, we'd done nothing but exchange pleasantries. At my niece's christening, he sat beside me. Matteo had raced down the pews, so I'd dragged him over my lap. I still remembered Michael's gratitude and the stinging patch on my cheek when he kissed me.

"You look beautiful, Carmela."

The ghost of his lips seemed to press into me. I stamped on the growing flames. I would not be manipulated.

"Stop pretending to be nice. We both know it's an act, and I won't have it around me. *Ever*."

"Fine."

His hand fell, and the light in his gaze died. I could've laughed at how quickly he abandoned the façade if this weren't so depressing.

"You shouldn't be here."

"I'm less concerned about superstition and more worried my bride will misbehave at the ceremony." Michael pulled from the sun's brilliance and stepped into shadow. "We have a long day ahead of us. My family is here, including my kids. Matteo will do whatever he's told, but my daughter ...she's not happy."

No shit, Sherlock. "What do you expect? You dropped this marriage on her without warning. She'll hate you forever."

"She already hates me."

I can't imagine why. "What do you want?"

"When we're around my children, we call a cease-fire. No fighting. No insults. No slammed doors. With them, we are the perfect couple."

"What do I get in return?"

His brow ticked. "You won't be punished. Before your panties twist in a wad, remember that you freaked out over a few sex toys. You'll cave after five minutes."

He was such a prick to throw that in my face.

"Go to hell, Michael."

"It's up to you." He checked his watch with a flick of his wrist. "If I were in your position, I wouldn't consider it a worthy battle. I'll have you begging for mercy in a heartbeat, and all our bickering does is hurt two innocent kids who didn't ask for this."

I hated that he sounded so reasonable, but I had no intention of dragging those children into our mess. "Makes sense. You don't want a repeat performance of the last marriage."

He rolled his eyes. "Quite clever."

"Are we finished?"

"Not yet. I have something for you. Part one of your wedding gift, so to speak." Michael lazily gestured at the door. "Bring him in."

Oak doors swung inward, and a disheveled man stumbled inside. His hair stuck up on all sides. Once free of Michael's soldiers, he shook his jacket.

"*Get your fucking hands off me!*"

I stood. "Dad?"

He wore a double-breasted suit, the material bunching on his chest. A butterfly bandage stretched across a heavily bruised nose. He pivoted toward Michael, who smiled and waved.

"Ignacio," greeted Michael with a tight grin. "Glad you could make it."

"Why am I here, Costa?"

"To give away your daughter." Michael pressed into my side, his arm wrapping my waist. "Isn't she beautiful?"

Dad wheeled, his jaw dropping as he took me in, wedding dress and all. "Oh my God."

His wide-eyed horror told me he'd had no idea about any of this. Michael had detonated a bomb, danced in the flames, and pissed on the charred ashes.

"Naz, didn't you believe me?" He stared at my father, wearing a wolf-like smile. "I told you I was marrying her. Hell, I even gave you an invitation."

It dawned on my father, the tan draining from his face. "All this for a grudge?"

"Grudge," Michael deadpanned. "Putting it lightly, Ignacio. You killed my brother. You owe me a life, and I'd rather have your daughter's."

"You sick fuck. You son of a bitch!" Dad fisted his hair and moaned. "Carm, tell me he's lying. You're not marrying this man!"

I fought to keep calm. "Dad, it's for the best."

"Yes, it is." Michael's soft purr rolled over my ears as his hand slid up my back, displaying a reckless lack of boundaries that would've gotten him executed a few weeks ago. "I'll look out for her, Ignacio."

"You can't take my daughter from me!"

"I already have."

Michael grasped my neck, his fingers pressing into my throbbing pulse. His touch slipped to my shoulder, his palm heavy and hot. It burned several layers too deep, like his silky voice. Then he kissed the shell of my ear, and I ignited into a human torch.

Two guys slammed into Dad as he lunged for Michael, who watched my father lose his shit with a curl of his lips.

"Carmela, no! You don't have to do this. Don't ruin your life for me. He'll never give you what you want—"

Michael laughed. "Actually, I have every intention of fulfilling her wildest fantasies."

I faced the monster who'd used my father like a sharpening block. "You disgust me."

"Oh, come on, Carmela. It's fun."

"Have it at someone else's expense, or I'll make today unbearable for you."

"I don't respond well to threats."

"You think you're my dream guy? You're making this harder than it needs to be, you selfish son of a bitch." The gloves were coming off if he thought I'd play nice. "Leave my dad alone."

Michael's playful smile indicated I wasn't in any position to bark out orders. He held all the power. "Ignacio, this will be the last your family sees of your daughter. I expect you to behave. If you don't, I'll remove you from the ceremony, and you'll cut your time with Carmela that much shorter. The only reason you're breathing is because I allow it. I can change my mind anytime."

Dad struggled against the soldiers holding him. His forehead bulged with throbbing veins. He seemed on the verge of a breakdown.

I cupped his cheeks. Dad choked with a sob. The men restraining him let go, and he sagged into my arms.

Michael's indifferent stare raked my skin. "I'll give you five minutes."

My vision swam with tears before Michael exited. When he was gone, Dad wiped his eyes.

"I can't believe what he did to you. I wish we had longer than five minutes." I shook as he pulled me into a hug. "It'll—it'll be okay. He—he hasn't touched me or anything."

"This isn't forever," he said quickly. "I'll get you out—I swear. Once Alessio returns—"

"Daddy, *no*. Don't involve him." I clung to his shoulders. "Mia and Alessio deserve to be happy. Besides, you have no idea where they are."

Gang violence had spiraled out of control since the new year. It was confined to other gangsters, and my brother-in-law was still a very high-profile target, even after he'd stepped down from an active role. Shortly before my sister Mia fled Boston with him, she'd begged me to come.

I'd refused.

Someone had to watch my stubborn father, whose resistance to leave verged on suicidal. There was nothing for him here. He was no longer a *don*, but he went into a rage at the suggestion of running, and I'd stopped bringing it up. My dad wouldn't be driven from his home, so I'd dug a trench and planned to ride out the storm.

"Michael will change his mind. It just might be a while." I gave him a peck on his cheek. "I love you. Stay safe."

"I love you, too. You make a beautiful bride, honey." His tone wavered and broke. "It wasn't supposed to be like this."

He balled my head into his chest, my heart wrenching as I seized his jacket.

The door swung open, and Michael breezed in, the gust of crisp spring air blowing the warmth from the room.

"I gave you five minutes. You've had ten." He beckoned my dad with a flick of his fingers. "Let's go."

"Give him hell, Carmela."

My soul shattered as they shoved him out of sight and shrank into a bitter husk when I met Michael's frigid gaze.

Give him hell.

———

CLEAR SKIES REIGNED INSTEAD of the promised storms. Boston's streets were miraculously free of traffic. Sunshine poured through the stained glass, caressing the aisles with colored light. It was something out of a dream with Mariette's flower crown, the tulip aisle markers, the carpet of orange-pink petals, the pillars overflowing with roses, my mother sobbing in the front row, and *Michael*.

Michael's glowing smile was ripped from wedding magazines. He looked as happy as his son, who wore a matching suit. He'd plucked the rings from the silk pillow raised by his four-year-old, and slid the band over my finger. Then he took my face and we kissed, his soft lips stroking me with blistering heat.

The gesture was surely perfunctory for the photographer, who praised us endlessly—"what a *gorgeous* couple." Everyone lavished us with admiration. My relatives were charmed by Michael, who let his son cut the cake. My maid-of-honor, one of Michael's cousins, gave a generic speech. Single women congratulated me on "taming the playboy."

It was a sideshow.

Michael and I sat with the bridal party, my father surrounded by Costa soldiers. He'd sworn not to make a scene, but the cost was a hard blow to his pride. Dad fisted the tablecloth and didn't touch the six-course meal, ignoring the waves of duck confit, black truffle risotto, and buttered Maine lobster. I'd never seen him ignore food. That bothered me more than anything about this stupid wedding.

Those who weren't drunk were getting tipsy at the white linen tables. My guest list seemed to prove Boston's seething underbelly. City hall officials mingled with wiseguys. Politicians hovered near the thick circle surrounding the acting boss of the family, Vinn Costa. Michael had spent the evening networking as I hung on his elbow. Countless business cards filled his wallet before we finally sat to eat.

Michael looked pleased. Our marriage had scored him a fuck-load of new contacts. He devoured his lobster while I took in my surroundings.

"So tell me about yourself."

"You want to get to know me at our *wedding*?"

He shrugged. "Might as well."

Jesus, he was a piece of work.

"You must have hobbies. Pinterest. *Barre*."

He obviously thought I was a vapid idiot.

"Music."

Singing was more precise. I used to sit at the top of the staircase and practice Whitney Houston's version of the national anthem. I was a regular at The Rickshaw, a bar ten minutes from my former place, but with the streets as dangerous as they were, karaoke night was out of the question. Music soothed my soul. I listened to do-wop, blues, pop, anything with a rhythm.

"Fascinating." His knife banged into my plate. "Eat. Your body needs fuel."

Where the hell did he get off on lecturing me?

"You've killed my appetite."

"Remember our agreement, Carmela."

I shrugged. "Nobody can hear us."

"They can *see* you." Michael gripped my chair and leaned in, his eyes flashing. "Best behavior means smile. Look at me without scowling. Act like you don't want me dead."

He didn't give a damn about me. The indifference behind his words stabbed deeper than if he'd yelled. The earth had opened and swallowed me whole.

"Is there nothing left of the man I liked, or am I stuck with this asshole forever?"

"Insulting me falls under misbehaving. *Strike one.*"

"Touch a hair on my dad, and I'll pay you back in spades."

"Threatening me? That's strike two." Michael took my chin and gave me a chaste kiss. "Keep it up. You'll regret it when we're alone."

I fisted my dress. I wasn't sure what did it—his velvety voice or the kiss—but I couldn't breathe until he'd pulled away.

"What does that mean?"

"Your father won't suffer. You will."

The sultry tone suggested it would happen in the bedroom. My fingernails pierced lace as Michael beamed, tapping my dish.

"It's a party, Carmela. Lighten up."

It's a nightmare.

Michael dragged my meal to his side and cut my lobster. He jabbed a chunk of meat and hovered it near me. I parted my mouth, and it slid inside. Michael radiated greed as I bit down. The tines slipped from my lips, and the lobster's buttery warmth melted over my tongue.

"Shit. Not again." He growled his displeasure as Matteo ran across the dance floor, chasing a crying girl. "This fucking kid."

"What is it?"

Michael shook his head, standing. He approached his four-year-old, who stopped in his tracks and begged to be picked up. Wearing an expression of deep disapproval, Michael knelt beside him.

"Teo, what did you do to her?"

"Nothing." A shy grin carved into Matteo's little face.

"Don't lie. Did you kiss her?" Michael guessed the worst from Matteo's continued silence, and took his arm. "What did I tell you? Kissing is only for grown-ups, like getting married."

I snorted, and Michael shot me a black look.

I couldn't help it. The absurdity of the day's events had reached a new level. Michael was pretending to be all about boundaries. That was rich. Motherfucker blackmailed *me* into a marriage, but the irony seemed to be lost on him.

Michael's frown deepened. "Apologize to her. Now, Teo."

Matteo stuck his fingers in his hair and faced the child clinging to her father's pants. "Sorry, Ashley."

"It's all good, buddy." The girl's father, a blond man in a double-breasted suit, grabbed Michael's son. "Give your Uncle Julian a hug."

Uncle?

He didn't seem related to Michael. Julian's fair features screamed Nordic, the polar opposite of my husband. He wore his brassy waves in a tidy man-bun, and the golden stubble covered his neck and cheeks. He was likely in his mid-thirties. He had to be Serena's brother, which meant the entire family was probably here.

A twinge hit my gut as I imagined them sitting through the ceremony that ignored his late wife, erasing her so thoroughly it was as though she'd never existed.

"Carmela, this is Julian," Michael deadpanned. "Julian, Carmela."

"We're glad you could make it." I shook his hand. "Are you having fun?"

"Yes, it's been fantastic." Julian offered a polite smile. "Congratulations to you both."

"Thank you," I said, forcing a grin.

"I can't believe I got the invitation a week ago." Curiosity seared in Julian's gaze. "Why did you send them so last minute?"

"Because I just popped the question." Michael's arm slid around my waist, and he squeezed my hip. "We've known each other for a while. This was a long time coming. Isn't that right, baby?"

That was my cue to lean into my husband and kiss him, which I did, bumping my lips clumsily on his cheek.

Julian raised his brow. "I had no idea you were seeing someone."

"Well, I wouldn't call it *dating*." Michael's voice lost its airy quality. "More like animal magnetism."

I dug into his midriff. "*Michael.*"

Michael's wicked laughter boomed through me.

Julian glossed past that over-share, smiling. "How did you meet?"

"At a restaurant. She was the hottest thing I'd ever seen, and all I saw was her neck."

He traced it with his knuckle, starting with the hollow under my ear. My skin burned almost as hot as my rage. Talking like this to Serena's brother was insensitive as hell. He shouldn't be rubbing me in Julian's face.

"Michael. You're embarrassing me."

"Okay, fine. I'll tell him how I proposed." Michael's attention flicked to Julian, who had gone quiet. "My kids helped. My four-year-old popped the question while I kneeled. I thought I stood a better chance if I involved them."

Two could play this game.

"They wore matching suits. It was *adorable*." I fondled Michael's tie, grinning. "He was in tears before he'd finished asking me to marry him. It was so sweet."

"No shit? Huh. I can't imagine Michael crying over anyone."

"Neither would I."

Both men exchanged venomous looks, which Julian broke with a sigh.

"You and Carmela should come over. Or she and I could get together for playdates with my daughter." Julian glanced at the toddler nuzzling his slacks. "Say hi, Ashley!"

"Nice to meet you, honey!" I reached toward the girl, but she turned away. "Aww, she's precious. I'd love to have a—"

"Carmela's schedule is filled for the next few weeks." Michael took his son from Julian. "Too bad."

"Yeah."

Julian's tone was resigned, but he seemed to burn with frustration as Michael handed Matteo to his au pair. He clapped Julian's shoulder and flashed him a condescending smirk.

"Enjoy the party, and don't steal the silver."

Julian's mouth twisted, and he stepped back, taking his daughter's hand. "Let's see if there's more cake."

I watched them leave, my stomach churning with the undigested wine and lobster. "Why did you do that?"

"Because he needed to be put in his place."

"Did you have to be such a jerk?"

"No, but it has its perks. You look good with color in your cheeks." Michael's stare was like a lightning rod. "Also, strike *three*."

"For *what*?"

"You scoffed at my kid."

"No, I was laughing at *you*. You are ridiculous. A man who forces a woman into marriage has no business teaching anybody about boundaries. He watches you with women. You're the reason the apple doesn't fall far from the tree."

A dark shadow rippled across Michael's features. He hadn't stopped smiling, but the shadows dragged his grin into a taut leer.

His fingers bit into my side. "Time to go home. *Come*."

I dug in my heels. "I am not a dog. I do not fetch, heel, or *beg*."

"Fetch? No. But you will beg."

My breathing hitched. "You said I wasn't a slave."

"That doesn't mean I can't play with you."

SEVEN
CARMELA

TRAPPED.

I couldn't escape him here. For the entire night, I had Michael's undivided attention. He'd hired a sitter for the kids, and we'd headed straight for his bedroom. Heat tiptoed along my spine like a flame-tipped finger rolling down. The evening would end here, and there was no avoiding the moment we slipped into bed.

I had a lot of experience with sex.

Most of it wasn't positive.

I sealed my fate once I said, "I do," but my throat closed when I pictured sleeping with Michael. The *safe* guy, a man with a cloyingly sweet smile that dragged every woman in the vicinity to their knees. The one my sister had nudged in my direction.

I should've recognized the lie.

Michael used good manners and warmth like a shield that reflected suspicion. Everybody trusted him, my sister included. But the façade he worked so hard to maintain seemed to be gone, purged by his brother's death.

Now there was a void.

I wiped my palms and disappeared in the bathroom, yanking the pins from my hair, shaking off the stupid flowers, and removing pearl drop earrings. I scrubbed off the pound of foundation. I needed out of this ridiculous dress, but I couldn't reach the back.

"Carmela."

Damn it.

I rejoined Michael in the bedroom, who watched me with a sour look. His fingers whitened on the glass. It hit the metal bar cart as he set the drink down. Then he approached, stopping inches away. His unflinching glare bored into me.

He wanted an apology.

He wouldn't get one.

Michael said nothing, but he didn't have to. My pulse throbbed as he lifted a strand of hair from my face. It slipped from him, and then he bunched my mane into a ponytail and swept it to my other side. Cold stung my neck as he unzipped, his knuckle grazing my skin. His command brushed my cheeks with heat.

"Take off your dress."

I didn't budge.

"*Do what you want with me.* Your words, right?"

I could've called him things I'd hurled at Nick—sick, twisted, cruel, *broken*. Michael was just like my ex-boyfriend. He took advantage of vulnerable women, except he'd find out I had no boundaries left to damage.

Nothing he did could hurt me.

I moved the straps from my shoulders. The delicate lace slid off my curves and pooled at my feet. Gooseflesh raised in rows across my arms as I wrapped myself, waiting for a degrading comment about my body.

He closed the distance between us, his waist nudging mine.

"Everything. Off."

I unsnapped my bra and flung it aside. I treated my panties and heels with the same disregard, and then I imagined a shoreline. Blue was the calming color. It would fill my vision as he pushed me onto the bed and shoved himself inside me. I waited, expecting him to walk into the blue.

Michael didn't move.

Why wasn't he touching me? What was happening?

I shifted my attention to his tented slacks and cream button-up to his heated gaze. He wasn't looking anywhere but my eyes, and that sent a shock down my spine.

Get on with it, you bastard. "What are you doing?"

"Taking my time."

I didn't want this dragged out. "Why?"

"I'm not interested in your fear. Just your submission."

"You don't have either."

"When will you realize that you've won? Your father gets to live. You saved him. You're married to me."

I'd escaped Nick only to be tortured by another villain.

How was that winning? "That's a punishment, not a reward."

"You could've done a lot worse. The world is filled with terrible men." Michael's hand cupped my cheek. "But I'm not one of them. Far from it."

His burning palm distracted me from the lie in his words.

"How can you say that, with your rap sheet?"

"I'm a rebel, not a monster."

"Yeah, you're up there with James Dean." I shook my head, sighing. "You've been arrested for assault."

"Who hasn't?"

I snorted. "*Me.*"

"No shit? That's surprising, given your reputation for ball-busting."

Was this lighthearted banter supposed to put me at ease?

"I would kick yours, but that'll just excite you, and I'm not into kicking a man's nuts for his sexual gratification."

"I like the way your mind works, but I'm not a masochist."

"Right. You like hurting *other* people."

"Don't get it twisted, sweetheart. I don't hurt women. I spank them. I fuck them. I leave them aching and wanting for more, and soon, you'll know what that feels like."

"I'm not attracted to you."

"Are we pretending the last six months didn't happen?" His

bourbon eyes seemed to pull me closer as he spoke. "You wanted me, Carmela."

"Your arrogance is staggering."

"You dodged me every time I came around. At parties, holidays, your niece's christening. You ran off after the service. I looked for you."

I'd been overwhelmed with his attention, and I'd camped in my room like a fifteen-year-old. It wasn't my style. When men were out of line, when they annoyed me, I told them off.

"I was under the weather."

"Bullshit. You were hiding because I kissed your cheek." Michael turned his head, his lips brushing my ear. "That's called a crush."

My face burned, and I jerked away. "I don't have crushes, and even if I did, you're not who I thought you were."

"Never trust the guy who only smiles at you, Carmela."

Good advice—given way too late.

I couldn't stand talking to him. I'd been so transparent, and I hated that he rubbed it in. "Let's get this over with."

"No."

I swallowed my shock. "No?"

My hair stood on end as Michael held my gaze, the silence suffocating and hot, like steam. He seemed comfortable, not at all in a hurry, so controlled.

"This isn't like ripping off a Band-Aid. I fuck women because

I need to, because they need me," he said, his voice hardening. "A marriage with me doesn't have to be hell."

"I don't believe you."

"You will."

Buttons unsnapped as he yanked off his shirt. The fabric tugged over his sculpted shoulders. Tight, corded muscle rippled across arms covered with dark hair. A mad impulse begged me to explore the broad planes of his chest and the slabs of strength defining his back. Two dimples begging for my mouth peeked above Michael's slacks, which he unzipped and let fall, exposing muscular thighs and his briefs, tented with a massive erection. He kissed my cheek. "*Stay.*"

His warmth disappeared as he retreated to the nightstand. I froze, counting the fleur-de-lis on the wallpaper. Michael rummaged through the drawer and retrieved something that jangled. He returned with a small box wrapped in silver.

"Your second wedding gift."

It probably wasn't a bracelet.

He smirked as I pulled the bow. I sliced open the present, revealing a creamy band with a shiny buckle.

A collar.

He got me a fucking collar.

Shock rooted me to the ground as he swept my hair aside and bound the thick leather around my neck, slipping the straps through the buckle. I swallowed hard, fingering the metal loops. It wasn't too bad—like a thicker-than-average choker necklace.

Still holding me, he pressed his body into mine.

"*Come.*"

Michael hooked a finger through a hook. He tugged, and I stumbled toward the mattress. He walked backward, his smile growing with rapturous delight. He ripped the sheets and slid into bed, leading me forward.

My palms flattened onto the satin as I crawled on all fours, my cheeks burning. I focused on the shimmery glaze of the white under my hands, and not my building humiliation, which burst into flames with Michael's soft chuckle.

"Look at you, acting like the perfect submissive. And I thought you'd give me trouble."

I was getting fucked whether or not I wanted it.

I'd been through this before. Fighting him would cause me pain, and sex with Michael wouldn't kill me. Risking his anger might. I'd let him have me. He could toy with me all he wanted—I couldn't be defiled.

He sat on his knees, touching me lightly.

I sank into the bed as Michael hovered above, apparently speechless. After a few moments, I couldn't take it anymore. "What are you doing?"

"Drinking you in." Michael lowered himself, planting a searing kiss on my brow. "You're beautiful."

"You said that already."

"I meant it."

Whatever.

He pulled back, holding a feather. He ran it through his fingers, the barbs pleating.

I eyed it warily. "What's that for?"

"This."

He lowered it to my mouth. Tiny sensations brushed me like wisps of a brisk wind. The softest strokes caressed my skin in winding paths. He followed my shoulders, the sensation tickling. Then it reached more intimate areas, and my pulse hammered.

"This has been on my mind for too long. What I want to do with you—how I'd make you come."

He certainly was making me *feel*.

The feather swiped my breast. The tickle skated the curve, narrowing in tighter circles until stroking my nipple. Jolts struck me like lightning bolts. My nipple contracted, his antics feeding the fire I thought was forever doused.

It wasn't supposed to be good.

I wanted to fade from my body, to disappear.

Michael made that impossible. Shutting my eyes kicked my arousal higher because I imagined his fingers instead. I gave up, looking at the ceiling, but he touched my jaw, and my attention snapped to his gorgeous face.

"You're mine. I'm not letting you hide."

My hands fisted the sheets. "Please."

"Please, what?"

Stop.

Demanding that no longer made sense, because the agony I pictured didn't match what he did to me. Nobody had ever given me pleasure—it was always taken. Taken without consent, until I had nothing to offer, just squeezing it from me.

"Please...what?" he prompted.

"I—I don't know."

Everything was confused, but Michael's dimpled smirk suggested that he understood my dilemma.

"What's wrong, sweetheart?" he said in a tone filled with mock-concern. "Look at me."

"No."

"Scared of seeing something you like?"

My heart pounded as I met his slanted gaze, which was a mistake. I saw my desire reflected.

Michael seemed hell-bent on giving me ecstasy. He thumbed my lips, almost sinking through. The feather changed course, dipping south. He lowered himself, nuzzling my neck. Wet heat lashed me, and then he sucked.

I inhaled a sharp breath.

His smile pressed into my throat, the kisses becoming hungrier, wetter, *hotter*. He pushed into a spot that thrummed wildly with my pulse.

I shouldn't enjoy this.

What the hell?

The feather teased in tantalizing circles, down my cleavage, and around the other breast. Wherever it swept, I ached. I craved more pressure—more of this lightning filling me with so much glorious warmth.

No, this wasn't supposed to happen.

Pain and horror were all men like him knew how to give, and yet this was the opposite of everything I expected.

His ragged breathing brushed my skin. Michael grasped my hip, his grip smoothing into an intimate stroke that stole my air. He grabbed my ass.

I lay there, melting into the sheets. "What are you doing to me?"

"Making you ache for me, just like I promised."

It was working.

The feather skated my abdomen, tracking my hips, sliding around my thigh like the lightest finger, teasing my legs apart. My hand flew to his chest unbidden. He leaned into me as he stroked my clit. A bolt of desire hit me, the jolt of pleasure tearing through me, the first strike of a brewing storm.

I arched into him, gasping.

"That's right, baby. Just feel it."

Michael tossed the feather aside. He swept his palm over my body, sending a dark thrill to my pussy. He found my clit and rubbed it in slow circles.

A whimper escaped my lips.

I was caught in a storm's eye, surrounded by a whirlwind that blotted the sun. Michael was everywhere, and soon he'd be inside me, something that had terrified me moments before. Now I'd surrendered to him. There was no escape—no corner of my mind I could hide. I'd be aware of every thrust.

I slid up his pecs, raking through a sprinkling of hair shadowing his muscles. His pulse thundered under my touch. My gaze jumped to his flushed face, absent of arrogance. He seemed possessed by lust.

I can't believe I'm doing this.

His mouth scorched a path down my neck as his fingers moved faster. Arousal slicked my thighs, and he pressed harder, the pressure growing into a demand that begged to be released. He grazed my nipple. Liquid heat smothered me in toe-curling ecstasy as he nipped and sucked. Then he dipped into my pussy, gathering its wetness to my clit, not quite penetrating.

Animalistic noises burst from me. I fisted his brown locks, digging into his scalp with a force that seemed to encourage him. He sucked my nipple into a hardened point. Then turned his attention to the other breast.

"Jesus *fuck.*"

"He gets the credit?" he tutted, his voice measured. "So not fair."

"*Michael.*"

His eyes fluttered, and he smiled, as though savoring the sound of his name. I watched him tongue me, unable to focus on anything but that searing image. Then he ripped away, leaving me in a horrible void.

No, no, no.

"I think you're ready."

Was I?

My heart felt like it was exploding.

Michael straightened, tugging his briefs off. My pulse raced as my gaze followed his muscled stomach to the shadow of hair leading to a long silhouette.

He was putting *that* in me?

My mouth dried as he gripped his cock and stroked. He pressed it into me. The head rubbed my aching clit, electricity ricocheting into my body.

"You're—you're big."

Dimples carved into his face. "Don't worry. I'll go easy on you."

He lowered himself, pushing inside me.

His weight bore on me. I bit my lip as the broad pressure filled me, the sting chased by warmth as he pulled back and inched forward. His nose touched mine as his strokes deepened, making my breath hitch.

"Don't stop."

I squeezed his shoulders, stunned by the confession I never meant to make. Michael's chuckle tickled me before he claimed my mouth. Slow and sensual, like his rhythm. His lips fluttered on mine, sucking gently. He tasted like citrus and mint, fresh and lively.

I dragged him closer, deepening the kiss. His tongue swiped across, parting my lips. I groaned, and he chuckled. His pace picked up as he adjusted me, sinking in deep and fast. The sensation stabbed into my stomach. I couldn't breathe. Desperate sounds escaped me that he swallowed.

His arms bound me in a vise grip as he pounded me. Michael's guttural sighs sharpened into grunts. He yanked me, mouth crushing me as we dissolved into a frenzy. He fucked like he needed me, like his soul screamed to be inside of me as he rolled his hips and punched forward.

I clawed him, every stitch of skin burning for him. I jerked his hair. His lips devoured me in frantic strokes. His hand slipped between our bodies. Fingers pressed into my clit, lighting a fuse to my arousal. Suddenly he vanished, leaving me to throb with aching want as he pulled out, his warmth gone.

No.

Did I say that out loud?

Michael laughed, his smile ghosting my tits, my hips—

Oh my God.

He parted my thighs. His sigh billowed over my pussy before a slick heat stroked me. I melted as the towering furnace returned with a vengeance. His fingers dove into me, filling the void as he tongued my clit.

I turned into a bucking madwoman. He fucked me, my feelings building into a crescendo until he locked his mouth on me and sucked. Violent pressure tensed my abdominals as I orgasmed. I arched and convulsed. I cried out when he withdrew, but he returned a second later, his cock ramming into me.

He wrapped me in an embrace, our mouths crashing into each

other as he thrust. I grabbed his face, pulling him closer. His tongue slashed me, and I tasted myself, greedy for more.

He pounded me without restraint, fucking with a reckless passion as he devoured my gasps. His kiss broke as he fought to catch his breath. He touched his damp forehead to mine, his sighs deepening to satisfied groans. Then he pulled out and sat back. Michael grasped himself, stroking fast. His expression smoothed from tension as he finished on my navel. His lips twitched into a relaxed grin. He dropped to his side and seemed to admire the view. Then he caught his shirt and wiped me.

Pleasure blanketed me like a sun-kissed glow. My eyes fluttered, all of me sore in the best way.

He hooked his finger through the collar. He tugged, and I yielded, too tired to resist. I trembled as I hovered over him.

"*Lay down.*"

Anger rippled through me, a sting puncturing my bubble of happiness. So far, I'd come when beckoned, heeled, and lay down. The only thing left was begging.

Humiliating.

The leather cut into my skin. My arms buckled, and I fell onto his chest. Heat bloomed between my thighs. The hills of his muscles molded into mine. The space between us heated to an inferno.

He adjusted me, his arm weighing on me like an anchor. His other hand yanked the sheets over our bodies. The fabric glided on my stomach and settled like a thin membrane. Then he stroked my hair.

I endured it, wide-eyed.

"*Sleep.*"

His last command boomed through my back.

He sounded halfway there already.

What just happened?

Poison replaced the fire in my veins.

He'd teased that orgasm out of me. He'd ravished me, lit my soul ablaze, owned me, and made me beg to prove a point. Worst of all, my body had betrayed my common sense.

I pictured myself sliding out from the hot cage of his embrace and stealing across the room. Taking to the streets naked, *screaming*. Going to the police with my collared neck. They'd believe anything I told them. Then Michael would use his connections to make every charge I filed disappear. My dad would suffer.

He believed he could dominate me.

He was wrong.

And this twisted game would be one he'd forever regret.

EIGHT
CARMELA

THE NIGHTMARE WAS FAMILIAR.

My knees stung from kneeling on splintered wood. Nick's steel-toed boots creaked the boards, the only part of him I could see. He was proud of those boots. They made up his identity, like the leather cut stamped with his biker name, *Crash*.

Nick's dirty blond hair fell to his shoulders in a messy wave that I used to love touching. He wasn't the best-looking man, but he'd once held the key to my heart. He'd lured me in with honey-coated poison, and now I couldn't meet his eyes. I couldn't appreciate the sprinkling of freckles across his nose. His full mouth used to entice me until it spewed the most hateful garbage.

I used to picture us at the altar—him in his leather cut and me in a white dress. I'd given him my heart, and he'd grated it into a fine powder.

In my head, I defied him.

I called him *Trainwreck*. I did everything I could to stay sane, especially when he got this bad.

He'd beaten me in front of the clubhouse, the humiliation worse than the pain. I'd stopped looking at them for help. Anybody with a semblance of a conscience couldn't meet my eyes.

I was naked, helpless.

He stopped, his soles inches from my face. Crimson had soaked through the leather. "Lick it off me, Beauty."

"*No.*"

He fisted my hair. "Lick his blood off my shoes."

"I won't."

"Then I'll have to put your mouth to work some other way."

I met his slanted gaze, refusing to show him fear. "Fuck you, Nick."

"Poor choice of words."

I ripped his hands into shreds, struggling to break free. I screamed so hard that my voice cracked. He tore at his belt and unzipped his jeans. His cock slipped out. It bulged in his hands like a pale worm.

Think of the ocean.

I pictured an endless sapphire-blue horizon on white sand. Nick's steel-toed boots kicked the water as he walked, deep inside the blue, the waves lapping around his ankles. I was that ocean. I was the water he defiled. Filling my eyes with all that blue used to help, because he couldn't turn it black. He was just a speck of darkness—a flea. Smaller than a flea, an amoeba.

He couldn't hurt me.

It all faded to black.

I lay on a bed. Naked. A man's body pressed into mine.

He palmed my shoulder, shaking me.

"*Carmela—*"

I slapped him off and dove from the sheets, but they'd wrapped my torso. The gentle touch returned, and I slammed my elbow into his body.

He grunted.

I freed myself and spilled onto a pile of clothing. There must be a weapon *somewhere*. If I could gain the upper hand for a minute—

The lights flared on.

I whirled, looping a belt around my fist.

Michael stood beside me, massaging his bare chest. A red mark glared on his left side. His heavy-lidded gaze flicked to my hand, and then his lips curved.

"What are you going to do, flog me?"

The panic from the dream lingered like a suffocating fog. "*Stay away.*"

He grabbed his briefs and pulled them on. "Put down the belt, Carmela."

I tightened my grip on the leather. "Take a step toward me, and I'll hurt you."

"Go ahead. Your ass will be raw after I'm done with you."

"I'll fucking do it! Stay away from me!"

"Well, that put me in my place." Mischief gleamed in his eyes as he lurched forward.

I loosed the belt and let the buckle fly. It missed his face and gouged the wall. Michael seized the leather, wrapping the strap around his arms. He yanked. I slammed into his chest. He gathered my wrists in one fist and knotted them behind me. A sharp pain jolted my elbow when I twisted. I couldn't free myself.

This was familiar. Way too familiar.

"Stop—*stop!* Please!"

"*You* stop."

"You have to let me go!"

Michael cinched his arm around my waist and utterly immobilized me. "I will when you calm the fuck down."

I couldn't.

My senses were filled with Nick. I stomped his feet and sank my nails into his legs. He snapped my wrists, stopping me. I screamed. I couldn't break free. I was trapped.

"Let me go!"

"*Stop fighting me.*"

I jabbed my elbow into his abdomen, but it was like concrete. I shoved with my feet. His back hit the wall. His

laughter vibrated through my body. I slipped from his loos-
ened hold. He seized my arm and lazily yanked me into his
embrace, which wrapped around me like ropes. He dragged
me to the floor, one arm covering my torso, the other
cinching my legs.

No.

A scream caught in my throat.

"Breathe. I'm not going to hurt you." Michael crushed me
against his burning chest. *"Breathe."*

He tucked my head under his chin, and his earthy scent
surrounded me in a cloud of intoxicating bergamot and spiced
orange. Rough hands grazed my forehead. I flinched. My eyes
screwed shut as he palmed my head. I expected pain—a
stinging slap—but the soft pressure returned.

Soothing. Gentle.

What was he doing?

I recoiled even though it wasn't painful. My heart pounded as
I anticipated pain. I dug my elbow in his ribs, wrenching left
and right. My panic reached a crescendo, and the air
vanished. I sagged into his arms, numbed, giving up.

This was the part where I'd float above my body and disappear, but Michael pressed his mouth to my temple. I grimaced
and shuddered, but after two more kisses, my body melted.
The lump in my throat shrank as his metronome heart
thudded into my back, and his scent enveloped me in a fog
that embraced me like a tight hug. His knuckles grazed my
hair. Warmth bloomed where he kissed me. Suddenly, there
was nothing else, not his hands or his body, just the imprint of
his lips.

It felt so good.

My breathing slowed. This was Michael. And he wasn't restraining me.

I slapped his arm away and dove to the opposite corner.

Michael didn't follow. He remained on the floor, back against the wall, his face flushed. He looked more alive than he had all week. He watched me with restless greed, head propped on his hand. His hair stuck up in all directions. He smoothed it back into a loose wave.

"That was fun."

"*Fun?*" The word stuck to the back of my throat. "You almost gave me a panic attack."

"I was controlling the situation before it got out of hand." Michael's tone darkened, and the smile flattened. "I don't tolerate violence in my home."

"Really? What the hell is all this?"

"They're toys, and there's a huge difference."

A lump swelled in my throat. "You tie up women."

"Only those who want me to tie them up."

Michael fanned his flushed chest and gave me a look as though I'd made him too hot, and it replaced my fear with a dark thrill.

"You attacked me, Carmela. That's not okay."

"Are you lecturing me?"

"I'm telling you the rules."

I ground my fingers into the carpet. "You backed me into a corner."

"I'll let it slide because you were scared, but you can't do that again. I am not your punching bag."

"*All right.*"

My stomach roiled as I imagined what might've happened if I'd landed a hit on Michael. I had never thrown a punch before my ex. My lack of control brought home the fact that I was damaged.

Michael sat beside me. "Bad dream?"

I looked away from him.

"Seemed pretty intense."

I'd rather drink battery acid than tell *him*. "Drop it, Michael."

An awkward silence settled between us. Evidence from last night throbbed between my legs. Blemishes marked my chest that I covered, buttoning the shirt. Michael stretched out his legs, pissing me off with his casual elegance. He didn't deserve his good looks.

He dipped, kissing the shell of my ear.

I moved away from him. "Don't."

"What?" He sounded genuinely shocked.

"Kiss me. Touch me. Act like you give a shit. Ever again." My anger boiled over when his eyebrow lifted even further. "You owe me honesty, not manipulation."

"I'm completely lost."

Liar.

He knew what he was doing.

God, I was tired of being used.

He seized my hand as I stormed away.

"I had you floating on cloud nine last night. Don't pretend you hated it."

I didn't hate it, and that was the problem.

I couldn't be that vulnerable again. "Never again."

NINE
MICHAEL

YES, I was a monster.

I spent my youth in petty pursuits—sleeping with high-class escorts, married women, anyone who caught my eye—and I didn't care about the fallout. I robbed businesses. I killed. I helped lesser men cheat their way to the top, and no matter how many people I destroyed, there were always more idiots waiting in the wings. If a man had the money to buy them all, he could conquer the world.

At twenty-three, I became the youngest captain in the Costa Family. I led a crew of six men that helped me move cocaine from Montreal. My part-time gig involved managing Sanctum, an underground sex club filled with beautiful women. I was young, the girls were hot, and I snorted anything that wasn't nailed down.

Then I got a girl pregnant.

Suddenly, I was responsible for a life other than my own. I sold my penthouse apartment, moved to the burbs, and cleaned up my shit. Serena was a disaster, but if it weren't for my children, I'd be dead.

I owed them everything.

That single-minded devotion had crashed headlong into Carmela Ricci, the woman I'd married on a fucking whim.

My head pounded. I'd finished half a bottle of wine. I needed to fuck my wife, but she loathed me, and I hated being around her. Those weighted glares. Her sullen presence. With my kids, Carmela was pleasant, but her incongruous smiles dug at me. Her contempt burned into my sheets every night.

I couldn't stand being at home, so I stayed away as much as possible.

In the five days of my new marriage, Boston had seen a spree of grisly murders, attempted assassinations, and car bombings. I was in charge of damage control. The violence wasn't our doing, but a sock-puppet MC club called Rage Machine.

I took phone calls all day. My role as advisor to the acting boss meant I handled a lot of the diplomacy. Considering Vinn was piss-poor at dealing with people, most of the kowtowing fell to me. Everybody was outraged over a civilian's recent death—a missionary and father of three, which meant on top of everything, an entire Baptist congregation was out for blood.

Not good.

Civilian deaths meant a lockdown on business. Police cracked down hard, raiding Irish and Legion drug operations, which threatened our alliance with them because we no longer had Alessio's connections.

A chime echoed through my home, the persistent ringing hinting at my visitor's animosity. I glanced through the leaded windows. The glimmer of blonde hair and a tell-tale khaki wool coat set my alarms on high-alert.

Oh shit.

Brooke.

She was a working girl at Sanctum that I'd fucked around with last year after Serena's death. Brooke had big fake tits, a model-thin body, and loved kink. The perfect submissive. She dropped to her knees when I pointed at the floor, but she had one huge drawback.

Insanity.

I hurried downstairs and froze as my unsuspecting wife unlatched the door, having already buzzed Brooke in. It was like stopping to check out a car crash. I had to watch.

Sunshine spilled over Carmela's bronzed skin. Her lips pulled into a bright smile that faltered with Brooke's accusing glare.

"Hello, I'm Brooke." Her nasal, West Coast accent shot into my house. "So you're the wife."

"Carmela." She hesitated before shaking Brooke's hand. "Can I help you?"

"You can step aside. I need to talk to your husband."

Carmela didn't budge. She took up more space between Brooke and the threshold. I expected her to call for me, but Carmela didn't tear her gaze from the blonde.

"Who are you?"

"His girlfriend," Brooke said, lowering her shades. "Didn't he tell you?"

That crazy bitch.

Carmela crossed her arms, not taking the bait. "He wouldn't invite you to our place."

"You don't know that."

Carmela frowned. "What do you want?"

To wreck my home, obviously.

"To speak with Michael."

"Yeah, I don't think so."

I renewed my descent, amused by the whip-like crack in Carmela's voice. She was keeping a remarkably calm head. Her lack of giving a fuck made me swell with pride.

Brooke tapped her heel. "Honey, Michael and I—"

"*Mrs. Costa.*"

"Mrs. Costa. Michael and I go way back."

"I don't care," she deadpanned, closing the door. "This is my house. He's my husband. Get your own."

Brooke wedged her fist into the frame. "He'll be upset when he finds out you did this."

"I don't give a damn. March your fake Louboutins off my porch, or I'm calling the police."

Time to intervene.

I strode across the room. The snap of my soles on the wood echoed, and they glanced at me. My rage must've been obvious because Brooke staggered before I slammed the door shut.

"Daddy? Who's there?"

Shit.

Mariette stood several feet away, gaping at us. "Why was she so mad?"

"Nobody, hon. Just a crazy person." I caught Carmela's waist, her body folding into mine with zero resistance. "Sweetheart, why don't you fix the children a snack?"

Carmela may have played it cool in front of Brooke, but when the door closed, her eyes flashed at me.

"Why don't *you*?"

"I'll take care of the nutcase. Go on."

I grasped her chin and kissed her frown lines, then her cheek, and then her angry pout. A shock jumped into me with the slightest pressure of her lips.

Jesus, it was electric between us.

Jaded women like Brooke didn't hold a candle to my wife. Carmela's buttery-soft mouth melted into mine, tasting like vanilla, like the girls I'd chased in my early twenties, her purity as refreshing as iced tea. I angled my head and met her tentative kiss with a harsh stroke.

Carmela sank her nails into my side.

I pulled away, my heart thundering.

"I'll be in the kitchen." Carmela detached from me, red-faced and feral. She looked like she wanted to clock me.

I'd get shanked in my sleep.

Where the hell was my self-control?

I watched Carmela sweep Mariette from the foyer, zeroing in on my wife's ass. It took a moment to remember the psycho standing outside. I wrenched open the door.

Unsurprisingly, Brooke hadn't left.

"A nutcase? You'll *take care* of me?" she exploded as soon as I stepped out. "Who do you think you are?"

"A powerful man who can make your life miserable." I seized her arm and shoved her backward. "What are you doing here?"

"I heard you were married!"

So she'd decided to show up at my home like a lunatic. No fucking boundaries. I'd ghosted her after she wouldn't stop texting me. I'd blocked her number, twice. She'd bought another line just to harass me.

What was it with me and crazy chicks?

Did I have a sign embedded on my forehead?

Brooke's tearful gaze slid to my living room window, where Carmela observed, arms folded. "How could you marry *her*?"

"Watch your tone."

Her voice broke. "Are you in love with her?"

"Is that any of your business?"

"You can't be." She seemed tortured by the idea, which struck me as hilarious. "You wouldn't have fooled around with me."

"She wasn't in my life then, and blowing me on a semi-regular basis hardly gives you the right to be jealous. I never promised you anything."

Brooke's knees hit the ground. "Please."

A pretty girl on her knees was my weakness. It should've filled my cock with heat, but I was as limp as a rag doll.

"Get up."

"Make me," she purred.

"This isn't a scene. I was done with you months ago. You're lucky I don't kill you for ambushing me at my house and harassing my wife. Leave my property."

"You said you weren't over Serena!" She shot upright and nudged my chest. "Why would you say that?"

"I lied to get rid of you."

"You're a fucking bastard, Michael!"

This was what I deserved for letting down a woman easy. *I'm never sticking my dick in crazy, ever again.*

She resisted the pressure as I wheeled her toward the gate. "I'll tell everybody the truth about you!"

"You going to tell them the size, shape, and taste of my cock? Feel free to shout it from the rooftops."

"You traffic women into Sanctum. You're a *monster.*"

What a ridiculous lie.

I pushed her onto the sidewalk. "Goodbye, Brooke."

"I know about Serena! She used to be a Sanctum girl. You met her there and got her pregnant."

Why was she digging into my past?

"Careful, Brooke. Remember who you're talking to."

I clearly needed the same reminder.

Brooke was a danger whore. Me strangling her would probably be the highlight of her miserable life.

"You know what the girls think of you?" She clung to my arm, and I shook her off. "Some of them love you. Others believe you murdered your wife."

I slammed the wrought-iron gate and stalked to the house. Brooke's threats followed me in high-pitched screams.

She would reveal my crimes. She hated me. She'd take me down.

Get in line.

Serena overdosed in rehab. Everybody knew that.

Didn't they?

Brooke was lying. She'd thrown that in my face to rattle me, and it worked. The thought that I'd mistreated Serena for a single second during our dumpster-fire of a relationship left me so agitated that I charged into a pink and black blur.

I steadied Carmela with a hand on her waist. The sight of her froze my anger. She was stunning in the kimono. A wide sleeve fell when she clutched her chestnut waves, exposing a length of her slender, olive-skinned arm. My mouth went dry as I took in her curves filling the silk, the tempting shadow of her collarbone, the peaks of her breasts, the hollow at the base of her throat begging for a kiss.

"Carmela, she's nothing to me."

She tucked a strand behind her ear. "I don't care."

"You threatened to call the police."

Her brows pinched as she breezed from my side, heading to the living room. "That was for your benefit, not mine."

I yanked her into my arms.

She turned, red patches burning high on her cheeks. "*Michael*. Stop it."

"Not until you admit that you're pissed."

"Fine. I'm angry." She elbowed out of my grip, dropping her deadpan. "I'm trapped in this house with a man I loathe, who has mistresses and invites them over."

"Did you miss the part where I threw her ass out?"

Suspicion and fury darkened her gaze. "I will not tolerate another woman, Michael. I have my pride. If you're unfaithful, I'll leave you."

She thought I'd let her go?

Cute. "I'm not a cheater."

"Does it matter if I believe you?"

Yes, it fucking matters. "If you're going to hate me, I'd like to know I've earned it."

"You kidnapped my father. Stole my freedom and happiness. Trust me, it's earned."

She stepped around me.

I blocked her path. "The same applies to you."

"Excuse me?"

"I demand loyalty." I leaned in, her vanilla scent triggering a dozen memories from that night. "Like it or not, I'm your only option."

"You may be my husband, but *you don't* own me."

Carmela shoved me, much harder than Brooke's pathetic tap on my chest. The force sent me back a step.

The first real smile in days carved into my face. If she was this upset over cheating, she'd already bought into this marriage. I had no intention of messing with our life together, but Carmela's head?

That was fair game.

TEN

CARMELA

DON'T COME BACK.

I hovered over the send button. Was that line too ominous? I gave my email another read-through.

Dear Mia,

This will be my last message. I can't go into detail. I know that's vague, but it's not safe for us to communicate. You're better off wherever you are than here. Boston's streets are flooded with violence. It's only a matter of time before this city implodes. I'm only staying for Mom and Dad's sakes.

If I'm happy about anything, it's that you and Alessio escaped. I'm proud of you for making that leap of faith. It can't have been easy.

Please live life to the fullest.

I wish you, Alessio, and baby Lexy all the health and happiness. I love you.

Don't tell me where you are.

Don't come back.

C

She'd hop on the first flight to Boston if I used that. I selected the block of text, hit Delete, and began anew.

Dear Mia,

I'm sorry that Lexy is teething! Hopefully, she grows out of it fast. Poor thing! That video of her tantrum was adorbs. I have so many pics of Lexy on my phone that people ask if she's my baby.

As much as I adore updates, don't send any photos. Vinn asks about Alessio whenever he sees me. They're obsessed with finding you guys, and I know you're taking precautions, but it's not worth the risk.

Everybody's great! Mom and Dad are homebodies. Dad's into gardening. He's overzealous with the shears. Our rhododendrons are bare. Drives Mom nuts.

I'm doing well. I don't live in Boston-proper anymore, but guess what? I'm working full-time at Sanctum as a bartender.

Isn't that crazy? Michael gave me the job. And you're right. He is such a sweetheart! <3 <3 <3

Give kisses to baby Lexy from me!

Love,

C

The entire email was a crock of shit. I sent it anyway.

It got the point across without raising her suspicions, and I even laid the groundwork for a romance between Michael and me. She'd hate missing my wedding, but at least she wouldn't be blindsided if the news spread to their hideout. My sister would lose her mind if she knew what really happened.

I was sandwiched between twenty-something-year-olds tapping on laptops. I was getting used to my new routine, which was waking up early enough to make the kids breakfast under the watchful nannies. People followed me all day. Having a member of the staff hang over my shoulder as I made tuna salad sandwiches was off-putting.

I hated Michael, but his children were adorable.

It was impossible to frown when Matteo flung his arms around my neck every morning, or when Mariette declared me her best friend after a few days of giving her my undivided attention. They were a welcome distraction, but I was restless.

So I'd walked to the closest café during my time off with an escort, a surly, tall whip of a man named Vitale. He smoked outside despite the stink-eyes from customers. Rain sluiced the coffee shop's windows as I drank my tea, distracted by a video playing on a man's screen.

"Boston mayor calls state of emergency as gang violence terrorizes citizens. Up next in an hour: the Commission of Inquiry of Public Contracts in Construction exposes corruption in city hall—"

The voice cut off as he inserted a headphone into the laptop.

Movement behind the glass caught my eye. A man slid into view. I recognized Michael's blazer and stowed my cell. He approached Vitale, who tapped the storefront and pointed at me. Vitale snubbed the cigarette on his shoe and strolled away. Michael bent his head, met my gaze, and waved.

Hello, asshole.

He beamed as he entered the store. Female heads turned as he weaved through tables. His soft apology brushed my ears like silk when he bumped into a young woman, who blushed as he stepped around her. He was excellent at appearing harmless.

I stopped that train of thought.

I didn't need to think about his other talents.

He pulled out a chair and sat. "Is the tea at home not good enough?"

"I wanted a minute alone without you hovering over me like a gargoyle."

"Privacy must be hard to find in a nine-bedroom mansion sitting on a three-acre property." Michael cocked his head. "Anything you want to tell me?"

Shit. "Not really."

"Carmela. You're up to something."

"I must have nothing to do besides watch your kids and suck your cock."

A smile ticked across his cheek. "If only."

"Go to hell, Michael. I have a life."

"And who have you shared it with?"

Nobody.

I'd managed my dad's legitimate business since my early twenties. It was unorthodox, a don allowing his daughter so much control, but I liked managing the restaurant and casino. I'd always assumed Dad was grooming me. Then he set me straight. My *husband* would handle all that. My duty was to tie the knot with a stranger, Alessio Salvatore. It'd been arranged that we'd be married.

I was scared.

Then a predator swooped in while I was vulnerable.

"I had my family until you took them away."

"Yes, that murdering alcoholic you call a father, your mom, and Mia. Where is Mia, by the way?" Michael leaned over, his brows knitted in mock concern. "Did you file a missing persons report?"

"I haven't gotten around to it yet."

"Interesting. How long have they been gone? Three months?"

Give or take. "They're probably having the time of their lives in the Amazon where there's no cell phone reception."

He stared. "That's what you're going with?"

I drummed the table, wishing my husband and his inconvenient questions would disappear. "It's a possibility."

"Alessio in the jungle, with the snakes, spiders, and bugs," he mused, laughing. "Have you met your brother-in-law? He's a guido, through and through. He's not hunkering down without an Italian deli in walking distance."

"It was a freaking joke. I have no idea where they are."

"I'm relieved that you still have a sense of humor, what with your sister being missing and all. I can't imagine. If it were me, I wouldn't rest until she was found. I'd lose my fucking mind. You must be worried sick."

Message received.

I kept my mouth shut and pried my mug from Michael. "I'm fine."

"Oh, honey. I wonder about you sometimes." Michael patted my hand. "You may fold under questioning."

Fuck, fuck, fuck.

I stood, cramming the phone into my bag. I flung my purse over my shoulder, nearly hitting Michael's face. I bulldozed past the queue of caffeine addicts and almost crashed into a woman balancing four coffees on a tray.

Michael caught up, catching the door on his elbow. "Hit a nerve?"

"Don't."

Michael pinched my wrist, dragging me to a halt. "I'm not an idiot, Carmela. The moment he stopped checking in, I knew. Everybody *knows.*"

"What do you want me to say? I have no clue where they are."

"I want the same thing as you—for Alessio to stay gone."

Like I believed that. "Whatever."

"I'm just saying, you don't have to lie."

"I'm not lying."

He grabbed my bicep and steered me to his side. "This is important. Vinn won't forget Alessio. The longer he stays away, the worse Vinn's retribution gets."

Gooseflesh puckered where he held my arm. "What are you suggesting?"

"If Vinn discovers my *wife* hid Alessio's location this whole time, he'll assume I helped you. That would be very bad for both of us."

Vinn was yet another Nick. What could he do to me that hadn't been done already?

"I'm not afraid of Vinn. He's a gangster with a chip on his shoulder. I've met his type. They're all the same."

"Maybe your spine is made of steel, but I doubt you want orphaning my two kids on your conscience."

I bit my lip. "Vinn wouldn't do that to you."

"There's nothing my cousin wouldn't do."

Michael had to be bluffing. The Costa boss wouldn't kill Michael, a made man, without good reason. Then again, I'd heard things about Vinn. Alessio called him Mussolini, among other degrading names.

"Either I bring you home and tie you up, or you tell me the truth."

It was on the tip of my tongue to challenge him, but it wouldn't make a difference.

Michael knew.

I had to tell him something. "They asked me to come with them."

"When?"

"Before they left. I decided to stay, and we said our goodbyes. I have no idea where they are, Michael. I swear to God."

Michael took my face, his hands gliding over my cheeks. He searched me, eyes dancing over my features. "Are you in contact with them?"

"*No.*"

He sighed, not looking convinced. "I'll give you the benefit of the doubt, but you better not be lying, Carmela."

My insides still boiled from his threat, and I wanted to strike back. "You're lucky your kids don't take after you."

He raised his brow. "Matteo is practically my clone."

"In looks, maybe. You couldn't be more different in personality."

"How so?"

"He's sweet. You're horrible. He's sensitive. You're a cold bastard. He cares about people. You don't."

Michael smiled. "He's just more adept at manipulating you."

"He's *four.*"

"That's old enough to know how to get you on his side. He knows you have a soft heart, and he's taking advantage."

"Don't project your motives onto your son."

"Everything is black and white with you, isn't it? Good or bad. He's innocent. I'm corrupt. That's not the way the world works." Michael palmed my shoulders, leading me across the parking lot. "Stop thinking of me as a villain. I'm your husband."

"Like being forced to sign papers in a church means anything."

"It does to me."

A darkness had slivered into his voice—a hint of the monster.

My spirits plummeted as he showed me to the car. "This marriage will never work."

"We got along fine on our wedding night." He opened the door, gesturing inside with his head. "Get in."

"You used me to prove a point."

"You're right. I proved that you want me just as much as I want you, and it's eating you up."

A raindrop smacked my cheek. Michael flicked it off before it rolled down, the gesture making my insides somersault.

"What were you doing here, Carmela? Planning your escape?"

"I'm not going anywhere. Your kids need help with you as their role model."

"Couldn't agree more."

ELEVEN

MICHAEL

Some women wanted children.

Others liked the *idea* of them.

Serena was the latter. She didn't realize how much she hated motherhood until the responsibility dropped in her lap. She was decent for a while, and then it got too hard. She stopped trying. My children paid the price for her coldhearted approach to parenting.

Carmela woke when she said she would. She took the kids to the park, made sure Mariette finished her homework, and helped my daughter prepare a memory box of Serena's things. When Mariette missed her mom, she opened it. Simple, and it *worked*. Mariette kept it under her bed.

After a couple of weeks with zero hiccups from Carmela, I relaxed. I checked in on her through the camera system, but not that often. She was nothing like Serena, and I frequently found new qualities to appreciate, like Carmela's utter lack of drama.

Several days ago, Mariette broke into our walk-in closet and found Carmela's makeup. She'd *accidentally* defaced one of Carmela's expensive purses. I'd spent hours dreading her meltdown, but when Carmela returned from her salon appointment, she shrugged off the damage. Mariette's confusion when Carmela hugged her stood out in my mind because I'd remembered feeling the same bewilderment.

Maybe I'd gotten used to crazy.

I never realized we could handle problems without a screaming match that took down the walls. Fucking and fighting—it was all I knew. Carmela showed me that there were more sane ways of existing.

I stepped outside.

A warm front had left us with mild weather. Dew clung to the grass, but it was drying in the vibrant sunshine. Yellow finches jumped from branches as I walked under the dogwood. The garden was turning green. Life ran through the dead-looking vines that snarled the property, blooming with thick leaves.

My gorgeous brunette sprawled on a blanket under the growing rosebushes. Her caramel-streaked hair gleamed where the dappled light stroked her. She lay on her side, wearing a bright pink cut-off over black leggings, whispering to my son in a sweet voice as she tried to coax him with tubs of Play-Doh.

My four-year-old shook his head and disappeared behind a tree. Smiling, Carmela rose to her feet and chased Matteo, who shrieked when her arms wrapped his middle. She tickled his chest and kissed his cheek. My son was beside himself with all the attention. He couldn't take his eyes off her.

Neither could I.

Carmela had rolled her ebony mane into a messy bun. Still, it didn't distract from her pillowy lips, the arching eyebrows, and her irresistible curves. I imagined her in heels and a swimsuit, posing next to a vintage car. Honestly, there wasn't much she could do without making my jaw drop.

Matteo's head turned. "Daddy!"

He ran, a blur of rainbow tie-dye, until he crashed into my knees. My chest tightened as he locked my legs in a vise grip. When I bent over, he threw his arms around me. I hoisted him to my hip, lamenting the day he'd be too big to hold. Tears misted his lashes.

"You okay, buddy?"

"He was a second ago." Carmela joined my side in a breeze of floral scents, rubbing Matteo's back. "Maybe he needs a nap."

"Nah. He has preschool soon."

Matteo disengaged from me, sobbing. His pain rammed into my stomach like a swift kick. It wasn't the usual I-skinned-my-knee crying. Matteo probably had no idea what to make of Carmela's undivided attention. My poor kid had never really had a mother.

He looked on the verge of a meltdown, and Carmela's affection seemed to do the trick. He bawled, hiding his face in my neck.

"What happened?" Carmela smoothed his hair, looking stricken. "What's the matter, honey?"

Matteo shook his head.

I patted his shoulder as my shirt collar became soaked. I sank onto the steps leading to my house as he curled on my lap, bawling. Every time Carmela touched Matteo, he howled louder.

Carmela appeared to take it as a personal failure. She stepped away, her glow draining from her features. "What did I do wrong?"

"Nothing." I sagged with relief when a car rolled to the curb and honked. "Look, your ride to school is here!"

Matteo faced it, hiccupping. He slid off me, his tears glistening. His crying stopped when he spotted the black Lexus.

A bewildered Carmela handed over his things. We walked Matteo to the driver, who packed him inside. He waved at Carmela and me. She waved back, beaming. When the car disappeared down the block, her smile vanished.

She hadn't let go of my hand. "Why is he so upset?"

"Four-year-olds cry about everything."

She still gazed in the car's direction. "He gets overwhelmed easily."

"That's courtesy of their dearly departed mother."

"What happened?" Carmela squeezed my fingers, her voice husky. "Did she hit them?"

A white van in a parking lot burned in my mind. The echoes of their screaming crashed through the birdsong, siphoning the warmth from the world until the coldness seeped into my chest.

I pulled from her grip and strode inside.

Carmela was clearly horrified. She was already assuming the worst, and I couldn't bear her pity. I'd done what I could to minimize the damage Serena had caused, but nothing ever alleviated the guilt.

"Michael?"

I bristled. "Don't push it."

"I'm not asking for the gory details. I just want the general idea of what they went through. If they've been abused—"

"Unless you're ready to spill the darkest moments of *your* life, *leave it alone.*" I seized the shopping tote I'd left on the kitchen table and pushed it in her arms. "I got you a present."

Carmela set it aside, glaring at me.

"Open it."

Her lips flattened as she yanked the tissue paper, pulling out a Burberry bag.

I'd found a store and searched for the bag my daughter had ruined, but they no longer carried that model, so I'd bought something similar. I had no fucking clue about purses. An employee picked it.

"What's this for?"

"Mariette destroyed yours. I thought you'd like a replacement."

Carmela dropped it on the granite, softening. "You didn't have to do this, Michael."

"I wanted to."

"I appreciate the gesture," she said bracingly. "But I don't care about the damned purse. You can't throw gifts at me and expect your problems to disappear."

Well, it had worked for the last wife.

"Don't ask questions you can't handle the answer to."

"Who says I can't?"

Because she was as pure as the driven snow. "Life isn't a fairy-tale. The answers aren't always pretty."

"Believe me, I know."

"How could you possibly understand?"

Carmela shot me a look filled with poison.

"Something you want to say?"

She held up a hand. "Don't tempt me."

"You're dying to have a go, so do it. Get it out of your system."

"I like your kids, but I do not like *you*." Carmela seized a dish-cloth from a drawer and wiped crumbs from the counter. "And I don't think I ever will."

Not surprising. "Keep going."

"You're a bully," she boomed, throwing the rag in the sink. "A joyless asshole. You're lonely. You're hurting over your brother and Serena."

"You couldn't be more wrong."

She cocked her head and smiled. "About her or the rest of it?"

I'd kick her out if my children didn't already love her. "How am I joyless?"

"You dodge family events. You don't want to join the band or the pajama dance party—"

"Banging on pots and pans is not music."

She glared at me. "It's fun."

"It's rupturing my eardrums."

"I'm helping your ungrateful ass, which you'd notice if you stopped behaving like a jerk!"

Carmela blew air in a steady stream, the only sign that she was distressed beyond the slight pink of her cheeks. I'd known no one with more grace. Beautiful, even when she gazed at me like slime under her heel.

I pulled her close. "Do you hate me, Carmela?"

Some of the fire in her eyes dimmed.

"You're giving me little reason not to."

"I'm trying to change that."

She glanced at the purse. "Why?"

"Looking at you is torture, but not touching you is *killing* me."

Her hourglass curves filled my hands, triggering a dozen images of us tangled in the sheets. Carmela's flush had spread to her neck and chest, and I dipped, kissing her cheek. Her lips parted, and she let out the smallest sigh.

"Should I tell you what I think of you?"

Her nostrils flared. "I'm good, thanks. I've had my fill of truth."

"I might surprise you."

"I don't need to hear it."

"The man before me left a deep wound." I traced an invisible scar over her heart. "You're hurting. You're lonely. And you'll be eating from my hand soon...because only I can give what you want most in the world."

She lifted her head, bewildered.

Nothing was more exciting than a strong woman surrendering control—that collapse of every layer of defense until all that remained was their true essence. The key to Carmela's soul wasn't hard—I'd discovered it within a few minutes of conversation.

She had yet to figure me out.

TWELVE
MICHAEL

I WAS A GANGSTER, not a diplomat.

But I was expected to fix our fraying relationship with Legion MC. The bikers didn't understand why we couldn't call off police raids anymore. They wanted a bigger cut. They demanded this and *that* while they terrorized Boston with their sock-puppet club, Rage Machine. The president of Legion had requested a meeting, so we booked an event venue where violence was unlikely to break out, a brick dining hall lined with elk tapestries.

Rich people and their majestic animals.

The Ivy League school, Bourton, was not the ideal place to discuss business, but it was neutral ground. Nobody would be tempted to open fire on a college campus. Nico had donated so much cash that all we had to do was mention him. Plus, the food wasn't bad.

My olive branch included free barbecue, which the biker scum would devour like rats. Steam spiraled from the heated trays that'd been picked through minutes before the president arrived. Carmela and I sat against the wall, surrounded by suits. She wore a pink dress with a plunging neckline, and I couldn't look at her without imagining my mouth on her tits. Eventually, I'd have to find Vinn, but I had zero desire to detach from the brightest thing in the room.

She was in a testy mood, probably because she kept catching me ogling her cleavage. She tapped my chin, forcing my gaze to crash into her deep browns for the third time.

"Where's your self-restraint?"

Almost dead. "I'm restraining myself right now."

Carmela rolled her winged eyes, dismissing me. She drank her Prosecco, her neck tipped in a graceful arch.

"You act like you never moaned my name during sex."

She choked, her lips shining with alcohol. I imagined claiming her pout and sucking it dry, or better yet, spilling more of that golden liquid between her breasts and licking them clean.

Our wedding night was never far away. Every smoking-hot minute of handling Carmela was fresh in my mind. She had a gorgeous body. The taste of her invaded my senses when I jerked off. She'd infused my blood with reckless lust that wouldn't shut up.

Carmela set the glass down. "Can we not talk about—"

"I love the sound of you coming. I wonder what noise you'll make when I fuck your mouth."

Carmela ground her teeth. "Not going to happen."

"Yeah, I guess finishing in your mouth is a waste of cum."

She threw me a suspicious look. "What's *that* supposed to mean?"

I was dropping anvil-sized hints, hoping the pieces would click in her brain. All she had to do was *ask*—my answer would be *yes*.

I leaned across the table, fighting to keep my voice even, to be patient. "You know what it means."

"No, I don't."

Perhaps she was that obtuse. "Jesus."

"Either explain or shut up."

"I can't. That's not doing you any favors." My knuckles glided under her neck, pressing into her throbbing pulse. "Figure out what you want."

"My family."

This was a waste of time. If she wasn't ready to accept it, forcing her down the path would inflict more damage.

She flinched when I kissed her forehead and darkened as though clouds shifted overhead. "I'm owed your trust, but you won't leave me alone with the kids."

"I will. Someday. Don't I deserve points for that?"

Apparently not.

Her face crumpled as she ripped from my hands and stalked away, disappearing into the crowd. A stone sank in my stomach as heads turned to watch the blur of pink march across the marble floor.

A couple of facts became apparent.

One—Carmela had a mental block the size of Texas.

Two—I wished I were on her good side.

It was out of character for me. Carmela could assume whatever she wanted about me. I was trying to get laid. It'd be a win-win situation. She needed to snap out of her denial.

Maybe that would never happen.

I couldn't trust her, and she'd never see past the bastard who had tortured her father. After Serena, I sure as hell wouldn't invest myself in another relationship. Marrying Carmela was for my children, and maybe a little for my career. She wouldn't love me, and that was fine—the hooker who loved me was *insane*.

Carmela would love my kids.

That was all that mattered.

My mood nosedived as a broad shoulder nudged mine.

Vinn scraped a seat and stole Carmela's vacated spot. He settled into the chair, which groaned with his weight. His clean-shaven appearance and black suit channeled an Italian James Bond. I still wasn't used to seeing my cousin in suits. He was more of a hoodie and jeans guy, but he had to dress the part.

He flung an arm across my shoulders. "Trouble in paradise?"

"We're great."

"Oh, Mike. What did you expect? You kidnapped her dad. Everything she says and does is under duress."

"Did I ask your goddamned opinion?"

"If you had, I would've told you not to marry a stranger. Why *did* you do it?"

"She checks off the boxes on my list."

"So do a million other girls."

Vinn's stare bored into me, but I had no interest in listening to him mock me for the next half hour when I gave him the real reason.

"I don't regret it." I finished my drink, the heat hitting my throat. "She makes Mariette and Matteo happy, and that's all that matters."

"You almost sound like you believe that."

"Mind your own business."

"Fine. Have you asked about Alessio?"

I dug into my glass. "She has no idea where he is."

"You think she's telling the truth?"

"Yeah, I've access to her emails."

Which was a lie, but I planned on hacking them eventually.

Vinn rubbed his temples, his forehead rippling with an uncharacteristic show of strain.

"Alessio will come back." I pictured him in a Hawaiian button-up and board shorts, and snorted. "He's too Italian to be content with grocery store cold cuts that taste like ass. He'll miss his espressos, cannolis, prosciutto di parma, and he'll come back."

"I swear to God—he lost his fucking marbles once that kid was born."

"Someday, it'll happen to you, too." I patted his bicep. "Then you'll understand why I married Carmela."

"I'm not having kids, ever, and you marrying Carmela will always be crazy." He gestured across the room. "Speaking of, you might want to save her."

"What?"

He pointed at a drunk Anthony, who swayed as he chatted with my wife. Anthony was the son of Nico Costa, the actual boss of the family who was serving a five-year sentence in jail. Anthony was an alumnus of this ridiculous school. He'd graduated with a bachelor's in psychology and had done nothing with his life but party and abuse drugs. We used to hang out all the time until I wised up and ditched the cocaine.

All I'd needed was the right motivator—fatherhood.

I had hoped he'd have a come-to-Jesus moment, but the man was thirty-four.

My chair pushed back before I realized I'd stood. Bodies blocked my way to Carmela, whose smile widened as Anthony leaned in with a conspiratorial wink. He wore a Bourton blazer over slacks and looked surprisingly put together, given his state. That was the danger with Anthony. At first glance, it was hard to tell he was so troubled.

He caught my eye and toasted the air.

"Mikey!"

I groaned at the nickname. "Hey, Anthony."

"*Tony*, man. It's Tony. How many times do I have to remind you?"

"At least a few more."

I buried my grin and grabbed Carmela's waist, distracted by the skintight fabric hugging her hips. I cinched her to my side. Then I pressed my mouth under her chin, kissing that delectable spot.

Carmela beamed, sliding her arms in my jacket.

"You two are so cute." Anthony jostled his drink, the ice clinking the glass. "Makes me want to vomit."

Pissant. "Pretty sure that's the Jägerbomb."

Anthony drank, frowning. "What do you *see* in him?"

Your jealousy's showing, you snide little fuck.

I held in the comment because I was eager to hear what she'd say.

"Plenty." Carmela placed a hand on my chest and stared at me. "Michael has a great sense of humor. He respects me. He's loyal—he lays everything on the line for family."

"Any plans for children?"

I peeked at Carmela, who seemed unwilling to answer. She swallowed hard and glanced at me.

"Carmela's dying for a baby." I smirked at my wife, whose face registered naked shock. "We'll get to that soon, won't we?"

Anthony sipped his cocktail. "I've never met a guy who wanted kids."

"Nonsense. What about Alessio?"

"He's a weirdo—doesn't count." Anthony shrugged, slurring his words. "Seems to be something men put up with to keep a woman."

"Not for me."

Anthony shot me a black look.

"That's what I love about you," Carmela gushed in a sweet tone she reserved for Mariette. "You are an amazing father."

Did she mean it?

She'd said it before, but never with a caress in her voice. It hit me in the only place I was vulnerable. I had to know if she was messing with me, but I couldn't read anything in her expression.

Carmela's hands glided up my throat. She stopped, her mouth centimeters away.

I leaned in, my heart hammering—

Anthony made a juvenile noise, cleaving through our energy. He murmured a goodbye before stomping off.

I could've hurled my glass at his head.

Carmela slipped out of my jacket and stepped back, her cheeks pink. "He's a character."

"He's a pain in my fucking ass." I growled, checking my watch. "Damn. I have a meeting I couldn't care less about, but when I return you're sitting in my lap all night."

"Won't that give you an erection?"

Probably. "Try not to break too many hearts."

THIRTEEN
CARMELA

I HATED WISEGUY PARTIES.

My dad couldn't stand that I was twenty-seven and unmarried, so every few months he'd invite all the single mafiosos for a barbecue. Mom bore the brunt of the cooking, so I'd helped roll the dough for the tomato pie and kept the liquor flowing for the greedy sons of bitches.

They'd packed my parents' home like vermin—fat, power-hungry, cheese-eating rats. Some were old enough to be my father. Men with pot bellies. Guys who talked too loud and leered at me with disgusting grins.

I felt like I was reliving the past at this party with all the Costa soldiers and their wives. There were no families. It was mind-numbingly boring, and I didn't have Matteo and Mariette to keep me company.

I nursed my Prosecco, unable to shake Michael and the things he'd said. *Carmela's dying for a baby.* I'd never so much as hinted at that, despite it being one hundred percent true.

What the hell was he playing at?

Men wearing leather drifted through the crowd, heading for the buffet. My pulse galloped as six-foot giant with a ginger beard loaded his plate with steak. Tattoos decorated his arms, and a Legion MC patch covered his chest.

Nick's gang.

My stomach filled with ice.

Michael had mentioned it was a get-together with his partners, but I had no idea that meant *Legion*. Nick could be here.

I had to leave. I opened my phone and called him, but it went straight to voicemail. My thoughts raced. I was better off at the house than here. Staying put me at risk of bumping into Nick, who likely still lived in a fantasy land where I was his loving girlfriend and he didn't repulse me.

I pushed people aside in my haste, bursting from the service exit behind the kitchens.

Frigid air stung my feet and legs. Men lounged against the brick, smoking. Leather cuts flashed into view as I hurried past.

A wolf whistle cut me to the bone.

"Lift up your dress. Show us that pussy."

"Want a ride, baby?"

The familiar baritone poured gasoline on the flames. The universe couldn't be that cruel.

"What's your name, beautiful?" A man peeled from the wall, flicking his cigarette. "Hold up."

I picked up my pace, my heels cracking the pavement. A lightbox glowed ahead. If I reached it, I could call campus security—

"Hey, I'm talking to you." Heavy footsteps thumped the concrete with a jingle of metal. "Baby, hold on."

He pawed my shoulder as something drifted into my nose.

Cloves.

I used to connect the scent with home, but now it reminded me of death. The smell came from Nick's ebony cigarettes. So many times, I'd watched him light up. Before our love story turned into *Fatal Attraction,* I'd bought boxes and slipped them in places for him to find.

"I said, hold the fuck on." His playfulness evaporated as he dug into my forearm. His mouth twisted into a scowl that smoothed over when I spun around. "*Beauty.*"

He looked the same as he did months ago, still wearing his golden hair in a messy California wave. A snarl of one-percenter imagery wrapped his sleeves in vivid, black ink. A dark shadow covered his jaw and cheeks. He kept his beard short because it grew in patchy chunks. Nick cupped my face, his eyes glazed with lust.

"Hi, Nick."

"*Hi, Nick.* That's all I get?"

Nick's broad hand settled over my chest as he pushed, with way too much force. When he'd hurt me, he fed me a line of bullshit. *I don't know my strength, babe.* Michael's imperial frame was just as strong, and he'd never injured me.

I had the feeling he'd scoff at a man who used that excuse.

"Nick, it hurts."

Nick hissed, crushing me against the wall. His fingers glided up my neck, and squeezed my artery. I slumped, my heart pounding, my lungs struggling. He loved keeping me on the edge of suffocation.

"Nick, stop."

"Where have you been? I've searched everywhere."

He pinched, cutting off my tether to life. Nick watched me gulp for air, his lips curled in sadistic greed. His mouth caught mine, hungry, devouring. A tide of vomit threatened as his tongue slashed my lips open. He tasted like his disgusting cigarettes, the clove spice invading my senses. He kissed me as black spots ate my vision. He released me, the rush of oxygen flooding my body with vigor.

I yanked to the side. "Get off me."

"I'm not done with you, Beauty."

"Back away."

"You want to talk?" He retreated several inches. He sighed, zeroing in on my cleavage. "Start by explaining yourself."

"I've been busy."

"Doing what, running out on me?"

Nick had no idea I was married. If he found out, he'd crush my throat. A faint tingle shot down my spine. I'd been prepared to die for a long time. I wished he'd just do it.

At least I'd be free of him.

Suspicion darkened his gaze. "Carmela."

"I'm here with someone else."

"You're messing with me." His finger stabbed my neck. He drew a line as though mimicking a blade, his nail scoring my flesh. "You must be. I'm a jealous man. You know I take no prisoners."

"We broke up."

"I never agreed to that. You walked out on me, and ever since then we've been playing this cat-and-mouse game." He slipped under my dress, sliding up my thighs to cup my ass. "I find you. We fight. We fuck. Then you run. I'll admit, it was fun for a while, but now I need you back."

I ripped him off me. "Nick, it's over."

"The hell it is. I love you."

No, no, no. "I don't feel the same anymore."

Nick yanked me off the wall. "You can't mean that."

"I do. We weren't good together."

"Bullshit. We have what everybody in the world wants."

"Which is what?"

"Love."

He wasn't capable of empathy, and I didn't love him. Maybe I thought I did in the beginning, but I was so naïve. His over-protectiveness, the grand gestures, the over-the-top displays of affection, the lavish gifts—they were a hollow imitation of love.

"You're my old lady." Nick tapped on his bicep, to the black-and-white rose. "You're in my heart, Carmela. In my soul. I'm tired of banging girls who look like you but aren't you. I want you every day, not once in a while."

As though a tattoo proved anything but his obsession.

"You beat me constantly."

He rolled his eyes. "You're exaggerating."

"I'm not. You hurt me so often that it took weeks to heal from everything you did."

"You are crazy—"

"You raped me in front of your brothers."

"I warned you. I told you that a relationship with me would be intense. *You said you didn't care.*"

"I had no idea what I was getting myself into."

"If I was a monster, it was because you pushed me."

"I never want to see you again." I wrenched from his grasp and rubbed at the red mark. "We're over."

"No." Nick shook his head, his expression maddening. "You will get over this."

I headed toward the service entrance, and Nick's toxic presence followed, demanding my attention.

"Don't you fucking turn away." He seized my left arm, scowling at something.

I balled my fist. Too late.

"What the fuck?" He brushed his thumb over my wedding ring, his voice rising into a shout. "What did you do!"

"Nick—"

"You're married?" He let my hand fall as though he was gutted. "How could you?"

"How could I find happiness? How dare I be with someone who doesn't hit me? He treats me like a human being and not a blow-up doll, which is all you've ever done."

"You slept with me two months ago!"

"What was I supposed to do? Fight you? You broke into my house. You're sick. Crawl into a hole and die." My throat tightened as I staved off the images from our last encounter. "I fucking hate you. I hate you so much."

"Carmela—"

"No. You had your chance, and you ruined it."

A heavy silence filled the space between us, broken only by his brothers, who were cat-calling another woman.

A bitter smile staggered across his face. "Who is it, Carmela?"

"None of your business."

"Give me his name. You said you loved me. You wanted us to marry and have kids, or did I *imagine* that? Lying bitch. You whore." Nick's shouts attracted attention from the employees gathered by the door. "Who the fuck is it?"

"Michael Costa."

"Michael Costa." Nick's voice lowered to a deadly simmer. "I've never seen you together, and suddenly you're married to that dago wop?"

"Yes, and thank God, he's nothing like you."

His hand whirled, and my cheek exploded with pain. My palms hit the concrete, the rocks digging into my skin.

Ahead, a group of men in smocks approached. One of them spoke on the phone, glaring at Nick, who squared his shoulders and whistled at his brothers. Normally, Nick wouldn't think twice about blowing them apart, but we stood on a college campus. He backed off, his eyes reduced to malevolent slits.

"Lady, you okay?" A forty-something dark-skinned man helped me upright. "Should we call the police?"

"No. I'm good."

The concerned men formed a circle around me as I reentered the venue.

"Are you sure you're okay?"

"I'm fine."

I must've repeated that phrase thousands of times in the weeks after I escaped Nick, when everybody saw that I was a shell of my former self. Bumping into Nick didn't rattle me. My hands were shaking because it was cold.

I was fine, except for the foulness that was Nick sitting heavy in my stomach. It churned violently. Acid shot up my throat.

I shoved people aside and hung over a trash can. The bitterness raked my tongue as I purged. I always vomited when Nick left. Every single time. It didn't matter that he never got the chance to rape me, because he'd find me and do it again, and again, and this would never stop.

The rage that consumed me could've blotted out the sun.

"I disappear for a few minutes, and this happens." Michael's warmth stroked my back, and suddenly a napkin hovered near my lips. "You all right?"

"No."

When I straightened, Michael's smile thinned and the tan drained from his face. "What the hell happened?"

"My ex-boyfriend is here. He hit me."

"What the fuck? Are you *serious*?"

"We had a really bad relationship, but we broke up a while ago." I brushed the mark on my cheek. "He's with Legion. He found out I'm married, and he was very upset."

"I see." Michael's voice chilled to subzero as his arms wrapped me in heat. "Where is the prick?"

"Outside."

He tucked my head under his chin, stroking my hair. "I'll send you home with Vitale. Take a bath. Do something relaxing."

"I don't want to be alone."

"I'll be right behind you. Promise." He gestured at Vitale, who peeled himself off the wall. "What's his name?"

"Crash."

FOURTEEN
MICHAEL

THE NAME SOUNDED FAMILIAR.

All biker handles blended together because they were stupid fucking names—Axel, Diesel, Crash. Was Mommy's Accident taken?

"Bad relationship" meant beatings and rape. A lot of Carmela's behavior now made perfect sense. Red flags I should've noticed smacked me in the face.

Men who hit women were a half-step above pedophiles. Crash was garbage. He terrorized her to feel big, because his ego was fragile. I'd find that piece of shit. I'd drag him into my car, shove him in a dark cell, and spend a few days inflicting unimaginable pain on him.

I'd sent Carmela home with Vitale. She was a mess. It took a while to calm her, and then I'd amassed the troops. Six Costa enforcers—brutes with hard-ons for fighting—and then we'd interviewed the staff. They gave me a much more harrowing account.

"He did what?"

My voice smoked with rage, and the atmosphere pulsed with fury. Everyone wanted to beat up bikers. When I was little, my brother would drink and rave about MC guys corrupting nice Italian girls. A deep mistrust of one-percenters was in our blood. Costas were protective of our own. Nothing enraged us more than bikers' filthy hands on our women.

"He choked her," the forty-something caterer repeated. "She tried to run, but the asshole wouldn't let her. He called her a whore. Slapped her."

A hush descended over the room.

Men had died for lesser offenses, but what Crash had done was egregious. He'd assaulted my wife. I was Vinn's right hand—was this guy out of his mind?

His fate was sealed. He'd die slowly.

"Where is he?"

He frowned, his mouth thinning. "You seem like a decent man. You don't want to be mixed up in that kind of trouble."

"Buddy, I am trouble." I patted his back and shoved a fifty in his pocket. "Thanks for the information. I'd appreciate it if you kept what you saw to yourself."

As soon as he'd vanished from the kitchen, someone smashed their fist into the wall.

"We should kill them all!"

Agreed.

I faced the hungry wolves desperate for a fight. "Nobody is

firing their weapon. Understand? The last thing I need is the governor on my ass about a school shooting."

They nodded.

"I'm serious. Somebody better keep a calm head, because I don't know if I can."

"Let's fuck him up, boss."

My shoulder rammed into the service exit, and it blew open into a darkened alley between two buildings. A dumpster sat to my left, and trash littered the ground. Bikers lounged against the brick wall, smoking, their Harleys parked in a row. I spilled into the cool darkness, my enforcers covering my six as I approached the men wearing leather cuts.

"Crash!"

They angled their heads at me. I had no idea which was him. Carmela had described him as blond and tall.

"Which one of you is Crash?"

"I am."

A soft voice beckoned me toward a man with a linebacker body. Black ink wrapped his sleeves, and he wore faded leather over a Metallica T-shirt. He was in his mid-twenties, his light features reminding me of Julian. His hair was swept back. A dusting of a golden beard clung to his jaw. The rounded cheeks gave him a baby-faced innocence that clashed with the biker outfit. He looked like a kid who'd watched too much *Sons of Anarchy*. He smoked an ebony cigarette, which he flicked in my direction. Red sparks danced across the pavement.

"So you're the dago that married my girl."

He was begging to die.

"And you're the chrome-humping rapist."

His friends slid from the shadows, reaching for their weapons. He raised a palm, and they stopped. "Is that what she says I am?"

"She never mentions you."

"Because you can't compare." Crash's mouth curved into an arrogant smirk. "She's sparing your feelings because you don't do it for her. I know my woman. She doesn't want a nice guy."

"What makes you think I'm nice?"

"You're not an alpha male. You're a beta bitch, and you're not what she wants. You'll give her up."

"Over my dead fucking body."

He shrugged. "There's no way I'd let you live after tasting my woman's pussy."

It was as though a blood splatter had blinded me. I seized my knife. I swung, burying the blade. It pierced his leather and struck something hard. There was no gush of warmth.

The fucker wore armor.

His knuckles smashed my head. Two more punches caught my jaw. I staggered. My enforcers launched at the bikers, armed with knives and blackjacks. I rammed my shoulder into Crash's stomach, pinning him against the dumpster. He hammered me. A blow to my kidneys knocked me down.

Fucking asshole.

I gritted my teeth and socked his gut. He unsheathed a blade and sliced, forcing me to jump. I blocked his blows with my forearms until a wild stab seared into my skin. I grunted as heat spilled into my palm. His knife whistled the air. I avoided it, ducking and diving. I grabbed his wrist, twisted, and wrenched the handle. Then I kicked his leg out.

His knee slammed into the concrete, and I grappled him. I couldn't get a hold on him. I dropped my weapon. I jerked him into a chokehold. He pushed with his feet, attempting to dislodge me. He thrust my chin and punched. Agony burst through my insides. Nausea radiated from the fire in my groin.

I let him go, gasping.

He lunged.

I took a bottle rolled under the dumpster and swung it like a golf club. It shattered on his cheek, glass raining the pavement. Crash swore and stumbled. I seized his jacket and tugged him to the ground. I smashed his face into the shards, introducing my knuckles to his eyes, his nose, beating every exposed inch. I scraped the broken bits and shoved them in his mouth.

"Choke on it."

Crash rolled on his side, vomiting.

"Stop!"

Dimly, I recognized my cousin's baritone as rough hands seized my arms. They yanked. My elbow cracked into a jaw. I was ripped off Crash. Another body tackled me, knocking me backward. I roared as Crash crawled upright, spitting crimson.

"Let me the fuck go!"

A red-haired Legion member patted Crash's shoulder. "You okay, man?"

"Get off me." Crash pushed him. He scooped a knife from the floor. His brothers waylaid him. Four of them subdued him, but he was like a rabid tiger. He slashed the ginger beard's chest, slicing his leather cut. Then the president stepped into the fight, slamming his fist into Crash's skull.

He dropped. His palms hit the asphalt.

"I gave you a goddamned order." The president of Legion stood beside Vinn, whose stony features betrayed nothing. "What the hell's going on?"

Crash slowly got to his feet, his bleeding lips stretched into a leer. "Costa and I had a disagreement."

"He assaulted my wife. I have witnesses. I demand his life."

"Carmela belonged to me before she was yours." Crash twisted the blade in his palm. "Give her back."

"If you have to make demands for a girl, she's not yours."

"You stole her—"

"I *proposed*. She said yes." I laughed, pointed at the president's shocked face. "Even he thinks you're insane."

"Two months ago, I was fucking her. We were together!"

"And then she ghosted your ass. Too bad." I'd carve this motherfucker and blowtorch his lying mouth. "Maybe you should've offered her more than your small dick."

"I will rip you apart, Costa. I'll destroy your world and everybody in it."

This dumb fuck didn't realize I'd marked him for slaughter.

"You'll never get the chance."

"That's enough." Vinn shoved me, his actions clashing with his tempered voice. "Not here, Mike. Look where we are."

I didn't tear my gaze from Crash. "I'm killing the bastard."

"*Not here.*"

The president motioned to his men, who dragged Crash to the bikes. As much as I wanted to end this here, I couldn't execute him on a college campus. A gunshot victim on Ivy League grounds would attract national attention. This wasn't the way to dispose of Carmela's ex.

I *would* kill him.

Soon.

WE HELD AN EMERGENCY MEETING. Vinn played the diplomat with Legion's president, who insisted that his road captain made an error in judgment. It was like Crash hadn't groped and hit my wife. He expected us to shake hands and forget, which would never happen. According to Vinn, this was not the first time Legion had been soft with Crash. Then I screamed into the receiver and threatened to cut off their drug supply, and he caved. We were free to murder Crash, provided we could find him.

He was probably holed up in a motel, licking his wounds. If it weren't for Vinn, Crash would've died on a gurney in between spitting out chunks of glass. His pride was shattered. Carmela had rejected him, and I'd beaten his ass.

He had to die.

Eventually, I cooled down. I visited the ER to get stitched up. It was past midnight when I got home. My heartbeat jacked, I climbed the steps to our bedroom.

Light bled under the door.

Shit. She was awake.

I hesitated before entering.

Carmela whirled. She'd cleaned up, but red marks etched her cheeks as though she'd gripped them for hours. She wore nothing but the black T-shirt I used for sleeping. She stalked toward me, her eyes burning.

"You bastard. Why didn't you call me!" Carmela grabbed me, her forehead pulsing with a throbbing vein. "I've been out of my mind with worry. You didn't return my calls. I didn't know if I should contact hospitals or the morgue or—"

"Look, I'm sorry. I thought you'd be asleep."

"Sleep? Are you insane?" Carmela swelled like a bullfrog, clutching my blazer. "You crazy son of a bitch."

She enveloped me in a bear hug and dissolved into sobs. Breath caught in her lungs as she struggled to inhale.

It killed me.

I'd never seen her fall apart. My words stuck in my throat as she clung to me.

"Sorry." I cradled her shoulder, burying my nose in her sweet scent. "I didn't mean to upset you."

"What happened?"

"I fought him. It didn't end on good terms."

"Don't be vague."

"He sliced my arm, so I shoved glass in his mouth. He's still alive—"

"Oh my God," she moaned, fingering the bandage. "You're insane."

"It's all right. Just a scratch."

Carmela crumpled as she unfastened the knot at my neck and pushed the jacket from my shoulders. She gazed at the strip of white wrapping my arm, her voice husky with regret. "I'm so sorry, Michael."

"I'd do it again. And again. Carmela, breathe. You're safe."

Carmela shook her head, so agitated she couldn't exhale without shaking violently. "I hate him. I wish he'd disappear."

Working on it. "How long has he been an issue?"

"A couple of years."

"*Years?*"

"Sometimes he leaves me alone for a few weeks. I move constantly. I rent apartments under pseudonyms. I do everything I can to avoid him. He always manages to find me."

I didn't know where to begin. "How did you meet this guy?"

"A bar." She closed her eyes. "I thought I was in love. We were together for a while. I ran away to be with him, but after a few months of living with him, it turned into a horror show. I left him, but he hasn't left me."

"You could've asked me for help. You were at my house on Christmas. We hung out all the time. I would've handled him for you."

"You have two adorable children."

"What do they have to do with anything?"

Everything.

My stomach dropped as Carmela slumped onto the mattress, depression descending over her like a cloak.

"You were such a nice guy. I couldn't bring him in your lives."

Nothing she'd said tonight devastated me more. "You're worth it, Carmela. I don't care what kind of trouble you're in."

Her head sank.

"Crash is the reason you never gave me the time of day. Isn't he?"

Carmela burrowed into bed and pulled the quilt to her forehead. It only slightly muffled her crying, and her agony pained me more than my throbbing wound.

I sat beside her, peeling the comforter to stroke her ebony tresses.

"Do you want company?"

She nodded.

I stripped, sliding in next to her. Carmela flung her arm over my chest and snuggled close, her warmth burning me.

I smoothed her sleeve. "So what's with the shirt?"

"It smelled like you."

She stared ahead, her expression blank.

I pressed my lips to her cheek, and as we touched she made a desperate sound, a sharp inhale that sliced into my chest. I turned my head and caught her lips. The salt from her tears slid over my tongue. I kissed her harder, determined to stop that awful, gut-wrenching sound.

She sighed, melting into the sheets. Her touch drifted to my face as she leaned into the kiss. Her arms coiled over me as she deepened it. She was so eager, sucking, biting, her delectable pout claiming every corner of my mouth.

My hands skimmed her thighs. She ground into me. I ripped off her shirt in a whirl of black cotton and tangled hair. My cock stiffened as she wriggled into a position that squished her breasts against me. I kneaded her ass, following the curve to a waist, up her velvety skin. My thumbs brushed the side of her breast. I cupped her tits, and she crashed her mouth into mine. I grabbed her hip and switched our positions.

Carmela's brunette waves splayed over white satin. Her tongue slashed my lips, invading my senses with vanilla. My instincts screamed to answer her softness with bruising force, but I yanked the reins on my arousal.

I liked rough sex.

I tied girls in compromised positions. I spanked them and forced them to beg for orgasms. I loved it, and I made sure they did, too. When I was frustrated—when life got too stressful—I fucked women.

But Carmela needed a gentle man right now.

I was the furthest from that, but I could try. I counted to ten. I closed my eyes and clenched my teeth. Carmela's hand wandered below my midriff. She rolled over my cock and squeezed. Her passion stirred a primal urge that screamed one word—*Dominate*. It was more than a desire—an imperative to control snared my limbs and made my cock hard.

I had to stop.

I flipped onto my back, away from her. Carmela followed, her touch red-hot as she drifted to my briefs. I moved her hand to where my heart thundered. She shook from my grasp, raising my lust to a five-story fire.

I pulled her off me.

"What's wrong?"

I stumbled out of bed. "I'm sorry. I can't be what you need."

Hurt flashed across Carmela's beautiful face.

This is too intense.

FIFTEEN
CARMELA

I'd never love again.

I'd barely survived my last relationship. Love was an indiscriminate killer of hearts, and mine was broken beyond repair. But Michael's fight with Nick had thrown that into doubt.

He'd stood up for me.

He'd shoved glass down Nick's throat without skipping a beat. Michael hadn't wasted time with twenty questions. He'd believed me and acted swiftly.

That meant everything to me.

I told myself Michael was defending his pride, not me, but I couldn't separate his actions from the safety they'd given me. And maybe I didn't love him, but there was room in my heart for his children.

I loved them.

Matteo was such a sweet kid. He hugged me at every opportunity, said hilarious things, and hero-worshipped Michael. His daughter was more complicated. Her fierce independence challenged me. She was prone to slamming doors and I-hate-yous. She was guarded, like her father.

The responsibility over both kids made me feel needed, but however much I lost myself in this new role, I couldn't forget that Nick was out there.

Giant oaks towered above us like giants as we strolled the deep green lawn toward the playground. Mariette raced ahead, hooting with pleasure as she hurled herself onto a swing. Matteo's legs dashed for the plastic tree house. He beat the bongo drum and twisted the gear wheel.

Michael's hawk-like gaze zeroed in on his kids. Sleep lines etched his face, but other than that, he seemed normal. An untamed scruff covered his jaw and neck, and his mocha waves were half-tamed. When his amber eyes flicked at me, my heart jumped.

"What is it?"

I smiled. "Want coffee?"

His attention slid to the children. "Sure, I like it with—"

"Milk and enough sugar for a diabetic coma. I know."

He raised his brows as I wandered toward the espresso stand.

Dew clung to the grass, slicking my ankles as sunshine broke through the murky sky. It was a beautiful spring morning. Cherry blossoms floated on the wind, clinging to my hair. The crisp air bit my cheeks. As I mixed Michael's coffee, I examined the lightness in my chest—*happiness*.

I joined Michael's side, handing him the cup. "I put in four sugars."

"Perfect." He frowned at it, as though he suspected poison, but he drank anyway. "Thanks."

"You have a sweet tooth," I said when he shot me a probing look. "Peppermint candy in all your pockets. And I found your hidden stash in the walk-in closet."

"I didn't realize you watched me." He wasn't angry. He looked flattered. "Are you after my heart, Carmela?"

"With a lousy cup of joe?"

"It's not bad." Michael's smile widened. "What else do you think you know?"

"You're eating all the children's snacks. Don't you have any shame?"

"*None.*"

"What a monster."

"I gave them life. The least they can do is give me their Snack Packs." Michael's fingers skimmed my leggings and pinched my ass. "Is that all you've got?"

"Your favorite vegetable is broccoli. You have a thing for plaid suits. You use a butter knife to cut meat. I could go on and on, but it doesn't matter. Your quirks don't offer any insight to who you are as a person. And I want to know my husband."

Michael acted like he was half-listening, his gaze hyper-focused on the kids, but he stilled.

"Tell me about your parents."

"Dad's dead," he said baldly. "Passed away when I was five. The guy you met at our wedding is my mom's boyfriend."

"Sorry about your father."

"I don't remember him. The funeral stuck in my mind, but other than that...he's a stranger."

So he grew up without a dad. That pitted my stomach with sadness. "What happened after he died? Who helped raised you?"

"Daniel." All the light seemed to disappear within Michael. "My brother was fifteen."

"That's a ton of pressure for a teenager."

"Yeah, but he did the best he could. He packed lunches and walked me to school. Bought all the candy I wanted. When I got older, he'd take me to arcades and slap a ten-dollar roll of quarters in my hand. That was a lot of money in those days. Especially for a kid. Daniel wasn't perfect. He wasn't even nice, but he was the closest thing I had to a dad."

Clouds rolled overhead, blocking the sun. He shook off his melancholy, the smile returning to his face.

"Life with me isn't so bad, is it?"

"It's not torture."

"Easy on the praise, honey. When you let loose those compliments, my knees knock together."

I took his shoulder and kissed his brow.

He stared at me, toying with the empty cup.

"Do I make you nervous?" I asked.

He snorted. "No."

"Ever since I told you about Crash, you've been different."

"I'm trying to be gentle. I'm not making excuses or getting out of anything. I'm telling you the truth." He leaned in, his breath tickling my cheek. "I don't have a pause button, sweetheart. When we're hot and heavy, it's tough to stop."

"I never asked you to change."

"I married you to build a better life. If I give in to my impulses, I *will hurt you*. And I can't live with that."

"You don't know that for sure."

"It's a risk I'm not selfish enough to take. I want you to be happy."

He couldn't mean that.

My heart drank it in anyway. I'd waited for *someone* to appreciate me. Nobody had ever seen my worth. They never cared to look beyond my face and body.

"You're lying."

"Then why did I marry you?"

I had no answer.

Michael no longer resembled the monster I'd met in his mansion. Piece by piece fell, like a badly fitting costume over a beautiful man. He'd sucked me in like a black hole, pulling me into his dark orbit.

He's lying.

I didn't care. I needed this.

I dragged him by his lapels, kissing him hard.

Michael let a shocked laugh into my mouth. A rumble vibrated in his throat, the sound deepening as I crushed him against a tree. His growl settled between my thighs as he flipped me around.

He palmed my back before I hit the wood. Our bodies molded together. His lip caught mine with a flash of teeth that nipped before a liquid heat swiped me. He devoured me in a slow, agonizing stroke while he glided down in silky caresses.

I pulled away, just enough to be warmed by his lazy smile. "Is this what you're like when you don't hate me?"

"I never hated you, Carmela."

"I don't hate you, either."

"Thank fuck."

He tipped forward, claiming me again. He was softer than last time, his tongue flicking my lip in such a wanton display we were seconds from being called out.

"I want you. The *real* you." I brushed his hair, fingers tangled in his hair. "Not the man you pretended to be."

SIXTEEN

CARMELA

I BELTED OUT AN ITALIAN BALLAD. The high notes strained my voice because the singer was a soprano, and I was a first alto. I'd lowered the key two half-steps but it was still too much, so I switched to a Patsy Cline song.

As the last lyrics of "She's Got You" faded, clapping burst from a room. My stomach tightened as I followed the sound into the office, where my husband lounged in the darkness. A sliver of light slashed his face into a diagonal slice, illuminating the faint outline of his silhouette. He sat on the couch, feet raised on the coffee table. He brought his hands together.

"*Bravissimo.*"

Patches of heat burned my cheeks. I had no problem singing in front of strangers. Michael was another story. "You're home early."

"I had a complication."

He was nothing more than a shape, which gave me no insight into his mood. He seemed to guess mine from the silence.

"Everything's fine. Keep singing."

"I can't when you're here."

"You think I'll laugh?"

My anxiety had more to do with his presence, which rippled toward me like dark tendrils, snaring me no matter where I hid. He'd always been overwhelming in a similar way to Nick. Michael was a different flavor of monster. I wanted to know how far he could be pushed.

"It's okay. I'm finished with practice."

Michael cocked his head. "How come I never hear you?"

"I do it when you're gone."

"We're married. You don't have to hide from me anymore."

He wouldn't let this go.

"I'm not hiding. I sing to Matteo sometimes."

"That kid has you wrapped around his pinkie." Not that Michael minded, judging from the softness in his voice. "Now he has *me* reading him five stories a night."

"I can't help it. I love him."

It slipped out before I could swallow the confession.

Love was a dangerous word. Nick had done unspeakable things in its name, and men like Michael considered their sons extensions of themselves. Zero degrees of separation existed between him and Matteo. He'd assume I loved *him*. He would use it against me.

What the hell was wrong with me?

"Are you telling the truth?" Suspicion laced Michael's tone. "Or are you flattering me?"

"I don't care about flattering you."

"I believe that."

That hung between us, heating the air. Then Michael interrupted the silence with a whip-like command.

"*Come.*"

I crossed my arms. "Ask nicely."

Michael drummed the couch before conceding. "Please."

I was surprised he caved so easily. I approached him, sinking into the space beside him. Michael's head turned.

"Why?"

"Why what?"

Michael went rigid, as though guarding himself from a strike. "Why do you love them?"

"I-I don't know. I just do." I stared at Michael, who was impossible to read in the dark. "They're cute children, and I bond quickly."

"I could never feel that way about somebody else's kids. I'm indifferent to everyone but me and mine."

"I'm not that heartless."

"Because you don't have one of your own."

That dug into me like acid. "Thanks for the reminder, asshole."

"Carmela, I'm okay with trying."

My stomach tensed.

A *baby*.

He couldn't have meant that.

He grabbed my wrist, pulling me down before I'd risen from the sofa. "I could give you a baby."

"Are you fucking with me?"

"No, but I'd like to be fucking you."

"Don't joke. Not about this."

"I'm not. I tried to tell you weeks ago. I've hinted at it heavily, but your skull is thicker than my cousin's. You can't believe anything good about me."

"You want a baby." I was still stuck on that bombshell. "With me."

"Why wouldn't I?"

"Well, for starters, you already have two. What would you do with another?"

"There are perks to having kids with you, Carmela. Besides the obvious." Michael's thigh pressed into mine. "Matteo is half-Italian. He'll never follow in my footsteps, but our sons will."

Oh my God. "What if we have girls?"

"Then you'll braid their hair and I'll build them dollhouses."

"And if we have a son?"

"I'll groom him into this life. I need somebody to take over when I'm old." Michael leaned over, softening. "You have to be okay with that."

I expected nothing less from a man like him, though it stung my heart. "What about Teo?"

"What about him?"

"Are you planning the same for him?"

Michael shook his head. "The kid is too sensitive."

"He's perfect!"

"I know. It's not a criticism. I love how nice he is, but I have to face facts. You were right. We're not alike. Plus, as only half guido, he'll never be made. I can't ask him to join something that'll never accept him."

This conversation was crazy.

"We are not even pregnant."

"I'd rather clear the air now. It's up to you. I'm happy either way."

This was insanity. "You're fine with doctor's appointments and changing diapers and—"

"Do you want a baby or not?"

Was that a serious question?

"*Of course*. I've always wanted to be a mom." I gasped as Michael's attention drifted to the zipper at my neck. "What are you—"

"Let's make a baby."

Michael unzipped my dress, his hand slipping down my back. As the cotton peeled from my body, he pulled my bra straps down, chasing them with hot kisses. His mouth was ecstasy. He palmed my breast, his tongue following his thumb's movements. Michael stroked up my leg, the swell of pleasure knocking me off balance.

I threaded my fingers through his soft hair, and Michael rewarded me with a sharp nip. He dragged me onto his lap. My thighs splayed over his as he cradled me like a doll.

I ripped into his shirt, trailing his chest, sliding over the slabs of muscle. Desire lodged in my throat like a fist. I undressed him, wetness soaking the fabric.

"What is this?"

"Blood," he murmured. "But it's mine, don't worry."

"Shit. I'll grab bandages."

"I have all the healing I need right here." He kissed me, and then he brushed the seam of my panties. "And *here*."

Oh *God*. "What do you get out of this?"

"I fuck you however I want."

A dark thrill shot through my veins at his clipped tone.

It was a warning.

One I should heed, because he was covered in blood. Something deadly stirred in him, but he wouldn't unleash it until I consented. A heavy silence stole the air as I considered surrendering control.

"Anything for a baby."

He took my wrists, his grip biting. "*Carmela.*"

"I'm willing to meet you halfway."

"That doesn't exist. There is all the way or nothing."

"Keep going." I grabbed his hand and guided it lower. "It's my choice."

Michael seized my chin and gave me a hard kiss. He slipped from my grasp and ripped off my bra. Then he pushed my dress, sliding the thong off, his strokes roughened. A fire bloomed where his lips pressed into me, and his tongue stroked with liquid heat.

With every stitch of clothing shoved off my feet, Michael cradled me in his arms. Slowly, he unbuckled himself. Leather slapped his slacks as he pulled his belt free. He held it taut and brushed my jaw.

"I can't be gentle. When I fuck, it's rough. It's intense. It's the opposite of your needs. You have to know that this isn't malice. I just can't hold back. I'm trying to be a good husband."

"It's all right. I can handle you."

"I'll destroy your limits, Carmela. All of them. If you're not feeling that, you better march your ass out of here."

"I want you, too."

He narrowed his grip. "You don't mean that. You can't."

"I said *yes*—"

"*That's enough out of you.*"

He kissed me.

It was so brutal, he cut off my air. I tasted his earthy essence as he slashed my mouth open. He angled his head, the stroke crushing me. He pecked my cupid's bow, and then my bottom lip.

He looped the belt around my waist. It slid up my abdomen, tightening, cutting off my mobility. It slipped under my breasts, and stroked my nipples. He tightened it, flattening my tits.

Weeks of watching his children hadn't dulled the urge to have a baby. My heart burst with jealousy when his kids piled on his lap. I'd started to resent him, thinking there was no way he'd ever agree. There was nothing I wouldn't give for that experience.

I wanted this.

I could do this.

As he restrained me, my world got silent and dark. I drifted into a state of numbness. I sagged in his arms, giving up.

Michael made a triumphant sound and leaned forward, his smile pressing into my cold lips. He pulled away.

"*No.* You don't get to disappear."

He hauled me upright. He thrust me backward, hands drifting to my ass. Then he lifted me.

My legs hit the desk.

He scooped under my thighs and pushed me onto the hard surface. Paperweights and folders scattered as he shoved everything off. Then he flattened me on the wood. He retreated and strolled to the curtains, yanking them aside. Light streamed into the room.

I gasped.

Patches of crimson had stained his sleeves. He ripped off his shirt, his lips curled into a feral smirk. There was no lightness in him. The monster had come out to play.

He kneeled, shoving my knees apart as his head disappeared between them. His mouth seared my pussy, and he sucked. Delicious warmth stroked my clit. Back and forth, he licked. Intense heat seared my cheeks as I groaned. Convulsions down my leg as he puckered, dragging me into him.

Sweet Jesus, it was hot.

All of me smoldered. I wriggled on my stomach, desperate to clench and chase his teasing, but Michael's grip never yielded.

He struck my ass.

I burned at the blow, but he soothed it with a pass of his hand. Then he hit me again.

And *again.*

Each time, harder. Not enough to make me scream—to test my boundaries to their limit. But even if he never relieved the raw skin, his tongue was there, licking and fucking me. I didn't give a damn about being spanked if he kept using his mouth. So long as it swirled in my wetness, which coated my thighs. I shouted, unable to bear the sharp frustration, the agony of not being able to ride him.

Suddenly, he ripped away.

No!

I cried out as he left, on the brink of self-destruction from the pounding ache that needed something to fill—

Michael's slacks crumpled to the floor. He pressed into my legs, as he took my waist. His cock rolled over my clit, slicked with my arousal. He yanked me by the tether, his voice seething with lust.

"You love this. Don't you?" He gripped my face and taunted me with a fierce tap. "I asked you a question."

"Yes."

"I'm going to fuck you really hard." His grip slid to my throat. "Remember what I said, Carmela."

Which part?

He entered me with a brutal thrust. His cock rammed home, allowing me no time to adjust as he squeezed, cutting my oxygen. A buzzing emptiness filled my head as he rutted me. It was overwhelming, the gliding, slick length massaging my sparks into a roaring inferno. I fought to breathe, taking in less air, and yet I ground against him. I pushed back, not at all eager to numb out.

He felt too damned good.

A needy moan burst from my clenched lips.

Michael rolled his hips and gave it to me harder. A blow cracked over my ass, the vibration tingling my pussy. Euphoria tingled my mouth. It glowed around the fingers slowing my air. It rode his cock, which knocked out what remained of my oxygen.

More.

My chest burned as I attempted to inhale. My orgasm was building, tightening. He settled into a frenzied rhythm. His palm moved between us as he rubbed circles into my clit, the gentle touch sparking electricity into my core.

He pinned me. The hold on my throat let go, and my orgasm crashed into me like a semi. A desperate cry launched from me. I gasped, throttled by a deep thrust as he finished inside me. Heat jetted my walls as his muscles spasmed, his hand still rubbing.

He'd promised to destroy my limits and he had. My barriers lay in shambles, all of them obliterated by Michael.

And I was beyond happy.

An aphrodisiac like I'd never known blanketed me as Michael peeled me off the desk. He unbuckled me, and my arms went limp. Dragging me into his chest, he fell onto the couch. He tucked my head under his and held me, the madness purged from him, no more deadly than a teddy bear.

I fingered my neck, in awe of the ache between my legs.

Why did his domination feel so liberating?

Why did I want him to do it *again*?

Michael brushed my hair, wiping the tears tracking my cheeks. "Under my control will be your favorite place. I promise."

I WOULD HAVE A BABY.

I wasn't pregnant, but it was only a matter of time. We'd made love three more times that day, Michael waking me up in the middle of the night, his erection pressing into my back. I'd already downloaded an app to track my cycle and had figured out when I was ovulating. I shared the calendar with Michael, who'd agreed to block out those days for us. His support was more than I'd hoped for.

I was cautiously optimistic.

I looked forward to Michael coming home, and not just for the amazing sex. I missed him. It happened after I woke up one morning to an empty bed. A void had gaped in my chest. I snuggled the pillow on his side for an hour before it dawned on me what the emptiness meant—I was catching *feelings*.

Shit, shit, *shit*.

With Nick, it was love-at-first-sight. I fell for him hard, and his obsession had dug into me with hooked barbs. We didn't know how to treat each other well. We never had twenty-four hours without a blow-up argument, screaming, fighting, and angry sex. Tearing him off me had hurt me, deeply.

Michael and I never really fought. He didn't have annoying habits. His world sprawled over a vast landscape. He wasn't an emotional basket case. The man wanted to fuck his wife, play with his children, and do repairs. In the weeks I'd been here, he'd repainted the fence, re-grouted the bathroom, fixed kitchen cabinets, and the list went on. He was always looking for something to mend, almost as though it calmed him.

I liked that he was self-reliant and he tipped his staff generously, and that he wasn't too good to check the rat traps in the crawlspace. His routine may have been predictable, but I'd been aching for stability.

Maybe this would work.

I smiled as I checked on the rack of lamb sizzling in the oven. The children played outside. Michael had invited his family over for Easter, and we'd spent the morning preparing an egg hunt in the backyard. Instead of drinking with the adults, Michael was playing babysitter. Children piled on his back, demanding his attention. He dyed eggs with his son and corralled the kids when it was time for a snack. Michael was never happier than when he was with Mariette and Matteo. It was sweet to watch, and it also stabbed at me somewhere deep.

Only one thing was missing from the perfect picture—my family.

Mia was gone. My parents—banned for life. We'd never celebrate a holiday together. I'd never hold my niece, and to top it all off, Matteo had developed a distressing habit of running away from me.

I chased him into the granite kitchen, a stitch stabbing my side from chasing his little ass. He shrieked as he collided into Michael, whose wine spilled over the rim.

He set it down and sucked his fingers. "Where are you going?"

"Chase me!"

"No. Dinner will be ready soon." Michael kneeled, wiping grass off Matteo's shirt. "Wash your hands before you eat."

"I was going to make him do that, but he keeps taking off." I snatched at Matteo, who escaped between his father's legs and shot into another room. "See?"

Michael glanced over his shoulder, shrugging. "He does that."

"Am I doing something wrong? We were getting along, and now...it's like he *hates* me."

Michael's soft laugh dipped into my belly. "Definitely not."

"Do they like me?"

"They're crazy about you."

"They'll always love you more. You've been there all their lives."

"Give it time, Carmela. Love isn't earned overnight."

I knew I had unrealistic expectations, but it was hard to detach from children that I took care of every day. I sang them songs. Read them stories. We watched movies, played games, cuddled.

Michael grabbed my arm when I headed for Matteo. "Speaking as an overprotective asshole, you're taking your role a little too seriously. The house is packed with adults. Nothing will happen to him."

"I walked in here and picked up your kid without anyone noticing."

"*I* noticed." He raised a brow. "Everyone will think you like my kids more than me."

"Well, I do."

"How can I change that?" His touch glided to my hand, the gentleness filling me with steam.

"You can't compete with Matteo."

"I know, and I'm not even going to try, but at least tell me you're breaking down." Michael's tone made me feel plunged in liquid heat. "Because you're sure growing on me."

"Your kids are happier, and you're getting your dick wet. Isn't that all you wanted?"

"I want so many things from you, Carmela. It's impossible to boil them down to just a couple." Michael's fingers brushed my cheek, and then my neck. "You sure you're okay?"

"I told you a million times, yes."

I'd slipped under Michael's spell.

The commands delivered in that voice. His possession over my body. The passion.

I'd loved it all.

The belts, ropes, and toys that baffled me in the beginning now seemed laughably harmless. I saw them for what they were—bits of nylon and cowhide. Only the person who wielded them could hurt me.

That wasn't Michael.

"Are you okay?" I asked, facing him.

"I don't know. All this fucking is wearing me out."

He winked.

I rolled my eyes, but didn't fight when he gathered me in his arms. I sank into his impossibly warm embrace and tried not to smile at all the happiness bursting from inside me.

"I'm just checking in, Michael. Marriage is a two-way street, or so they say."

"I could do with a blowjob." He laughed as I dug into his back. "All right, fine. There is something I want."

"What?"

Warmth slid around my waist as he pulled me close. His mouth grazed my jaw. Several more kisses seared my face and ear before his ragged whisper cut through my muddled feelings.

"Go on a date with me."

SEVENTEEN
MICHAEL

HAPPINESS WAS A FICKLE THING.

In my twenties, I chased it with a series of ridiculous goalposts. I'll be happy when I make two million dollars a year. I'll be satisfied when I bang three girls at the same time. I'll be content when I'm not trapped in a dead marriage with a woman I hate.

You get the picture.

It set me up for disappointment because the goalposts never stopped moving further away. It wasn't until I destroyed them that I found joy in everyday things—a cup of coffee, rain washing the pavement, fucking Carmela.

It had been a perfect morning.

Perfect, like Carmela's lingering kiss when I tried to say goodbye. Sweet and hot. She didn't want to let go of me, and leaving her felt wrong. She'd given me everything I'd wanted, and it'd made me optimistic.

Maybe this could work.

Maybe we'd be like those obnoxiously cheerful couples I usually hated.

I was riding high after she'd ridden me all night, and I'd never been so exhausted. My face cracked with a ridiculous grin as I strolled into Sanctum, my underground sex club.

The club was all black accented with gold, and everywhere was jammed with beautiful women and guys thirsty for high-class ass. Girls wearing animal silk masks and designer lingerie hung like ornaments beside their male companions. A naked woman sat on all fours, balancing a tray of drinks on her back as two men chatted. Others did a striptease. People fucked on chaises and sofas, in rooms with doors opened.

Pure hedonism. Madness.

I'd been known to indulge, but those days were over. Familiar faces smiled at me, but I ignored them. I'd never been so indifferent to naked women. I made a beeline for the round entrance. The doors yawned into a room flickering with orange light from a glass wall fireplace. Obsidian furniture packed the space, the barely visible silhouettes shimmering. Silver grout around brick shimmered. This area was invitation-only. It was where we kept our A-listers, Saudi princes, British royalty, anybody who needed more privacy.

I spotted a stoic man standing outside a booth along with Julian's flash of blond hair. His expression said he was bored out of his mind. He tapped on his smartphone, his pale gaze meeting mine when I approached.

"Hey, Michael."

I grunted. "How long has he been here?"

"All night."

I glanced inside the booth. Anthony's hair spilled over the leather, his eyes closed and his lips curled in lazy contentment. "Is he high?"

"Probably."

Fucking Anthony.

The dad in me wanted to fix him, to guide him by the hand and teach him things. Mostly, I wished I could strangle him. He was a pain in the ass, like my four-year-old could sometimes be, except I didn't love Anthony unconditionally.

The booth was a mess. Empty bottles, glassware, mounds of powder littered the marble table. The idiot thought he was Scarface. The girls helped themselves to lines of coke as I stomped inside.

"There are no drugs allowed in this club."

Leticia straightened, rubbing her nose. "Wha—Michael? Oh shit." She elbowed the other woman, a new hire. "Michael, we're so sorry. We didn't—he offered."

"Get out."

They scampered.

"*Michael.* What a surprise." Anthony pushed himself upright. "Have a seat—join me. Want a hit?"

He knew damned well I was off cocaine.

"I have two kids at home."

"You're just as boring as Alessio." Anthony patted his jacket, recovering a pack of cigarettes. He stuck one between his lips and searched for a lighter. "Never mind. How've you been?"

"Pissed off."

"Why?"

"For starters? I'm here instead of knocking up my wife."

Anthony grimaced. "Jesus Christ, man."

"I have enough on my plate without you. I spent the day talking to our partners. Trying to convince them you'll stay out of trouble. You're killing me, Anthony. You really are. *What are you doing?*"

"Having a cigarette."

"There's no smoking in here." I plucked it out of his mouth and crushed it. "And I don't allow drugs at Sanctum. Not now —not ever."

Anthony grinned as he gave me a heavy-lidded stare. "You're the boss."

I cuffed him across the face, and the gleam in Anthony's eyes burned brighter. "Don't talk back to me."

"Who the hell do you think you are—my *dad*? We're the same age."

"Act like a child, and I'll treat you like one."

Anthony raked his hair, behaving as though he was on the verge of a meltdown. "Fuck you, Michael. I have an addiction."

"How many trips to rehab do you need?"

"You don't understand."

"Why do you keep doing this? Is it a cry for help? A drawn-out suicide attempt? Do you want to die?"

His voice darkened. "No."

"I don't believe you."

"No," he sulked. "I don't want to die."

"Then prove it. Stop doing this shit to yourself." I grabbed his arm, marveling at how much weight he'd lost. "Go home and lay low."

"Give me something to do, and I swear I'll dump the coke and —and the clubs."

I was all for giving the dipshit some responsibility, but Nico was adamant about keeping his son out of the mafia.

"Absolutely not."

"I'm the next in line! I should be acting boss, not Vinn."

"One, you're a train wreck. Nobody will follow your orders. Two, this isn't England. You don't just *inherit* the throne. Three, you'll get killed if you hang out in public. Every gangster in Boston is gunning for you."

Anthony seized the bottle of vodka and brought the neck to his lips. I yanked it from his grip and resisted the urge to crack him over the head. I pulled him out of the booth and shoved him into a bodyguard's arms.

"I promised your father I'd keep you alive, but you seem hellbent on killing yourself, so I'm cutting you off. No more visits to Sanctum."

"*Fine.* I'll freeload somewhere else."

Talking to him was a waste of time.

I faced his bodyguard, who had bags hanging under his eyes. "I'm hiring more guys to help you. I want him surrounded day and night. No drugs. No alcohol. No fucking clubs."

"You got it."

I waved my hand, indicating they should go.

Anthony shot me a look filled with poison as they dragged him to the exit, and then I turned to Julian. He watched Anthony leave, laughing when he tried to grab a hooker on his way out.

"Useless junkie."

That bothered me, coming from him. "When you see Anthony with drugs, you call me immediately. Not after he's snorted a felony's worth of cocaine."

"Michael, you're fighting a losing battle. This kid's going to die."

"If that idiot dies, Nico will murder all of us." I beckoned at Julian, who followed me into a private room. "I need you to do something."

"Sure. What is it?"

Julian's deadpan grated at me. He was probably annoyed that I delegated my shitty tasks to him, like babysitting Anthony. He'd lost his job a year ago. I took pity on him and offered him work because Serena had begged me. Somehow, he was still in my fucking life.

"I want you to manage this club's black-tie events."

Julian leaned back, sighing. "What do I know about event planning?"

"Throw a party every other Friday to induct more suckers into Sanctum. The less I'm here, the better."

"I get it. Happy wife, happy life." Julian sank his head onto his palm. "I'll do it, but only if we have regular play dates. I want a relationship with my sister's children."

And I'd rather he disappeared. "All right."

"How's everything at home?"

"We're fine."

"Okay," he said bracingly. "Carmela seemed upset at your wedding. I thought that was odd. Then I asked around, and nobody knows when you started dating."

"Do you have a question?"

Julian hesitated. "Why did you propose?"

"I told you. I've known her for a while. We reconnected at my daughter's birthday, and by the end, I wanted to marry her."

"So you proposed, and she agreed. Just like that."

"Yeah, asshole."

"Relax, I'm not picking a fight. You and Serena weren't a great match. I'd hate for history to repeat itself."

"Shut the fuck up."

I stood and yanked the door, gesturing outside.

That was the thing about Julian. He was a sarcastic bastard underneath all that fake concern. I loathed the whole family. Now the fucker had gotten into my head.

Carmela did seem too good to be true.

She was amazing with the kids and drama-free. She'd respected everything I'd asked—no fighting—which never happened with Serena. I thought I'd have to throw credit cards at her and tolerate weekend retreats at Nantucket, but all she wanted to do was garden. Carmela ripped up the grass and built planter boxes while I was at work. Tomato plants now lined the east wall. The other day, I caught her clipping a flyer.

Who the fuck did I marry?

She was a rich girl who used coupons. A beauty who shoved her hands in dirt. She was a walking contradiction, and I couldn't figure her out.

It bothered me.

I stared at my laptop as Julian left, the door closing softly. When the latch clicked, I opened the lid. I pulled a web browser and typed the credentials into her email. I'd hacked it weeks ago, but I'd held off from violating her privacy.

I shouldn't.

But I had to.

A festering boil bubbled in my stomach as I searched her inbox, finding nothing but promotional messages. Then I dove into her Sent folder, determined to leave no stone unturned, and what I saw gutted me.

Fuck me.

My lips curled as I read every message, including the one claiming I'd hired Carmela. Within seconds, I'd stripped the camera information from Alessio's pictures and discovered his location. Vacationing in the Amazon, my ass. He was in Boca Raton, Florida.

Sloppy.

She'd whitewashed the content of these emails to keep her sister hidden, but that didn't bother me.

She'd lied to my face.

She swore she had no idea where they were.

Did I not explain how important it was to bring him back?

I stared at the text until the black lines bled into white, and a sickening rage engulfed my body. My impulse to make Carmela's life easier vanished.

Carmela had no idea who she married.

I replied to the email:

Michael forced me to marry him. Help me.

EIGHTEEN
CARMELA

MICHAEL FISTED MY HAIR. His gasps billowed my neck as his body rocked like a wave. His muscles glided under my hands, sweat slicking his tanned skin like oil. He plastered his face into my collar. He sucked and bit down, hard.

He burst with a wordless groan.

Something wild in Michael exploded when he fucked me. Maybe it was his orgasms, the way they sounded like a wound, or his hold on my wrists as he came. A low growl rumbled through his chest. His thighs twitched with spasms as he spilled inside me. His breathing calmed. He released me, the darkness purged from him.

I loved having sex with him.

But I cherished the moments when he melted into me, kissing. He was so sensual it made braving the flames worth it. Tonight, though, his kisses stung me with white-hot bites.

"Daddy! *Daddy!*"

Michael broke from me, groaning. He yanked sheets over our bodies as Matteo crashed into the room, dressed in his jammies. He vaulted onto the mattress and threw himself onto Michael's back.

Michael cringed. "Buddy, give us a minute."

"What are you doing to Caramel?" Matteo cinched his arms around Michael's neck. "*Carmela.*"

"Grown-up things. Teo, go play with your sister."

"I wanna sleep with Carmela."

Michael gave his son a wry grin. "If you were any other guy, that'd be a hard pass."

"There's too many people on this bed," Matteo roared as he flung himself between us. "Daddy, you can sleep on the floor."

"*What?*"

I covered my face and laughed.

Michael pulled on boxers before dragging Matteo off. I went into the bathroom. Michael joined me, hugging me from behind. His heart hammered as he folded me in his sweat-streaked body.

"My sweet caramel."

A rush of warmth accompanied those words. "Still want to go out?"

"Hell yes. I hired a sitter."

I showered, slipped into a cocktail dress, and did my makeup. When I finished, I rejoined him.

Michael combed his hair, eyes on the mirror. His forehead rippled with a deep frown, and then he glanced at me. The glance turned into a stare and his lips curled into something feral. He dropped the comb and approached me like a hunter stalking prey.

"Aren't you a temptation. Ditch the mom jeans and wear this every day."

"When have you ever seen me in pants?"

"I don't pay attention to your clothes. Only when your outfit gets me so hard, my brain stops working." His finger prodded my chin until I'd met his gaze. "Wait outside."

"Why?"

"Can't go to dinner with a loaded gun."

He pushed me toward the door and swatted my ass. Twenty minutes later, Michael emerged from the bedroom. He'd shaved his face, slicked his hair on the sides, and put on a navy blazer over black slacks.

We went downstairs, said goodbye to the nanny, and packed into his Audi, my stomach leaping with excitement.

"Where are you taking me?"

"Somewhere you'll like," he deadpanned as we pulled from the driveway. "Traffic sucks."

"Did you make reservations?"

"No need."

Interesting. "Now I'm wondering if I overdressed."

Michael's hand glided up my thigh, his touch burning through the fabric. "You look fine with a capital F."

"You're handsome, too. I'm happy we're doing this."

"Me too. You know what? We're due for a family vacation. I'm considering Florida."

"Disney World? Yeah, that'd be great."

He shook his head. "Not Orlando—Miami. Palm Beach. Boca Raton, maybe."

My heart galloped ahead. "Sure."

Michael frowned. "What's the matter?"

"I'm fine—I'm just thinking."

"Thinking what, honey?"

Honey. "Are you feeling all right? You seem different."

He shot me a puzzled look that made me doubt myself.

The discussion ended as we stopped at a familiar road. He got out of the Audi and tossed the keys to the valet. Then he took my hand, smiling so broadly that I must've imagined things.

I read the restaurant's name on the glowing awning and gasped.

"This is my dad's place!"

"I know."

"How?" I hadn't been inside in months. "I practically grew up here."

Michael smiled at the building, as though he was lost in

nostalgia. "It was one of the property titles your dad trans-ferred to me."

"We're eating here?"

"Unless you don't want to."

"No, this is perfect. Thank you, Michael."

It was as though the weirdness in the car never happened. I balled my fingers in his jacket and kissed him. He was unyielding at first. A stone structure that breathed but emanated zero warmth.

Then he opened his mouth.

"Of course, baby. I thought you'd might like to eat here before I tear it down."

NINETEEN
MICHAEL

CARMELA GAPED at me like I'd shot her dog. White light paled Carmela's golden skin as we stopped under the awning. The glow faded from her smile.

"What do you mean, tear it down?"

"Boston doesn't need another Italian restaurant. I've done some market research in the area, and guess what's in high demand? *Weed shops.*"

"*What?*" Her voice was like a thunderclap.

"I'm turning this place into a marijuana dispensary." I savored the devastation on her face. "Cash only. Perfect for money laundering."

"So, you're getting rid of my father's clean business to build a pot store that the FBI will raid." Carmela's eyes radiated with unrestrained fury. "That is the dumbest idea ever."

"I'm thinking of calling it Starbuds."

"Why would you get into that business? There's so much regulation."

"We'll self-regulate. I'll bribe city officials to glance the other way." I palmed her shoulder and wheeled her toward the building. "I'll paint it gray with a green trim. I'll gut the kitchen. Donate the furniture to homeless shelters."

"You're not destroying my fucking restaurant."

"I own the title. I can do anything I want."

Before she opened her mouth, the hostess took our coats and showed us to a table.

Brick surrounded the dining room. Espresso-brown padded booths were shoved against the wall, next to rustic wooden tables. Cast-iron lamps hung over them, the white glow bouncing off the patent leather. Sheer black curtains draped over windows. It was the same aesthetic as my house.

A jazz quartet played music on a tiny stage. It was sonorous, boring shit. The space was packed with young couples. It was gorgeous. Ignacio had invested a fortune in remodeling.

I seized the wine list as we sat, scowling. "These prices are a racket."

"Look around, Michael. People love coming here." Carmela leaned over the table. "*I* love it here."

"Then I suggest you order everything because I'm shutting it down."

"Why would you do that?"

Because you're a fucking liar. "I'm expanding into new business opportunities."

"Do it on one of your properties!"

"There you go again," I teased, reading the short menu. "Honey, we're married. What's yours is mine."

"So you won't mind if I ruin your home?"

"Have at it."

"I don't understand." Her voice trembled, the sound stabbing me. "Why are you doing this?"

"This restaurant is nothing to me, but it's something to you. I'll close it down. I don't give a damn."

"What the hell is wrong with you?"

A lot.

"Nothing. I like seeing you hot and bothered." I faced the grimacing waiter. "We'll have it all."

"Sir, we don't make smaller portions—"

"You know who I am. Bring me the whole goddamn menu, or you're fired."

The man paled. "Right."

Carmela set the glass down, fingers pinching the stem as though she wished it was my neck. "You touch a brick, and I swear to God, Michael."

"You'll put salt in my coffee? Key my car? Destroy my sex toys?" I enjoyed watching her squirm. "They can be replaced."

"I can think of a few things on your body you'd miss."

"You don't have it in you." I leaned forward, patting her hand. "Plus, I'd truss you up before you got a knife anywhere near my balls."

"You better sleep with one eye open."

"I'll tie you to the bed frame. *Problem solved.*"

The waiter approached with our appetizers—bruschetta, grilled octopus, and burrata. Carmela beamed at the server, which caused him to linger until I shot him a pointed glare. She dove into the bruschetta and piled on cheese, her face suffused with greed as she ate.

She moaned. "So good."

"You're ridiculous."

"Michael, try it."

I did.

I sank my teeth into the ciabatta glazed with basil. The sharp, nutty flavor yanked me to the Mediterranean, where I had a fantastic bowl of pesto. Nothing in the States had ever compared. All I saw were the turquoise waters and white umbrellas of Portofino. The vision faded behind Carmela, who watched me with a knowing grin.

"It tastes just like Italy, doesn't it?"

I tried not to enjoy it. "It's not bad."

"The secret's in the pine nuts. Most places import them from China. Cheaper, but the flavor profile's not the same. You have to go to the source. The Mediterranean."

I thrust the half-eaten appetizer away, hating that she'd gotten to me through food, of all things. "Portofino."

"See?" Carmela seized on that, glowing. "This isn't *just* another Italian restaurant, Michael. You have no idea how hard I pushed for those nuts. They cost a fortune, but they're worth it. You can't eat them without your taste buds exploding."

"What are you, the head chef?"

"I managed this place for a while. I worked in a lot of Dad's businesses." Carmela picked up her fork and scrubbed at a watermark. "I'd come here, work the lunch and dinner shifts, and attend meetings with his builders."

"Builders?"

"Yeah, Dad wanted a brewery and tasting room. It was an enormous project—lots of permits. Dealing with construction was a nightmare. I had to be on them for every minor thing."

"What's in a brewery besides four walls and concrete?"

"Bureaucracy. It took forever."

A smile ticked over my cheek. A scrappy woman existed underneath all that beauty. I was drawn to her because of her tits and ass. I liked curves, and she had plenty. I never thought she'd done something with her life besides spend her dad's paper.

Now I knew better.

She wasn't a crushing wallflower or a high-maintenance brat. She was a hustler. A girl who toiled twelve hours a day just to keep busy. She sounded like me. This new side of her pitted my stomach with dread.

I needed to destroy this woman before she killed me.

I beckoned her. "Come."

Irritation flicked across her gaze. "What do you want?"

Could she do anything without arguing?

"I'm giving you a chance to save your daddy's restaurant."

She slid off the chair, her big eyes widening with hope that I'd crush.

"Since you're a renaissance woman, it should be easy for you to entertain this crowd. Follow me."

Her cheeks pinked as I wove through the tables, making a beeline for the stage. I unfolded a hundred-dollar bill and approached the man singing in the microphone.

I waved money in his face.

"We don't do song requests—"

"Get off. Let my wife sing." I tucked the cash in his hand. When he raised his brow, I shoved in several more bills. "Fuck off."

He stepped aside, the music grinding to a halt. The patrons didn't glance our way.

Carmela gaped at me. "Michael, what are you doing?"

"You are tonight's entertainment." I gestured at the hipsters neck-deep in their Bolognese and wine. "Get this whole room to clap, and I won't bulldoze this place."

"Fine."

Fine?

Carmela smiled like I'd handed her a trophy, and faced the guy behind the keyboard. "Can you play 'Valerie' in E-flat?"

By the time I returned to my seat, Carmela had already wiped herself of emotion. She seemed calm—in her element. She adjusted the microphone stand as though she'd done it thousands of times before.

The band picked up with a jazzy, upbeat tempo. Once people locked eyes on the magnetic woman on stage, nobody looked away. Carmela belted the lyrics. I didn't recognize it, but voices joined in the chorus.

She was perfect. She never stumbled over a lyric. She sounded great, and before the tune ended, half the place shouted the chorus. People clapped when she finished—even the fucking barman. The guitarist palmed her shoulder, mouthing *good job*. She replaced the microphone, beaming like she'd taken a hit of ecstasy. Heads followed my smoking-hot brunette to our table, where the jealous stares of men raked my back.

Carmela bounced with a liveliness I never saw before. The torch-like intensity of her confidence blinded me. "I win. You lose."

I didn't care.

I was awestruck. "You were amazing."

Carmela sank into her chair, her cheeks flushing.

"Where the hell did you learn to perform?" I dragged my seat so that we sat beside each other. "How did you *do* that?"

"Everybody likes 'Valerie.' It's a popular record." Carmela

shrugged, picking at the fried calamari. "I've had a lot of practice. I used to sing karaoke."

"You seemed really happy up there."

"I was. Singing is my passion. If I had to do it over again, I would've joined a band."

"Why can't you?"

"I wouldn't even know where to begin."

"You made a room of strangers ecstatic. They're still watching you. Maybe you belong on stage, Carmela."

Carmela looked how she did outside. The bruschetta crumbled in her fingers. She wiped them on her napkin, wide-eyed.

"What do you mean?"

"You could do gigs at my club. I throw black-tie events every month. Interested?"

"Oh my God, yes. Yes, I'd *love* to."

I turned to the food, but she grabbed my wrist.

Her eyes blazing, she pressed her mouth into mine. She kissed me in a way she never had before. An electric current passed through me, her aggression stirring my cock, awakening feelings that should've stayed dormant.

We parted. She crushed her lips into my cheek until I half-heartedly pushed her away.

"All right, settle down."

"I can't help it. It's what I've always wanted."

I toasted her. "To your new career."

She melted. "Thank you."

"No skin off my back."

"I owe you. I wouldn't have put myself out there if it weren't for you."

"Are you kidding? I thought you'd fall on your face."

She sipped her wine. "Joke's on you."

I couldn't stay mad at her. "I got my ass handed to me."

"I like a man who admits defeat."

"Yeah, well. I admire a woman who proves me wrong."

Carmela's cheeks went pink. "I never know where I stand with you."

I dabbed her finger in the pesto sauce and licked it off. "Let's go home. I'll show you."

CARMELA WOULDN'T LEAVE my head.

I imagined her tits filling my hands, her ruby-red lips milking my cock, how I woke up with her thighs splayed over me, and how she'd tasted mild and sweet. Her mouth and pussy—the way I'd gone back and forth. She'd loved it so much I'd done it again this morning.

I'd also taken a picture of Carmela, fast asleep in my sheets. I looked at it as often as a teenage boy with a crush.

Giving her a gig at Sanctum wasn't an act of love. I was placating the wife. Feeding her a fantasy. I didn't even mind being upstaged at my challenge. I respected her for turning the tables on me without throwing a fit. She had a lot more guts than I gave her credit for, and I liked her as a role model for Matteo. He needed a mom who didn't throw tantrums. Yeah, she'd fucking lied, but that was a week into our new marriage, and she was protecting Mia. I could forgive that.

During the post-orgasmic bliss of last night and the haze between waking, I was at peace. That's how I stayed until I arrived at Sanctum.

Julian wanted to be anywhere but here.

His face was pinched with fatigue, his normally clean-shaven jaw glistening with stubble, and I had to talk to him about his wrinkled shirt. An employee of Sanctum couldn't look like he'd just rolled out of bed.

"Is there a reason you can't pick up an iron?"

His mouth twisted. "My kid was sick, and the nanny was late. She had a car accident, so I didn't have time. Is that all right with you?"

"Your eyes are bloodshot."

"From working nights." Julian raked his hair and sighed. "Can't complain about the scenery, though."

I'd never explained that I met his sister here. He had no idea she was a hooker. Serena told her clueless family that she was an actuary, which was hilarious because the only numbers she knew were the grams of heroin to get high.

I was courting disaster by having Julian at Sanctum. Someone would bring up Serena, and the truth would wreck him.

"I did it for years. Suck it up and don't get hustled by the girls." I glanced at the calendar hanging on the wall. "I need you to do me a favor."

Julian sagged into the chair and released a gigantic sigh. His attitude was ungrateful, considering I'd paid for the clothes on his fucking back.

"Perhaps you need another reminder of why you work for me."

Julian's lips thinned before he pushed out a barely audible no. "You don't have to be such an asshole."

Julian's short-lived defiance flared out like a dud. That was the way he was—an easily cowed loser who folded at the slightest pressure. His entire family was full of weak character.

"My wife will perform at our black-tie events from now on. Give her anything she needs. Turns out, she's a phenomenal singer." A faint glow of pride warmed my chest. "She can do whatever she wants, so long as the vibe is good, and people are signing up for memberships."

"Your wife is working here?"

"I warned her about this place." That didn't mean I trusted the horndogs from hitting on Carmela. "Keep an eye on her."

"Okay."

"There's something else." I slid a large mug shot of Carmela's ex across the table. "Be on the lookout for this man."

"Who is he?"

"Biker scum. He goes by Crash." I tapped the photo, dragging his attention to me. "This is important. You see him, you call me. *Immediately*. If he attempts to leave, stall him. Give him everything. Comp his drinks and girls. Drop to your knees and suck his cock. Don't let him leave. Got it?"

"Michael, I'm not a gangster. I've no interest in being involved. You should use one of your soldiers—"

"Man the fuck up. I'm not asking you to kill him. Just make him stay."

I doubted Crash would show up here, but I had to prepare for any possibility.

"All right."

"If Carmela is here, get her somewhere safe. She can't run into this guy. Understand?"

"What's this about?"

"The less you know, the better." Julian opened his mouth, but I waved him off like a Sanctum girl. "And change your fucking shirt. I have extras in my closet."

Julian mumbled something indistinct as he shuffled from the room. My gaze fell on Nick Smith's dead-eyed mug shot. I'd put a hefty price on his head. It was only a matter of time before someone gave him up.

Since Carmela told me the whole story, I'd been consumed with vengeance. The gossip surrounding Carmela and Alessio's breakup never mentioned a biker or an eight-month captivity. Alessio had kept every sickening detail on the down-low, discouraging any mention of Carmela.

He'd glossed over the incident so thoroughly I'd pushed it from my mind. She claimed he'd done it to spare her humiliation, but that was bullshit. Alessio was a selfish dick. He didn't want to look bad.

Why hadn't he killed Crash?

Why the fuck didn't he fight harder for Carmela?

I needed Alessio back.

I had a lot of *questions*.

TWENTY

CARMELA

I STEPPED OFF THE STAGE.

Bartenders applauded between serving drinks. Men whistled and clapped. Although I'd stumbled through a few of the lyrics from sheer nerves, I'd finished my first set.

Unreal.

Boundless energy zipped through my body as I made a beeline for the ebony bar. I was just the opener for the main act, but that suited me. I needed the practice. Singing in a dive was nothing, but performing at a high-class establishment sawed through my spine.

My hands shook as I reached inside my purse.

"You need a drink." A masked stranger thrust a tumbler filled with amber liquid near my elbow. He was old enough to be my grandfather. "What's your name?"

"Carmela, and she's married." Julian's grave tone cut the air as he pushed into my side, channeling a jealous husband vibe.

"My mistake," the man said, turning away.

My husband's ex-brother-in-law raked his thick blond waves.

"You could've let me handle him."

"Yeah, but Michael gave me specific instructions. Some guys can get super creepy." A wide grin staggered across Julian's handsome face. "I had my doubts, but you were amazing."

A ripple of warmth ran through me. "Really?"

"You've got pipes, girl."

"I might change the key for '*Someone to Watch Over Me*.' I think it was too low."

"No, you're perfect. Your voice is clear as a bell." He leaned against the counter, ignoring a naked blonde making eyes at him. "You're too classy for this place."

"Eventually, I'll upgrade to more intimate lounges, but this is a decent start."

I didn't mind that it was a sex club. Nobody would bump into me here, so it didn't matter if I screwed up, and Julian was amenable to my requests. We hadn't spent much time together aside from the occasional one-hour playdate, but he was easygoing.

I didn't know why Michael had such an issue with him.

"How's Michael treating you?"

"Good. The kids are great, too." I fingered my dress, unable to fight the rising flush from claiming my cheeks. "How's your daughter?"

"She's with her mom for the week." He rubbed the bridge of his nose and yawned. "Damn. Graveyard shift is tough. I have no idea how Michael did it for so long. He used to work nights while my sister took care of the kids. He'd sleep through the mornings, wake up around noon, and spend the day running after Mariette before having to do it all over again."

I sipped the drink as grief seemed to pour from Julian.

He blinked, his voice tight. "Does he ever mention Serena?"

"Never."

His lip curled. "*Of course.*"

Truthfully, I was dying for the whole story. I'd heard wild tales from Mia. "What was she like?"

"Beautiful. Like you, in that department. She had this ridiculous laugh. She could be warm and gracious, but she was also selfish. Entitled. Greedy."

"Michael hates talking about her."

"I'm sure he'd like to forget she existed, but those children are still half my sister."

I palmed his shoulder. "So you know, I'm not trying to replace her. I encourage the kids to talk about her. Mariette has a memory box. I want them to remember Serena."

He smiled, his eyes gleaming. "I hope he doesn't treat you the way he treated her."

"What does that mean?"

"They had a volatile relationship. Lots of fighting. I love my brother-in-law, but he can be harsh. My sister called me all the time, crying. If you need help, ask. I'm a phone call away."

"Thanks." My skin prickled at his somber tone. "I'll keep that in mind."

"What's that?" A jacketed arm slid across my waist, tugging me into a man's body. A bundle of tulips wrapped in cellophane slipped into my hands. Then a smoky voice tickled my ear. "*Bravissimo.*"

Heat blistered my lips as Michael's kiss burned me from the inside out, and then he faced Julian, radiating aggression.

"Is there a reason you're standing here?"

Julian sighed and murmured a goodbye. Michael watched him disappear in the sea of black jackets. His wolf-like stare followed Julian until I grabbed his tie.

"Why do you have to be so rude?"

He pinched my cheek. "He needs to be knocked down a peg."

"No, he doesn't. He's a nice guy."

"That's what you said about me in the beginning." Michael bumped his forehead on mine, grinning. "You still like nice guys?"

"I care about how you treat people. I don't want to be known as the wife of the jerk."

"You already are."

I growled. "Why do you hate Julian?"

"I don't respect him. He's a sarcastic, ungrateful fuck."

"Would it kill you to tone it down?"

"Probably not, but I won't."

He cupped my cheeks.

Heat rippled up my neck. "Why's that?"

"You like me how I am."

"Oh, I like you?"

He smiled. "Yeah."

He'd come a long way from my first night. He'd defended me from Nick. He'd gotten me gigs in a club. He would eventually give me a baby. He gave me hugs, texted silly emojis, cooked me breakfast, and showered me with small acts of kindness. Something warmer than affection coated my heart when he held me.

I lifted the flowers to my nose, inhaling their scent. "How did you know they're my favorite?"

"Easy. You picked them for our wedding."

"You remember that?"

"Hard to forget anything since you came into my life."

I tipped my head and kissed him. He met my pressure with a flurry of hot strokes. His sigh caressed my mouth. Then he pulled away, eyes closed as though he savored my taste. His expression broke into a lazy smile.

He hooked my elbow and dragged me from the guests mingling with half-naked women. He stepped into an empty, darkened hall where open doors beckoned into rooms.

"You're nice today."

"You and that damned word."

He grabbed my waist and pushed me into a room. A thrill rushed down my spine as he backed me against the wall. He slapped my arm against the concrete and fastened a leather cuff around my wrist.

"I'm crazy about you, Carmela. That's why I'm *nice*."

Sweet Jesus.

A second jolt shot through my ribs.

Did he mean that? Was this part of the sex? I assumed the playful banter started and ended in the bedroom—but he brought it to *Sanctum*. He looked at me like I'd hung the moon in the sky.

My mouth went dry as I put it together.

His passion reminded me of another man.

Nick.

TWENTY-ONE

MICHAEL

THE DEVIL MAKES US SIN, but we like twisting in his grip.

My mother said that all the time. I considered it hand-me-down nonsense, but I was never sober long enough to string two thoughts together. I didn't understand it until I stopped using. Once the withdrawal plunged me into constant migraines, all I could think about was taking more.

I couldn't function without drugs. I'd let them consume me, destroying everything I liked about myself. I never realized how badly I'd wrecked my body until I quit cocaine. The kids saved me from self-destruction, but another devil was waiting in the wings.

Vengeance.

I'd gotten Crash's number.

Common sense dictated I shouldn't contact the guy I would kill, but the PIs I'd hired weren't finding the fucker. I needed to know which rat-infested whorehouse he slept in so I could *throttle* him.

I wanted him angry.

I hoped he'd fuck up and show his face somewhere. I opened my burner phone and dialed. My thumb hit the green call button before I'd composed myself.

It rang once.

"Crash." A toneless voice answered.

"This is Michael."

"*Costa.* How'd you get this number?"

I smiled. "Don't worry about that."

"I got nothing to say to you."

I had plenty. "How's your mouth? Still healing?"

"Does it bother you she was sucking my cock two months before she said I do?"

"We never dated, so there's no blow to my pride. You know, she didn't want me, either." I wheeled in my chair, looking out the window. "But at least I was man enough to keep her."

"I didn't lose her."

"You did."

"Just because I like the chase—"

"I beat you. She married me."

"It's not over yet!" he bellowed like a wounded animal. "You're the fuckboy. I'm her forever."

"You've got that backward. She's wearing my ring. We're building a life together. We'll have a baby. You're a douchebag rapist. A burnout loser. Biker *scum.*"

"Give her back, you piece of shit!"

"I'll torch your bike and throw it into the Bay before I let you touch her."

"Shut your fucking mouth, or I'll kick your teeth down your throat and shut it for you—"

"I will find you," I growled into the receiver. "I'll slip into your house while you're sleeping and gut you. Before I do that, though, I'm banging my wife."

"I'll murder your whole guinea family you fucking dago—"

I ended the call. Then I cracked the case before hurling the destroyed phone at the wall. Threatening my loved ones hit a sore spot.

I left my office as Carmela's footsteps thumped the staircase. She disappeared into our bedroom. I creaked open the door, lured by the sound of the shower. My gaze landed on a pair of heels beside the bed, crumpled panties, a bra. I caressed the velvety pads, still warm from cradling her tits. My cock stiffened as a rush of heat surged to my groin, and then I marched to the bathroom.

Carmela stood behind the half-fogged glass. The spray washed her neck and shoulders. I drank in her tanned curves, every cleft and dimple, her teardrop breasts, the graceful arches that were forbidden to other men. I thought of Crash, how he'd once coveted the same woman and gained her trust, only to defile it and inflict harm on that body.

I needed to execute that bastard.

The door clicked as it latched.

Carmela's head turned. Her lips parted, taking me in before she faced the showerhead. She lathered soap, massaging her scalp, streams of white foam running where my hands ached to touch.

I ripped my shirt off and undid my belt, stepping out of my slacks and briefs. I stepped into the shower's steam. Carmela's brows twitched when I entered the jet of water.

Things were better between us.

I'd wake in a vanilla cloud, with her arm flung over my chest. Sometimes it was all I could do to not say the three words begging for release, but I'd only dented her armor. If I told her, she'd panic. Carmela's thick walls shot up whenever I hinted at having stronger feelings. It had something to do with Crash.

I massaged her shoulders.

Carmela let out a ragged sigh, backing into my embrace.

"I don't tell you how beautiful you are often enough." I caressed her olive skin and kissed her shoulder. "Biggest crime I've committed."

"You're such a cheeseball."

"And yet, you love my stupid jokes."

Carmela rolled her eyes and smiled, her dimples growing as she faced me. She threw her arms around my neck and kissed me, lashing me with electricity that jumped everywhere.

I caught her lips with a flash of tongue and teeth. I groped her curves, kissing the dent below her ear. The heat searing my insides was unbearable. It towered to an inferno as Carmela grasped my waist, teasing the edge of my cock as she drifted downward.

I turned off the water.

We stumbled into the bedroom. I snatched a towel and patted her down until Carmela gently tugged it from my hands and wrapped me.

"When's the last time someone took care of you?"

"I don't need—"

"I know. You don't need anyone." She seized my chin and ghosted my lips. "That's why I like you so much."

I need you.

She kissed me, cutting me off before I could utter my confession.

Carmela was the life in my veins, the fire in my soul, and once she was pregnant, she wouldn't leave me. I had to seal the deal.

She bit me, soothing the hurt with her tongue. She broke off, her sexy grin widening. Her nails raked my body as she descended to her knees. Blood drained from my brain as Carmela palmed my thighs.

I fisted her hair. "What are you waiting for?"

"You to tell me how you want it."

My cock twitched at the sight of her, naked and kneeling. "You shouldn't need directions."

Her touch tickled my balls before she gripped my shaft, sliding up and down. She stroked, massaging the stream of precum around the head. Her velvety skin teased me until I was ready to wreck her. She kissed the tip. Swiped me with wet heat.

A jolt shot into my groin. I rocked my hips and slid along her mouth. Her lips parted. She took me inside. I grazed her scalp as she leaned forward. Her tight warmth hugged me. Goddamn, she went deep.

I pulsed, trying not to come like I was eighteen and not thirty-four. Stamping down on the flames was next to impossible when she deepthroated me, her eyes locked on mine. She pulled away, gasping.

"Yeah, take a breather. That was hard work."

She laughed.

My chest tightened as she swallowed my cock. I traced the length of her neck, up the delicate arch, and under her jaw. Her muscles flexed. It was beautiful to watch. I was seduced by this dick-sucking Siren, who seemed determined to drain me.

"Slow down. You'll make me come."

She didn't. Carmela worked me vigorously, flashing that coy smile whenever she paused. She taunted me with the tickling of her tongue, her smooth cheeks, and her touch, gliding up and down my legs.

My fingers sank into her hair. I couldn't stand giving up control. Allowing her to pleasure me was more than I could bear. I would've fucked her face, but the desire melted once I met her gaze.

I couldn't.

Watching her in this position sawed into me because it forced me to confront my crimes. Innocence gleamed in those big brown eyes that trusted me. She'd given me everything.

And what had I done to her?

I stilled her with a hand on her shoulders. Then I hauled her upright and dragged her into my embrace.

"Why'd you stop me?"

I steered us toward the bed. "Because I'd rather do this."

"Was I doing it wrong?"

"You're perfect. Always perfect."

I lowered her onto the mattress. I slid between her thighs and pushed inside her. My lips met hers as my hips rocked, slow and sweet. Her legs cinched my waist. She sighed as I filled her deeply. She dug into me, but I resisted the temptation to rut her like a beast.

I wanted to make love to her.

When was the last time I'd done this? In my early twenties, I figured out I was into kink and never looked back. Vanilla did nothing for me. If I wasn't dominating a woman, I got bored. But I didn't feel like being rough.

I pulsed in and out, rolling over her slicked skin. I kissed her pout as heat webbed across my chest. My rhythm picked up, and Carmela arched. She gripped me and yanked me, but I didn't lose control. Her eyes searched me. Questions swam in her gaze—ones I wouldn't answer.

Not yet.

Our lovemaking reached a crescendo of rapid thrusts and sloppy kisses. Carmela's orgasm shook through her body. Her walls clenched me, massaging my cock until I came. I buried myself. A wave of euphoria leached the strength from my limbs as I spilled into her.

Carmela pressed her smile into my cheek and nipped my ear. "That was different."

"Vanilla." I grabbed a strand of her hair and inhaled.

"And you liked it?"

"Of course." I kissed her flushed face, surprised at the genuine worry in her voice. "You're always great."

"I just want you to be satisfied."

I was more than satisfied.

I was in love.

TWENTY-TWO

CARMELA

My life was a fairytale.

The storm clouds had blown away, and the horizon of my bright future awaited me. I waited for the snide asshole to return, but Michael seemed committed to being the perfect husband.

He felt different. I never woke up without his hand on my thigh or hip. He took longer to release me from hugs, and he dragged his feet whenever he had to leave, although that might've been because I cooked more often. I baked him sweets because he inhaled rolls of store-bought cookies, and I didn't want him eating crap filled with preservatives.

"Gotta go." Michael finished the snickerdoodle and kissed the kids' heads. "Later, babies."

"*Wait.*" I dipped a spoon in the pot on the stove and offered it to Michael. "Taste this."

Michael sipped. "What is it? Soup?"

I grimaced. "Spaghetti sauce. Don't tell me it's watery."

"A little," he admitted. "But it tastes great."

"I used too many vegetables."

How else would I make these kids eat properly? I couldn't believe how hard it was to get them to consume anything that wasn't a potato.

"It'll be fine. Let it simmer for a few hours."

Michael lingered when I caught his hands, marveling at the heat spinning my insides when he leaned forward, his mouth brushing mine like goose down—

"Stop kissing!" shrieked Mariette, who glowered at her dad. "You're always kissing. It's so gross."

Michael grabbed Mariette and planted a noisy kiss on her cheek. Then he rumpled her braid and headed out.

"Disgusting," she muttered, wiping her face.

They ate, and I washed dishes. The doorbell chimed as I cleaned the counters. I threw the rag in the sink and got the door, peering at the man lounging on the wrought-iron fence. His skin was as dark as mine, and he wore slim-fitted navy pants under a V-necked black T-shirt. He had thick ebony hair and angular features. His brooding demeanor oozed over the lawn. Relief flooded his expression as he straightened, beckoning.

"Alessio?" I stepped outside, gaping at what must've been a mirage. "What are you doing here?"

I rushed to the gate and yanked it open.

Alessio entered, raking his espresso-brown locks as he looked through me, at the mansion. "Is Michael here?"

"No, you just missed him." My eyes burned as Alessio scooped me into a fierce hug. "I can't believe you're here."

"Mia's at the house. Let's get the fuck out of here."

"What? Why?"

"Carmela, can we play twenty questions at my place? I want to leave before he shows up."

"Why are you even here?" I headed inside, frustrated when my brother-in-law stood in the garden. "Don't stand there. Come in."

"I'm not here to dawdle."

But he sank his hands into his pockets and followed me inside, his widened gaze flicking at the portraits on the walls, the children's drawings stuck on the fridge, and me.

"I read your message. I couldn't believe it, to be honest. I thought for sure someone hacked your email, so I spent the last few weeks reaching out to my old contacts...and they told me."

"I don't have a clue what you're talking about, but it was a mistake to *come back*. Take Mia and go." Every second he lingered put them in danger. "They're still looking for you!"

"I'm not leaving without you."

"Alessio, I'm fine. I'm breathing and everything." I slapped my sides, hating his pity. "Don't look at me like that."

"Honey, you asked me for help!"

"What?"

My former fiancé gaped at me as though I'd suffered brain damage. His brows knitted as I left his side, strolling into the living room. Both children sat on the couch, stabbing iPads. Their heads whipped around, and Matteo shrieked.

"*Zio!*"

Mariette elbowed her brother aside in her haste to tackle Alessio, whose shell-shocked expression never flickered. He looked like he was waking from a terrible dream. He patted Mariette's head.

"Hey, hon."

"Where've you been, *Zio?*"

Alessio's gaze swiveled to me, wide-eyed. "You didn't send it. He did."

"Send *what?*"

"The fucking email!" He dropped his voice at Mariette's scandalized gasp. "You—*he wrote*—that you were forced into marriage."

It clicked together when Alessio opened his cell and showed me the message.

Michael forced me to marry him. Help me.

I'd never typed those words. I would've committed Seppuku before dragging my sister and her husband back to Boston.

Michael did this.

He'd violated my privacy. He'd lured my brother-in-law into a trap, and he'd done it without consulting me. The betrayal sliced me to the bone. It stuck in my throat.

"You need to go. Right now." I grabbed his arms and squeezed. "You have no idea what you're up against."

"Yeah. Your parents are missing."

What? "They're at home!"

Alessio's face creased with sadness. "They disappeared weeks ago. Nobody has seen or heard from them."

My warmth vanished. The lights seemed to dim. My world shrank into a desolate landscape.

"No. That's impossible."

"Carmela, I was there. The lawn is overgrown. Their mailbox was so full the post office stopped delivering. They're gone." he said, incredulous. "Did you not know?"

I'LL RELEASE IGNACIO.

Michael's callous voice taunted me during the quick drive to Alessio's mansion, the kids chattering the whole way. I hadn't told Michael I'd left and I wasn't sure what to do. I was barely holding it together, my shoulders shaking, my gasps silenced by the music Alessio cranked up. His worried gaze swept over me once we parked in his driveway. Black escalades surrounded the Georgian-Revival home, but all the security wouldn't stop Michael.

Alessio hiked Matteo to his hip as we walked toward his house. Mariette flew through the kissing gate and launched up the steps, where my sister stood in white capris and a pink top. I broke into tears as the pint-sized brunette tore across the garden. She crashed into me, arms cinching my waist in a bear hug. We stumbled inside, laughing and crying as Alessio shepherded the children.

"Are you okay? Do you need anything?" Mia patted my shoulder as though searching for wounds. "Should we get a doctor?"

"I'm fine."

The next half hour felt like a replay of the weeks after I escaped my ex-boyfriend when my battered body was all they saw. They still looked at me like a broken thing, and it roiled my guts because I wasn't damaged. I'd survived Nick. I'd survive Michael, but *this* hurt like hell.

Mia's manicured nails dug into my shoulders as we settled into their playroom, which seemed covered in an inch of dust. "Why didn't you *tell* me? Why'd you pretend everything was okay?"

"Because you deserved to be happy."

"What about you?" she fretted, clasping my palm in her tiny one. "You think it makes me glad, knowing you were being tortured—"

"Michael never laid a hand on me."

Mia exchanged a glance with Alessio, who sat beside his wife. "It doesn't matter. He crossed the line."

"He said he'd let Dad go if I married him. I thought he'd follow through. I guess I was that desperate, but it was so *stupid* of me. I can't believe I trusted him."

He never released my father.

Dad was probably dead. And Mom? Who the fuck knew?

Devastation cut me to my knees. My hands slapped the floor as pain balled in my throat, bursting out in a scream. Mia flung herself on me, dissolving into tears as Alessio's appeals for calm were ignored.

My life was a lie.

He'd conned me, and I'd fallen for it, seduced by his charm and the promise of a baby.

How could he do this to me?

How could he be so cruel?

I broke into loud, unrestrained sobs, the sound echoing through the house. Mia clung to me, her low growl shaking with wrath. Nothing calmed me—not Alessio's promises or my sister's support—it wasn't until a small body pressed into my side that I fell silent. Fingers touched my cheeks as a soft voice pleaded.

"Don't cry, Mommy."

That word cleaved me in two, filling me with the sweetest joy and the sharpest agony. Michael must've encouraged Matteo to call me that, knowing what it'd mean to me. He'd manipulated me from the beginning.

I loved them too much.

I couldn't leave Michael without abandoning his kids.

"Sorry, honey." I wiped my face and forced a smile. "I'm sad because I haven't seen your auntie for a long time. It's okay. Go play with your sister."

Matteo's warm eyes filled me with grief. They were so like his father's. He returned to the pile of LEGOs and seized fistfuls of them, spraying Mariette with colorful blocks.

"I should text Michael."

"Carm, you shouldn't go back there." Mia gaped at Alessio, as though asking him for guidance. "We'll help you."

"I can't. They need me."

Alessio and Mia exchanged worried looks. "They'll survive. They have a team of nannies."

"I love them."

"You'll find someone else." Alessio lowered to his knees, softening. "You'll have kids of your own."

"No. I'm not leaving them."

A chime echoed from Alessio's pocket. He hissed into the receiver, and then he faced us. "He's here."

I sighed, standing.

"Stay with us. We have plenty of space."

"He'll never allow it." My insides collapsed as the front door creaked, the floor clipping with his youthful gait. "It's fine. I'll leave."

"No, it's not," Mia growled, seizing Alessio's jacket. "You can't let him take her away."

"I can't keep the man from his children!"

"No, you can't."

Michael's smoky cadence seemed to suck all the air as he

strolled through, poisoning the room with his presence. My husband surveyed Alessio with a curled lip.

"You look very tan. I guess Boca Raton agreed with you."

Alessio's jaw tensed. "What do you want?"

"My wife and kids. *Right now*."

"They should crash here for a few days."

"No. They belong with me. You ought to prepare for Vinn's arrival. He's on his way." Michael cocked his head and flashed me a sweet smile. "*Come*."

Mia balled her fists as Michael tugged his daughter along.

"Good to see you, Mia. Sorry you couldn't make the wedding. We'll share the photos with you."

They followed us to the door, Mia's face vivid with fear.

Alessio fisted my husband's sleeve. "You're dead to me."

Michael yanked from his grip. "Cool story, bro."

TWENTY-THREE
MICHAEL

CARMELA'S EYES SHOT FIRE.

As soon as I put the kids to bed, she'd stalked into the walk-in closet. She unzipped her dress and hurled the delicate fabric into the corner. She kicked off her heels, her mouthwatering curves on full display. Carmela slipped the bra straps from her shoulders. Her gaze burned with unshed tears as she removed every barrier, and my cock swelled, indifferent to her pain.

But I wasn't. "What are you doing?"

"Giving you what you want."

Carmela palmed my chest and shoved, hard enough to knock me backward. She didn't understand what her rage did to me, the dangerous impulses it stirred. "All you ever wanted was a body to use and a mind to *fuck with*."

"You know that's not true."

"I have no idea who you are anymore. Only that you're a liar and a disgrace to your children."

"That's why I married *you*. You're their moral compass." I stepped back, reining in my boiling feelings. "Carm, all I've done has been for us."

"You broke into my email!"

"I had a strong hunch you were lying when I asked you about your brother-in-law. Your story was laughably thin. Yeah, I read your emails. Want an apology? Look elsewhere."

"Fuck you."

"My children are more important than Alessio, and his absence threatened their safety. Do you read the news? It's getting worse out there. Partly because he left us without his contacts. I'm not sorry for manipulating Alessio."

"Because you're a bastard."

"You're not mad I hoodwinked *him*. You're upset because you think I betrayed you. I *didn't*. I've always been in your corner."

"You violated my privacy!"

Why was she stuck on one minor detail? "Go through my messages. I don't give a damn."

I tossed my phone onto the carpeted floor. I expected her to glance through my cell, but she shook her head like I was dangerous.

"I can't be with you."

My insides twisted. "Why?"

"Because it's not just the email. You lied about my dad. You were dishonest about everything. I feel stupid for believing in you. Marrying you was a huge mistake. I'm taking the kids for a few days."

"You want to rip out my heart, too? I can't live without them."

And that included her.

"Go to hell."

She choked, her words laced with so much bitterness that my skin tingled. She trembled, her hands balled into fists. Carmela was furious, and that gave me hope.

She cared.

So I confessed the last thing I was hiding.

"Carmela, I love you."

The color drained from her face. She seized a suitcase, turned it on its side, and packed it with stacks of clothing. Suddenly, she couldn't leave fast enough.

"I love you."

"*Stay away*."

I hadn't moved a muscle. "Why?"

"Because you're scaring me. You don't love me, Michael."

"I've never felt this way about *anyone*."

"That's called infatuation."

She was wrong.

I loved her.

The realization didn't come in a Hallmark-worthy moment with confetti and fireworks. It was a slow burn. Her picture was a screensaver on my fucking phone before I admitted it to myself. She was on my mind all the time, and I'd started to think crazy things.

"It's love."

"No, Michael. You love what I've *done* for you."

"Why can't it be both?"

"I'm saying it's not." She paced the walk-in closet, her teeth clenched so hard they ground together. "That's the problem with men like you."

"Why are you such in a hurry to dismiss my feelings?"

"The last man almost loved me *to death*."

"Carmela, I'm not him." I watched her freeze when I took her hand. "I love you. What do I have to do to prove it?"

"I-I don't know."

"Don't I show you that I care? Haven't I been there? I've given you everything you've asked for. What else do you need? Tell me, and it's yours."

"This is too intense." Patches of heat burned high on her cheeks. "I need a break from you."

But I didn't want a break. I wanted her in my arms, on the bed, the sofa, in my office, anywhere and everywhere. "You've lit a fire inside me. How am I supposed to put it out?"

"*Figure it out.*"

"I already have. I love you."

"Shut up." Tears squeezed from her eyes as she shook her head. "You don't love me!"

"Yes, I do. Because if I didn't? I would've killed your dad when he threatened to come after my children."

"He wouldn't do that!"

"He said it, Carmela." I rubbed my neck, remembering Ignacio's parting shots after our wedding. "I was all set to let him go, but then he ran his fucking mouth."

"What did you do with my parents?"

"I spared them. *For you.* I went against instinct and common sense because I love you."

"Where are they?"

"Italy. They're fine." I sighed as she trembled. "I kept it from you because I was worried you'd hate me."

"I do. I fucking hate you!"

Her indifference would've stung, but the rage got my blood flowing.

"Baby—"

Her hand whirled, crashing into my ear. My skin flared with the brutal slap, and Carmela uttered a horrified gasp, backing into the closet.

This was sick.

I shouldn't.

I grasped her wrist as she swung again, yanking her into my chest. I leaned forward, my nose touching hers. I swallowed her whispered *fuck you*, and claimed her mouth.

She shuddered as my lips stroked hers. She gasped, and I

deepened the kiss. My tongue chased her honeyed flavor as I kissed her harder—

Her fist crashed into my jaw.

I staggered back, stunned by the unexpected pain, and then I snatched her wrist. I pinned her against the wall, my heart hammering.

No violence.

"Apologize."

"No."

"Apologize, or I'll punish you."

"I'm sorry that your upbringing was so fucked up that you turned into a *sadistic* human being." Her passion broke as she dissolved into tears. "I'm sorry I trusted you. I'm sorry I thought we could raise a child. I'm sorry I ever laid eyes on you."

I grabbed the collar from the shelf and wrapped her neck. I latched it on before she'd tugged it off, and then I hissed in her ear.

"I'm not sorry for any of it."

The darkness burst forth. Everything I'd built to stave off my worst impulses crumbled. All that I'd locked away rushed toward Carmela.

I dragged her to the mattress. There was nothing loving about how I shoved her onto the bed. I climbed over her. Greed had consumed me. She tangled her fingers in my hair. She didn't pull or push. She watched me with a seething fury that was so fucking hot.

She tipped her head, taunting me with a half-open pout. Her skin baked with the heat of contempt. "I hate you."

"*Show me.* Use your mouth, not your words."

Carmela seized my jaw and smashed her lips into mine. I peeled off my jacket, and then the shirt. My belt slapped my slacks as I ripped it off. Carmela tore my body as every barrier disappeared. My naked chest molded into her tits as we made out with frenzied, biting kisses. Blood seeped onto my tongue, the metallic tang swimming with her sweet vanilla, a taste I'd corrupted.

She raked me. Her nails dug into my ass like tiny puncture wounds of hate. I welcomed the pain. She could batter me, scratch me bloody, or scream. It didn't matter.

I'd always love her.

Especially her tits. I licked them as she moaned. I swirled her nipple. Her grip softened. I kissed between her breasts, under her ribs, where her heartbeat slammed, and down her belly. I thrust her thighs apart, fingers gliding along her seam. I toyed with her as she lay still, fists digging into the sheets.

"Oh, now you want me?"

"*Shut up.*"

Her insolence shot a red-hot wave down my spine. She deserved to have my handprint permanently etched on her butt, so I flipped her and fisted her hair. I pulled the strands, forcing her to arch. Then I cracked my palm on her ass.

She twisted around, her cheeks blazing. "The fuck are you doing?"

"Disciplining my wife."

Carmela wrenched free. I seized her wrists and pinned them above her back dimples. She wriggled, immobilized by my weight. "Get off!"

"What did I say the night after our wedding?" I smacked her ass, relishing her pink flush. "Tell me the rule you broke."

"No violence!"

"You'll be so raw, you won't be able to sit for hours."

Carmela shuddered with each blow, her mouth twitching when I pinched and stroked the burn. She groaned. It didn't take long for her olive skin to blush. I glided up and down her thick curves. Carmela's gasp melted into a sigh.

"You'll have a nice reminder for a few days," I hissed into her ear. "Every time you see my hand, remember what happens when you disobey me."

Carmela's expression was dazed as I flipped her over and settled between her thighs. I dragged my cock down her clit, slipping into her wetness. I shoved her legs onto my shoulders and lowered myself. I pushed inside her, hard. Her breathing hitched as I anchored.

"Fuck you."

"I am. I'm fucking the hate right out of you." I pulled out and stabbed deep, and she gasped. "Hate me. Fight me. It doesn't matter. I'll always love you."

Her growl deepened into a rich groan. "I hate you."

And yet she kept pulling me closer, whimpering, chasing me with her soft lips. She hated me, but she couldn't get enough of me. She curled with me on the couch, in bed, everywhere.

Her influence had enriched my children's lives. She did so many things to make me love her.

So I did.

How was that a surprise?

Catching her throat, I squeezed while her heart hammered. My mouth crashed into hers. I pounded her hard, my thrusts shoving her backward. She glided up my arms, attacking me with kisses. She bit my shoulder. Her tongue wetted the sting.

I held her hips and rammed into her. Then my cock twitched, and a yell burst from me. My limbs shook. Euphoria tangled my body, as swift as alcohol rushing through veins. I kissed the tears skating her cheek as I pulsed back and forth.

Carmela was getting close. She rocked, meeting my thrusts. Her brows pinched as she clung to me. She dug her nails into me, her teeth clenched. She made a frustrated sound and grabbed my neck.

I gave her a Prince Charming kiss. Carmela met my gentle strokes with a furious passion. She clawed my ribs, convulsing around my cock. Spasms rippled over her face, like shock-waves of pleasure.

"I love you."

Her eyes still glazed with hurt. "Stop saying that."

"I'll keep repeating it until it sinks into your thick head."

Carmela ripped from my side. She dropped from the bed, snagged a robe, and tossed me a fearful glance before dashing outside. Her bare feet slapped the wood as she disappeared into another room. A lock slid into place.

I didn't chase her. It would take a while to regain her trust.

I wanted her to have everything.

But it had to be with me.

TWENTY-FOUR

CARMELA

I love you.

Every time the warmth from those words washed over me, my throat closed. I froze. My body seized with panic. Michael went ahead with life as though nothing had changed, but for me everything was different.

I love you.

This was my worst nightmare.

Nick's love had almost destroyed me. What would Michael's do?

Somehow, I'd forgotten that Michael's wrought-iron fencing wasn't a white-picket utopia. It had felt like a home. I'd started to appreciate his leather chairs and steel-gray sofas. The walls weren't so lifeless after I'd plastered the kids' paintings everywhere. My colorful throws had brightened the place, and once I'd switched out the pieces I'd hated with softer, more feminine furniture, I'd become comfortable.

I didn't see him much for the next few days. Alessio's return had consequences. There were city hall officials to court, gangsters to control, and an unruly public to soothe. Alessio's PR machine needed time to work.

I spent hours hanging out with my parents, who'd returned from Italy. Having everybody home was nice, but the undercurrent of tension kept me from relaxing. I'd told Dad and Alessio about Crash's return to my life. They were upset, especially my father. Dad broke down in tears. Alessio slammed his fist into the wall, shattering a picture frame.

I felt nothing but a vague annoyance. It was hard enough processing what'd happened without having to deal with other people's feelings, so I wandered the house until I heard them arguing with escalating voices.

Alessio stood with his back against the bookshelf, his black eyes pinched shut. "I didn't think Vinn would go after my family. I was *wrong*. I'm sorry."

Dad shook his graying head. "You fucked up, kid."

"I know." Alessio sank into a chair, rubbing his face. "Mia and I wanted out."

"That's a pipe dream. You don't have a father-figure anymore because he got locked up, so I'll give you advice. Get your shit together. You have a family."

"I was trying to make her happy—"

"My daughter's a young girl. But you? You knew better, you fucking *moron*."

I gaped at Dad.

Alessio glowered. "You're right."

There was no resentment behind his words, only resignation.

Dad made a derisive sound and stomped from the room. The walls trembled from a distant door slamming. Alessio stared at the floor, which left me in the awkward position of comforting my ex.

We had hated each other, but he'd come a long way from the angry gangster who used to be my fiancé. His love and devotion to my sister had changed my perception.

"It'll be okay." I squeezed his shoulder. "Mia will move on. She's not an idiot. She knows you can't just quit."

"She's a dreamer," he said, the roughness tamed from his voice. "Telling someone to give up on happily-ever-after is tough. There'll always be a crisis."

"She doesn't have to abandon all hope. Once she settles in, she'll realize that raising a child surrounded by family is better than doing it alone in Florida."

"Yeah, if it weren't for the constant violence." He shook his head, as though dislodging the memories. "Never mind. I'm back. If you could do me a favor and visit Mia I'd—*shit*."

"What?"

Alessio stalked to the window, glowering at the Audi rolling to the curb. "*Michael*."

A ripple of anger ran through me. "He shouldn't be here."

"You expected him to listen?"

"See you later."

Alessio grunted as he watched the street.

I trudged out of the house, not bothering to look for my dad. He was probably drinking heavily, and Mom was busy in the kitchen, cooking a feast for people who seemed unlikely to coexist.

Michael strolled the driveway, his hooded gaze softening when it landed on me. He balled me against his cashmere chest. Then he spotted Alessio, and he dug into my shoulders. He cupped my face and kissed me. It was a hard and possessive, the bruising pressure filling me with heat. His hand sailed down my spine until it rode my ass.

He acted so much like Nick.

It scared me.

"You're supposed to stay away from my parents.'"

"I can't get enough of you." Michael looped his grip around my waist as we headed toward his car. He kept glancing at Alessio, and then he flipped him off.

"Michael, *stop*."

"I'm kidding." Michael's smile faltered as he opened the passenger's side door. "I can't help but feel a little jealous. The man was engaged to you."

"He didn't care about me."

Michael made a doubtful sound.

"We were the worst couple. We hated each other." I settled into the leather cushion, shuddering at the idea of having Alessio for a husband. "He's okay, but I wouldn't want to live with him."

Michael sank into the driver's seat, fingering the key fob. "It's none of my business, but—"

"No, I didn't sleep with him."

"That wasn't what I was asking. What was your reaction when he married your sister?"

"Worry. I thought he was abusive." The irony of that never ceased to dig into my ribs. "I never wanted him. He's not my cup of tea."

"What is?"

The romcoms I'd binged led me to believe my dream guy was someone kind, funny, and romantic. What had I gone for? Psychotic. Damaged. *Obsessive.*

Michael started the car, smiling. He squeezed my thigh as we drove from the curb. "Well, you're my type."

"I know."

"No, you don't. I would tell you more often if you didn't scowl at me, but you're a beautiful woman. Alessio has eyes. He must've regretted letting you go."

"Michael, he didn't like me. Once he found me with Nick, he took off—" I stopped talking, but the damage was done.

"What?" Michael tapped the brakes and whipped his head around. "He found you?"

Oh shit.

"What do you mean, *he found you?*"

"Nothing." I waved my hand, my heart hammering. "Forget about it."

Michael pulled over on a suburban street, giving me his undivided attention. "I want to hear this."

"I'd rather not talk about it"

"You will." His words throbbed with restrained anger. "Right now."

The engine quieted as Michael turned the keys. I worried my lip as his stare bored into my skin.

"Today, Carmela."

"Fine. Alessio found me with Nick, about a month after I ran away."

He gaped at me. "You're *kidding*?"

"No. I begged him to leave, so he did."

"He found you at a clubhouse. With Crash. You can't be serious."

"I told him to go, Michael."

"I don't give a fuck. He left you there. *Alone*." Michael's voice almost disappeared. "This makes me sick."

"Why?"

"He should've realized what'd happen to you. He knew better." Michael's tone soured. "The son of a bitch went after your sister. That motherfucker!"

"Michael, *stop*. I'll never tell you anything if this is how you'll react."

"Sorry."

Michael dialed back the aggression and squeezed my hand. He said little during the ride. Once we got home, he flung the keys onto the counter.

"What's wrong with you?"

"Nothing," he deadpanned, but his hands balled into fists. "I'm fine."

Okay.

I strolled into our bedroom, and Michael's soft footsteps followed. He held a box. "I bought a test since you mentioned you felt under the weather."

"That was just one day." My throat tightened. "You want me to take this?"

"You don't have to, but aren't you curious?"

Hell yes.

I ripped it open and slipped into the bathroom. Michael caught the door before it shut. He lingered there, a sliver of a man. His expression was pensive as I peed on the stick.

"Well, what's it say?"

"I don't know yet." Electricity jolted my skin as I flushed the toilet and dropped it beside the sink. "I've never done this before."

"Me neither." Michael shrugged. "Both kids were...happy accidents."

"Didn't learn the first time?"

"I like being a dad. I was never against having more." Michael sat on the tub, flashing me a wicked smile. "And I'm still not."

"What if it says yes?"

The possibility was real, and now fear mingled with the excitement. There'd be no escaping Michael once I was pregnant. He'd be all over me, more than he was already.

Michael leaned forward. "We make an appointment with the doctor, find out how far along you are, and start arguing about baby names."

"I'm angry with you, Michael. Don't forget that. You're so lucky that my parents are safe and healthy. If anything had happened, I would've divorced your ass."

"Good luck finding an attorney to take your case," he quipped, his gaze sliding to the test. "What's it say?"

My stomach sank as I read it. Disappointment welled inside me, the bitterness clawing at my throat.

One line.

Not pregnant.

TWENTY-FIVE

MICHAEL

I needed Crash dead.

It was only a matter of time before Carmela got pregnant. Once that happened, I'd never sleep without one eye open. My tireless efforts to find the guy had gone nowhere, so I zipped back to Ignacio's house. Alessio's Lexus was still parked in Ignacio's driveway.

Good.

I was due for a talk with my new in-law. Watching them through that window gave me a nasty shock. I trusted my wife, but I couldn't ignore that they had a history, however brief and loveless.

My fist bashed the door.

Ignacio answered in track pants and a knit shirt, nursing a cocktail. He didn't seem to give a shit that his captor stood on his doorstep.

"What do you want?"

"Just a chat."

Ignacio grunted in annoyance and backed into his mansion, his insolent gaze sliding from me like I was a pesky stray cat. He didn't look to see if I followed. He strolled in, beckoning to his wife.

She beamed at me. "Hi, Michael!"

Maria had Carmela's shape, but Mia's wide-eyed innocence. She kissed my cheeks. Clearly, she had no idea I'd tortured her husband. Ignacio had fed her a bullshit story to explain his disappearance. I was there when he called her. I'd thought he was an idiot for wasting a phone call.

Now I understood.

He loved her. He'd do anything to keep her safe, even offer his home to the likes of me. If he hadn't murdered my brother, I would've admired this man. Carmela had inherited his courage. I hoped she'd pass it on to my future sons.

Ignacio slid an arm around my shoulders and smiled. "Maria, can you bring us something to eat?"

I waved a no-thanks. "Don't go through any trouble."

"It's no problem."

Maria flitted from the cupboards to the fridge, fetching this and that while her husband steered me into the dining room. She was just like my mom, gracious with guests and pushy with offers of food.

"What is it?" Ignacio drank, settling in his chair. "Come to break my balls about my other useless son-in-law?"

"I'm not useless."

"What have you done except *try* to make my life miserable?"

"I gave you a vacation at my Tuscan villa instead of a permanent one with Jesus."

He laughed bitterly.

"I'm here to talk about Crash."

Ignacio's expression darkened to midnight-black as Maria set down appetizers. "Why?"

"I want to know everything about him."

"Again. *Why?*"

"I'm taking care of him."

Ignacio snorted. "You expect me to believe that?"

"I don't care if you do. That's what I'm doing."

He sank into his wicker-backed chair, offering a vague smile at Maria, who disappeared into the kitchen. "Kill him, and you'll be my favorite son-in-law. All will be forgiven."

"I'm doing this for her, not you. She deserves justice."

"Huh." Ignacio ate from the charcuterie board, smiling. "Maybe you're not a worthless asshole."

"You have a fucking mouth, Naz."

"I'm not afraid of you."

No shit. "Why is that?"

"Because you're all bark."

"How many times did I beat you?"

Ignacio offered me prosciutto, which I declined. "If you wanted me dead, I'd be in a hole. Instead you sent me to Italy to get fat and drunk."

Ignacio chuckled, and it engulfed my body in fire. He grasped my wrist and yanked before I stood. "I'm breaking your balls, Mike."

"Don't call me *Mike*." That was what my brother called me, and I couldn't stand it from him. "I'm here to talk about Crash."

"I'll text all the information I have. It's not much. The PIs I hired got nothing useful, and Carm made me drop them."

I could've screamed.

All he had to do was put a tail on Carmela, and they would've found Crash months ago. It saddened me to think about how she'd suffered, putting on a brave smile for everyone while that dickhead terrorized her.

Ignacio raised his brow when I waved off a cornetto.

"No thanks. I'm not eating here for the next decade." I gathered my coat. "Let me know if anything else comes to mind."

On the way out, Maria accosted me with leftovers. I turned them down five times before she shoved ziti into my hands. The woman was pushy. Alessio's broad frame slid into the hall. He gave me a meaningful look and gestured outside. We said goodbye to the Riccis. Maria shouted down Alessio's refusal of ziti. Then we stood in the crisp air, cradling our Tupperware containers.

Alessio faced me, his stony features hardening. He was like a dark cloud. His gaze shot lightning bolts as though I'd showed him my dick.

"Are you mad that I married your ex?"

He was silent for so long that my skin crawled. "I'm pissed that you're fucking with my family. Carmela deserves better."

"I'm better than you."

I winked at him and strolled to my car, grinning when his footsteps scraped the pavement behind me.

"Michael, why did you marry her?"

"I don't owe you an explanation." I laughed when I opened the car door, and he slammed it shut. "What are you going to do? Punch me? You're not in a position to do anything except what I want, so fuck off."

He grabbed my shoulder. "Let her go."

"Carmela's no longer your concern." I shook from his grasp and dumped the ziti into a curbside trash. "She's mine."

"You forced her into this marriage. She's been through enough horror."

"Whose fault is that?"

Alessio's eyes shuttered like blinds on windows. "I never hurt her."

"You didn't care about her. You left her for *dead*."

I was hoping he'd deny it, but Alessio stuck his hand in his hair, which he did whenever he was overwhelmed.

"You abandoned her with that biker piece of shit."

"She wanted to stay with him, Mike."

I couldn't look at him the same ever again, not after falling in love with Carmela. "You left her alone in a clubhouse. What did you think would happen?"

"I had no idea he was dangerous."

"Stop lying." I shoved his chest, knocking him several steps backward. "You wanted the younger one."

"Careful, Mike. You don't want to say something you'll regret."

"Why, you'll take off again?"

He slapped the Tupperware on my car hood. "She doesn't hold it against me, so why do you?"

"Because you took a backseat while that nutcase was raping her! He's become a big problem because you failed to act. Jesus Christ, you're not the guy I thought you were."

"Neither are you. You've lost your way."

"Meaning what?"

"You have no clue what the hell you're talking about." Alessio raised his chin, sounding dead. "It's best you don't come around anymore."

A jagged edge cut into me, but I couldn't forgive Alessio.

I looked at him and saw a *coward*.

Good riddance. "You and I are done, but I'll be visiting my father-in-law."

I flung open the door and sank into the seat. Alessio hadn't moved from his spot. He stared ahead, his features frozen.

"Watch your toes, asshole."

I started the car and drove off. The plastic container flew off the roof and smashed, spilling ziti over the road.

Fuck him.

My wife's psychotic ex prowled the streets because Alessio had dropped the ball. He should've ended Crash's life. Instead he ran off with the *sister* and claimed it was love. Unbelievable.

My phone rang as I approached our driveway. "Yeah?"

Vinn's frantic voice boomed through the speaker. "Anthony's been kidnapped."

TWENTY-SIX
MICHAEL

He was taken while he walked his dog. They found his Husky rolled in a ditch, dead with a single gunshot wound. Anthony had dismissed his bodyguards. All they'd had to do was grab him.

Tubs of white-wrapped sweets packed the candy store's stockroom, which we used for meetings. I stuck my hand in a tin container and grabbed a few, tearing off the paper. Rich sugar coated my tongue.

Vinn sat at the table, his skin drained of color, his eyes listless. His pitch-black gaze flicked at me, his irises so dark they blended with his pupils.

"We're so fucked, Mike."

It wasn't like him to panic. "We can't dwell on the consequences."

"Uncle Nico will kill us. His son! His only fucking son was kidnapped under *my watch*."

"Yeah, it's bad."

"We're finished." Vinn kicked his chair aside, raging. "I will not die for that junkie!"

It was lucky I'd sent everyone out of the room.

Vinn seized the desk and hurled it into a rack. Saltwater taffy spilled over the floor. He unsheathed his Ka-Bar knife and shanked the cushion until stuffing poured from the gashes, and then he threw the chair at another rack, knocking tins off shelves in a massive, noisy crash.

"It'll be all right, buddy."

"No, it won't." He whirled at me, still holding the knife. "How are you so calm?"

"We're getting Anthony back."

Hope flashed across Vinn's face before it died in a nasty wreck. "Whoever did this is carving out Anthony's heart as we speak."

"I don't think so."

"You're way too optimistic."

"They killed Comet. Why not shoot Anthony, too?" I unwrapped a candy and popped it into my mouth. "If it was a hit, they wouldn't have dragged him off."

"Why haven't they contacted us with their demands?"

"They will. Trust me. Do we have any witnesses?"

"Just one." Vinn rubbed his forehead. "His neighbor said they were all dressed in black. They rolled up in an SUV. Shot the dog. Grabbed him. Gone."

"Where the hell were his bodyguards?" Alessio pushed off the walls and unfolded his arms. "Or did you idiots screw that up, too?"

I scrolled through my cell, checking for missed calls. "The dipshit dismisses them all the time."

Alessio raked his ebony mane, swearing. "I'll contact Judge Gilstrap and pull the camera footage from his street. Somebody will have to tell Nico."

Nobody wanted that job.

Alessio's hand wavered as he thumbed through his list of contacts.

Vinn grimaced. "I'll call him."

"No. Let me handle him." Alessio heaved a sigh. "He'll take it better coming from me, but we should have information for him besides 'your son was taken, and we have no idea where he is.'"

"We should lay low for a while. Check into a hotel and keep changing rooms." I needed to get the kids, *fuck*. "I'll call our people in prison. Nico will need more muscle."

A fist hammered the door, and Alessio let Vitale inside. He approached me, unlocking his phone. "We have a situation."

A gruesome image flashed on the screen. A nude woman curled on grass, blades tangled with her lengthy, black hair. Ligature marks wrapped her wrists and neck. Her glassy eyes stared skyward.

Elena.

A Sanctum girl, and the happiest hooker I'd ever met. She baked everyone cookies on Christmas. We'd fooled around a couple of times. Elena was one of the few girls that didn't latch on like a barnacle. She was nice.

Now she was dead.

I glanced at her abdomen. A dagger stuck from her ribs, with a note.

I HAVE YOUR PRINCE
GIVE HER BACK

The air vanished from my chest.

"They found her in Sanctum's parking lot." Vitale swiped his thumb, displaying additional views of the corpse. "We took care of her."

Vinn shuffled to my side. "I'm assuming you understand what the hell this means."

Sick fuck. "Yeah. It's a message for me, from Crash."

A tinkling of glass drew my attention to Alessio, who'd dropped his cell. The screen had splintered into shards.

"He wants my wife," I explained, facing Vinn. "He must've abducted Anthony hoping for an exchange. The takeaway here is Anthony is alive."

Vinn zoomed in on the photograph. "We need to bait a trap."

My throat tightened. "I'm not involving Carmela."

"I'm not suggesting that." Vinn gestured at Alessio, who glowered at him. "We send an email from Carmela to the psycho."

"It might work," Alessio muttered. "He's off his rocker."

"But not *stupid*." I shook my head. "We'll search for Rage Machine's clubhouse. We'll triple the reward for information. We won't involve my goddamned wife."

"What if we just—"

"*No*. She can't find out about this." My gaze wheeled from Alessio to Vinn. "We are not bringing Carmela into this."

"I agree. Family's off-limits," Alessio murmured with a hint of a sneer. "I'll take care of what we discussed."

He left, the door banging shut.

"Anthony will never survive this." Vinn's vacant stare swept over the mess. "Even if we get him out, he'll never be the same."

Too fucking bad.

I would keep her safe. Even if it meant Anthony had to be the sacrifice.

TWENTY-SEVEN
CARMELA

MATTEO RAN laps around the coffee table.

I stumbled as he crashed into my knees, upsetting the plate filled with cucumber and salami sandwiches. I groaned as one slipped off the edge and slapped the floor.

I sank into the L-shaped steel-blue couch as Matteo zoomed the living room. "Teo, settle down."

"No!"

I cleaned up the mess and passed the snacks to Mariette, who glowered at Matteo. "Honey, we're not watching the film until you sit."

Matteo bumped into the table, knocking over the popcorn.

Mariette scowled at him. "You're such a butthead."

"Your face is a butt!" he shrieked, his eyes welling with tears.

White rained on Matteo's head as she hurled fistfuls from the bowl. He launched. They tussled, Mariette subduing Matteo in a headlock.

I tossed a pillow at them. "Mariette."

She released Matteo, who dug into the cushions for spilled kernels and stuffed them in his mouth.

I grabbed his hand. "Teo, don't eat couch popcorn."

"Put on the movie!" Mariette roared, bouncing on the cushion. "Is Daddy coming?"

"Not sure." I frowned, glancing in the office's direction. "I'll get him. Mariette, watch your brother."

I'd seen very little of Michael. When he was home, he shut himself in the office all day. He refused meals. He stared into space, jaw locked in a tension that kept growing.

My life would never be perfect.

It hit me at Mia's place when Anthony Costa's toothy grin flashed across the evening news. His disappearance had consumed our husbands' lives; they'd temporarily put aside their feud to work together. Michael had deflected Anthony's kidnapping like he did all Costa business. *Everything was under control.*

Nothing ever was.

I'd grown up surrounded by violence. Mia and I had attended so many burials that we were on a first-name basis with funeral directors. My father shot a man in the back of the head in our backyard. Why did I think I could have two kids and a loving, supportive husband who was *not* homicidal?

I grabbed a sandwich and entered a room with white floorboards and concrete walls. A built-in bookshelf took up the left side. His desk sat in the middle.

Michael lounged in a leather chair, wearing a black sleeveless button-up over dark jeans. I'd never seen him in denim. It suited him. The way the pants clung to his thighs pricked my chest with heat. His suits slimmed him, but these made him look like a soccer player.

I knocked on the door. "It's movie night. The children are asking for you."

"Start without me."

His tone made me pause. Lately, he'd sounded so heavy. It was as though he exhaled lead. He frowned at the desk. His beard was overgrown.

"Brought you a snack." I slid the plate over the desk.

His lips tugged into a brief smile. "Thanks."

Michael barely glanced at it, which raised my alarm bells.

I took his shoulder. "What's wrong?"

He peeked at my hand, and then my face. "Why does something have to be wrong?"

"Because when guys refuse food, it's because the world is on fire."

"Not all men are the same."

"Are you okay?"

"Thinking about Anthony." Michael played with the sandwich. He grabbed a bite and set it down.

"Do you have any leads?"

"Not really."

I didn't know Anthony well, but I hoped he was all right. He'd seemed troubled but harmless. "Do you want to talk about it?"

"Nah."

"You seem upset."

"I'm worried, but otherwise I'm great. I'm content with my life." He pulled my wrist, reeling me closer. "Aren't you?"

That was a complicated question.

"Not while bosses' sons are being kidnapped."

"Forget him. *Are you happy?*"

I shouldn't be, but my honest answer was yes. Resenting him seemed petty, considering the facts. I'd already forgiven him in my heart. "I'd like to see my parents and sister more often."

He glared at the floor. "Then do it. Just don't expect me to tag along."

"Why?"

"Because they hate me, and I hate them."

"What do you have against Mia?"

"Nothing. It's Alessio I have a problem with." He soured, glaring at his desk. "He's a coward. Left you to die."

"I thought he was your best friend."

"Not anymore."

Michael's arm hooked my waist, and he drew me onto his lap. Heat rushed into my face as he held me tightly, his anger vibrating through my back.

"He's a dick. He abandoned you with that monster." Devastation flickered in his bourbon eyes. "He didn't give a damn about the consequences. He just left you there."

"You're being really harsh. I told him I was safe."

"You weren't, and he knew better. If you'd been my fiancée, I never would've done that."

Honestly, I held zero animosity toward Alessio. We were forced into an engagement we didn't want, and I'd run out on him. I'd fallen in love with another man. I'd had no desire to be chased by Alessio.

But flames licked my body when it was Michael.

I kissed him. Michael stiffened, and then he melted into me. Sparks danced across my skin as his fingers teased my waist. He slid me over the desk. His touch sailed up my dress, and he kissed me in long, torturous strokes that reminded me how much I loved being naked with him. It'd been forever—fuck—almost a week.

"Will we watch the movie, or are you kissing all night?" Mariette's dry voice cut into the room.

We jumped apart as Mariette crossed her arms. Michael chuckled as he pushed the straps over my tingling shoulders. Then he took my hand, and we strolled into the living room covered in popcorn. He brushed kernels off the couch before we sat together. Matteo dove into the crook of his arm.

It was dark and peaceful. Michael's heartbeat pulsed into my back. The swell of his breathing lulled me into closing my eyes. I sank into oblivion as he nuzzled my temple and whispered words that made my heart race.

"I love you."

I STILL WANTED A BABY.

The desire grew into a full-fledged obsession by the time I'd left Mia's house and arrived at our quiet, oak-lined street. It'd hit me hard as I'd played with my fourteen-month-old niece, who'd started walking.

The bubbles were almost gone. A floral scent saturated the lukewarm water. Heat lapped my neck as the soap fizzled. I'd disappeared into our bathroom, hoping he'd notice.

I didn't wait long.

As soon as he put the kids to bed, the doorknob twisted. Michael's Derby shoes slid into view, the rest of him hidden in the fogged mirror. The visual of my well-dressed husband stepping through steam tickled my skin with flames.

He approached the bath, wearing a smirk that licked my body.

The air was stifling, the bathwater boiling, and I couldn't stand it. My toe snagged the chain blocking the drain and knocked it out of place. Michael grabbed a towel, taking his sweet time.

He held it toward me. I reached.

Then he jerked it away.

"I didn't see that one coming."

"Then why did you try to grab it?" Michael grinned as he dried me off. He patted my face and soaked the drops clinging to my shoulders. He wrapped me, kneeling as he wiped my stomach and hips. The cotton ran down my legs. Judging from the smile that turned feral, he assumed I was game for more than playful banter.

He was right.

Michael stood, the cotton sliding into my hair. He massaged my head. "You want to fool around?"

"I need more than fucking you once in a while, Michael."

"We were going at it pretty often."

"That was before I found out you were a liar. You're not the man I was falling for."

"Perhaps I am. I never pretended to be good. Ask me a question."

"What?"

"You said you don't know who I am, so *ask*."

I couldn't think while his pulse bumped my naked skin. "Tell me about your life."

"I grew up poor. We didn't have two nickels to rub together after my father died, so my brother dropped out of school to work. I returned the favor when I was older—trips to Italy, gifts, that sort of thing."

"What were you like as a kid?"

"Like Matteo, but a lot meaner."

"So, you were his opposite."

"I was energetic. Always bouncing off the walls, causing trouble, wreaking havoc in classrooms because I couldn't sit quietly."

That side of him had passed on to Matteo.

Michael nudged me. "What about you?"

"My teenage years were uncomfortable. I had big boobs when I was ten, so I was fending off men from a young age. Dad never wanted me to date, so I didn't. He told me to save my purity for my husband, which had never made sense. Why did I have to be pure? He sure as hell wasn't."

Michael laughed. "I stopped being pure at fifteen. Did it in the backseat of my brother's car, which I stole to bang my girlfriend. He beat the shit out of me, but it was worth it."

"Your brother hit you?"

"Yep. He resented quitting school to watch us. We fought constantly. When I was thirteen, he stabbed me in the thigh. I would've bled to death if he hadn't wised up and called the ambulance."

I rubbed his bicep. "God, I'm so sorry."

"He was an asshole, but I still loved him."

Thinking of my father, I nodded. "Yeah, I know what you mean."

"Do you?"

I met his gaze, startled by his tone.

Did I *love* him?

He leaned in, the smell of him enveloping me like a fog.

"Michael, I want to keep trying."

The towel slackened. It struck the floor with a wet slap.

His palms scooped my face. "Thought you'd never ask."

"I just want a baby. I'm not saying that I—"

"*I don't care.*"

His grip settled on my hip. The other brushed my hair off my shoulder, and a violent shiver ripped through my skin. A feather-light stroke sailed down my abdomen as his breath skated my neck.

I whimpered.

Michael's chest and groin pressed into me. He turned my head toward him, fingers clasping my jaw as his other hand drifted across my legs.

I gasped as he grazed my clit. The gentle pressure slammed desire into a body that didn't worry about Michael's crimes.

His lips crashed into mine.

He rubbed my clit in brisk circles, sliding up and down my seam. I moaned, arching against him. He unzipped his slacks and took off the belt, which landed with a jingle. He pushed me onto the bathroom counter, rubbing me harder.

My hands smacked the mirror, my limbs on the verge of collapse. His cock slid inside. I groaned as he filled me.

It'd been too long. I needed this.

God, did he make me feel.

With Michael, surrendering never felt like giving up. Not when he ran his tongue down my neck and lashed my breasts like I was made of sugar. Or when he parted my thighs and drank from my pussy.

Pure bliss.

I felt worshipped.

He fisted my hair and fucked me. A thrill launched into my heart as I watched us in the foggy mirror. He was goddamned beautiful, a spectacle of masculine power as he removed his shirt. He lowered himself, his mouth twisting into a snarl as he transformed into a rutting beast.

He was so hard. It was like being impaled. I hissed, but Michael didn't take it easy on me.

He yanked me upright, his hand wrapping my throat. Michael's growl reverberated deep as he stabbed into me. He squeezed, and a lightning bolt of pleasure shot into me. My breathing ragged, I bucked against him. My muscles tensed. He hammered me faster. My hands slipped off the mirror. He caught me before I dropped. The last thrusts were like two swift blows as he groaned.

He let me go. The air flowed into my lungs. I came with a shuddering moan, the sound broken by his pounding hips. I slumped onto the counter, trembling. He dragged his knuckles through my hair. A rumble resonated in his chest.

"I fucking love you."

My eyes burned.

I wanted to say it back, but I needed the warmth that accompanied those words without the sting of fear.

I kissed him before realizing my mistake. Feeding his feelings was dangerous. I had to stop.

Sooner or later, they'd turn him mad as they had with Nick.

Love had ruined him.

And Michael—it would destroy him.

TWENTY-EIGHT
MICHAEL

Sundays used to be my favorite day.

Every weekend, I'd pack the kids into the car, and we'd head to Mom's. Serena was usually sober enough to make it through dinner, even though I had to micromanage her wine intake.

Daniel's empty seat weighed on my mind as we tucked into Mom's gravy. The mood was somber, probably because Carmela took Daniel's spot near the sliding glass door. I didn't have the heart to tell her she should've stayed home, but she insisted on coming. Carmela wanted everybody to get along.

I loved that about her, but it was naive. I would never trust Ignacio with my children. I wouldn't forgive Alessio or play nice with that *prick*.

My sister's fork shrieked the ceramic as she spiraled her pasta. Mom stared at her plate and drank. At least she hadn't burst into tears. Carmela coaxed Matteo into finishing his supper. His doctors wanted him to gain more weight, but he was a stubborn eater. Carmela had taken to blending vegetable soup.

"Don't you want to be as strong as Daddy?" Carmela squeezed his little biceps. "They won't grow if you don't eat. Come on. One more bite."

"No." Matteo shook his mess of curls. "Not hungry."

Carmela began anew with a different tactic, "You can't leave the table until you finish."

Liana watched with a lifted brow. My sister was a petite woman and practically a baby at only twenty years old. I considered her family, but we weren't related. Mom adopted her after a mob assassination orphaned Liana when she was four. Daniel had raised her with a much gentler hand.

Liana's gaze tore from Carmela. "Is Vinny coming?"

Not this again. "*Vinny.* He'd die if he heard you call him that."

Hope swirled in her blue eyes that I wished would disappear.

"It's what I've always called him."

"He's not Vinny. He's the boss." I ignored Carmela squeezing my thigh and speared a meatball. "Remember that."

"Is he on his way?"

God, she wouldn't let it go.

"No idea." I dunked a chunk of bread in the sauce. "Why?"

"He hasn't returned my calls."

Of course, he doesn't. "Baby girl. Put down the torch already. Vinn is not interested. Find somebody else before he breaks your heart again, and you become an old maid."

Judging by the sudden absence of clattering knives and forks, I'd crossed the line. Liana turned a shade of beet-red and glowered.

"He's not my boyfriend."

Good.

She knew damned well I didn't approve. He would never, ever share her feelings. Daniel would tell me to knock it off, but I was tired of watching her agonize over my heartless cousin.

Carmela seemed to want to fill in for my brother. She seized my knee, dug in, and dragged up my thigh.

Hello.

I grabbed her leg. Carmela's nails pierced my slacks. I pushed my chair back before she stabbed my balls.

"*Michele.* Your sister is just concerned." Mom used the Italian pronunciation of my name whenever I was a shit.

Too bad it never worked.

"So am I. She has a crush on our cousin."

"I don't have a crush," she seethed. "And we're not related, you jackass."

"Hey. *Language.*"

Mom took the bowl of gravy and passed it to Carmela, who heaped a second helping over her pasta. Liana shot away, disappearing in a blur of pink. Carmela grimaced into her glass of water, and Mariette raised her head, looking thoughtful.

"What's a jackass?"

"Great." I glared in Liana's direction, my voice rising into a shout. "You see what happens when you curse at the dinner table?"

Carmela's haughty disapproval deepened into disgust. "You're embarrassing me."

"*I am?*"

"Yes. Go apologize."

Fine.

I left my seat, sighing. My sister sulked in the kitchen, tearing a napkin into fourths, pacing, her blue gaze spilling with tears. She was so *sensitive*. I never knew what to say. Our age difference sometimes made it feel like we lived on different planets.

"Li, I'm sorry."

Liana crossed her arms.

"I don't like hurting you, but you know I'm right."

"Shut up and stay out of my life. You're not Daniel. You've never acted like a big brother."

Ouch. "I don't want you to make the same mistakes I did."

"Believe me. I won't. I watched you destroy yourself with Serena." Liana threw silverware into the dishwasher. "I miss Vinny. I wish he came by more often. That's all."

He'd stopped dropping in a year ago, after Nico promoted him to acting boss. She'd probably only showed because she hoped Vinn might come.

God. "Why don't you find yourself a nice guy?"

"Why can't you see a therapist for your rage issues? Or your drug problem? Or whatever hole you've dug yourself into *this* time. I don't need *your* advice. Mind your damned business."

Well, that went well.

I shut my mouth and left Liana. My mother took over looking after the kids as Carmela gathered plates.

I kissed her cheek.

Carmela's lips thinned. "You shouldn't have done that."

"*What?*"

"You're burning bridges with your sister."

My insides squirmed. "Vinn isn't good enough for her."

Her eyes flashed with disapproval. "Did you have to humiliate the poor girl?"

"I hate that she pines after Vinn." I helped her gather dishes, sighing. "She's loved him ever since they were children."

"So what? She's a young girl. Give her a break."

"That's why I want to keep her away from Vinn." I snorted. "He's too thick to put it together."

"Why not tell him?"

"That's not my place."

"But it's your place to stop her from dating the man she wants?"

"He is a violent man with a drug addiction." The cutlery rattled as I dumped them in a bowl. "I was married to someone similar. My sister is never going through that. *Period.* End-of-fucking-story."

"Vinn seems healthy."

"He's been sober for years, but still."

There was a lot more I could say, but I wouldn't.

I loved my cousin. I did, but I'd never trust him around my sister.

Carmela carried everything into the kitchen. "Deciding that for her won't work. Let her make her own mistakes."

"No fucking way."

My attention snapped toward the front door as a key scraped the lock. It swung open to admit a broad-shouldered man with a wide, chiseled jaw.

Fuck.

Carmela laughed as Vinn strolled inside, slipping the keys into his jacket sprinkled with rain.

Mom rushed to his side. "Sit down. Eat."

"Hi, *Zia* Lena."

"Are you hungry?"

"No, I'm good." He bowed, kissing the air beside her cheek. "I'm here to talk to Mike."

"You should eat. Sit." Mom gathered a mountain of pasta and grabbed his elbow, steering him into the dining room.

"I'm full."

"Refusing my mother is pointless," I shouted, wiping the plate Carmela had washed. "She won't leave you alone. Just say *yes*."

Vinn dropped into the seat, as Mom whisked over a napkin, water, and cutlery. Within a few seconds, she'd gathered enough food to feed a football team and shoved it at Vinn, who seemed to have cut his losses.

A stampede of feet cascaded down the stairs. Liana appeared in the doorway, beaming. I cringed as she bounced over. Carmela's grip dug into me, but I ignored her.

"Hey, Vinny. How've you been?" Liana slid her arm across his neck and hugged him. "I haven't seen you in ages."

Vinn glanced up, looking like he always did when confronted with the sheer force of my sister's affection—deeply uncomfortable. He patted her. "Fine."

Would it kill him to fake a little warmth?

Liana wasn't dissuaded from his one-word reply. "Did you read my texts?"

"Yeah, sorry...Been super busy."

Liana couldn't take a hint.

Vinn's gaze swept over my sister and found me. His eyes narrowed with a pointed *save-me-from-your-sister* plea, which I used to ignore because I loved how he squirmed. It stopped being funny when I realized Liana's childhood crush wasn't fading.

Six years ago when he joined the Marines, Liana had been a fucking mess. She'd called me every week, bawling. Vinn would get shot. He would die. She'd never see him again.

He returned home months later, kicked out after an incident he refused to discuss. Nobody would hire him after he was dishonorably discharged, so I got him a job as an enforcer. He booted his drug habit soon after, but he was never quite right again.

I rapped my knuckles on the wall. "Vinn and I need to talk business. Li, could you give us the room?"

Her arms disengaged from Vinn, who didn't seem to notice her disappointment or catch her lingering stare. They were two of the dumbest people I'd ever met.

I sank into the seat beside Vinn. "What's up?"

"Anthony's been kidnapped, and you're having Sunday dinner."

"I'm supposed to put my personal life on hold?" I seized Carmela's drink and drained it. "There will always be a crisis. Learn from Alessio, who never took five and burned out."

"Yeah, but nothing slipped past him."

"Except you kidnapping his wife."

He made an amused sound, already halfway finished with his meal. "Rage Machine."

"What about them?"

"Sock-puppet clubs are litmus tests for patched members. If they run through a gauntlet of vicious crimes, they're accepted into the main club, Legion. Seems to attract guys with zero brain cells." Vinn sighed and raked his ebony hair. "Anyway, guess who's the leader?"

"Crash?"

"President claims he's lost control of his little experiment, which means Legion is on its last legs. He'll get killed, and we don't have the numbers for a war."

"Then we import soldiers from the old country."

"That'll take time. Negotiations." Vinn picked his Bolognese without interest. "We should've murdered him while he was spitting glass."

Carmela walked in. I shot her a pointed glare, but she sat beside me.

"Honey, we're having a conversation."

"You're talking about Crash?" She cut through my denial, frowning. "I heard his goddamn name. Let me help. I have more reason to want him dead than either of you."

"What'll you do? March into his clubhouse and shoot him?" Vinn sneered, gesturing toward the kitchen. "Keep washing dishes."

I slugged his arm. "Don't be rude."

"I'm serious! Use me to draw him out!"

I hardened into stone. "Vinn, can you give us a second?"

He lumbered into the living room, where my sister accosted him. Their voices rumbled in the background, but I tore my attention from them and took Carmela's chin.

"How often do I have to repeat myself? Let me handle him."

"It doesn't feel right."

What does that mean?

Carmela ripped from my side, shoving the chair under the table. In a whirl of skirts, she disappeared into the bathroom. A sob echoed before the door shut. Carmela wasn't big on crying. She was such a pillar of strength—one of the many reasons I loved her—but something had crumbled her resolve.

I nudged the door open.

The curtain of hair almost hid her frown. She sniffed hard when I approached. She turned away, as though ashamed by her tears.

"I'll get him, Carmela. I—"

She whirled around. "Why were you talking about a war?"

"I was exaggerating."

"You're not helping by downplaying everything. You think I'm an idiot? I read the news. I know you're stressed out of your mind. And I'm not a fucking robot. If killing Nick means starting a huge conflict, I don't want it."

"This will never touch you or the kids."

She made a hopeless sound. "Michael, I'm worried about *you*."

Ah.

It occurred to me that Carmela had been awake all week when I got home, no matter what the hour. Maybe she *was* falling for me.

Finally. "When did this become about *my* life?"

"Shut up." She captured my mouth with a swipe of her tongue. Her arms looped my neck.

I kicked the door closed, and then I lifted her onto the counter. Carmela's eyes blazed as I stepped in between her legs.

"Let's test how quiet you can be."

TWENTY-NINE
CARMELA

"Higher, Mommy!"

I pushed Matteo on the swing. The mid-morning sun stroked my face with warmth. Sometimes bits of Michael flashed out in charming ways—the coy smiles, the playfulness—but his daughter was just like him.

Fiercely independent.

Uncompromising.

When Mariette called me *Caramel*, it was without Matteo's innocence or Michael's sweetness. I was the intruder. Matteo barely remembered his birth mother, but Mariette had years of memories. She was still grieving. She glowered whenever she caught her brother calling me *Mommy*. Michael stopped pretending to give a shit about Serena. It must've been gut-wrenching to watch her dad cozy up with a new woman.

"Stop pushing me!"

A pink-and-blue blur ran across the playground, howling as

Mariette stood at the top of the slide, arms folded over her sequined tiger T-shirt.

Oh, Mariette. "What did you do?"

"I told her to go home. She's stupid," she burst in a scathing tone. "We're playing pirates. Not *cheerleaders*."

"Honey, we don't use that word."

"Daddy does!"

"When you're thirty-four years old, you can say whatever you want. Until then, you'll follow the rules."

Mariette's lip curled, echoing her father's sneer. She ignored the kids jostling for the slide and zoomed down. Her trainers hit the gravel, and then she stalked to her brother, giving him a push on the swing. The heat bristling my chest softened as she played with Matteo.

At least *they* got along.

I waved at a three-year-old who crossed my path. Her wide eyes gaped at something over my shoulder.

A shadow rippled over me. Then a man's body pressed into me. He grabbed my waist and glided up, squeezing.

I smiled, leaning against Michael. "You're back."

"*I am.*"

My entire body went cold and dark.

That voice.

I slid my gaze from the kids to the man of my nightmares.

Nick stood in full biker regalia—plaid shirt under his leather cut, steel-toed boots, the gun half-hidden in his jeans. Sun rays stroked him in warm light. This harbinger of death was so out of place on a playground.

"Did you think I'd give up on you?"

He grasped my jaw.

No.

Nick's hard mouth crushed mine. He kissed me like a man ravaged with hunger. He shoved his tongue down my throat. Clove spice violated my senses as he swept me in breathless strokes that I didn't return.

I jabbed his ribs.

He stopped short of mauling me, his grin still intact. He didn't seem to care I hadn't reciprocated.

"Nick, you shouldn't be here."

"It's all right, babe. I'm taking you home." My insides recoiled as his attention shifted to Michael's children. "You'll never have to watch his brats again."

"Leave them out of this."

Mariette's fierce glare locked on Nick as she stepped from Matteo's swing. "You're not *Daddy*. You can't kiss her."

"I can do whatever the fuck I want."

"Nick, stop!" I yanked his leather cut, and when that failed, I shook him. "Nick. Look at me."

"So those are his kids, huh?"

"Nick, you don't have to do this. Don't hurt them. I'll do anything. I'll go wherever you want, please—"

"Relax, baby. I'm not hurting anyone."

"Leave them alone!"

Women in the playground glanced at Nick and walked away quickly. He pushed me off him, his eyes flashing as he approached.

"Mariette, run!"

She didn't budge.

Nick gave me an exasperated look as he reached into his side pocket and fished out a magazine. Then he knelt beside Mariette.

"I'm just giving them a present."

"Nick, please stop." I looked for our bodyguard, but he was nowhere in sight. "Please—"

He popped two rounds from the clip. He tucked one in Matteo's shirt and offered another to Mariette. "This one's yours."

You sick son of a bitch.

Mariette held out her shaking hand.

Nick dropped the bullet in her palm, and then he patted her cheek. "Tell your daddy it's from me. My name's Crash."

Agony tore my guts as Mariette burst into sobs.

Nick stood, his face blank. Then he grabbed my bicep. "Now, we can go."

"Wait. Let me say goodbye."

"You are such a bleeding heart." He sighed, shaking his head. "Make it fast."

I turned to Mariette. "Honey, I have to leave with Nick."

"Why?" she demanded.

"I need you to be brave. Stay close to your brother." I pressed my phone into her palm. "As soon as I'm gone, you find an adult. Call your father."

"You're leaving us?"

Her broken tone cleaved my soul. I took Mariette's hand and cinched it on Matteo's. The phone trembled in her grip. Tears slipped down her cheeks.

"Why are you going?"

"I don't want to." I wrapped them in a fierce hug. "I love you both so much."

I forced a smile. Their last memory of me wouldn't be tainted with horror, so I swallowed my anguish. I turned my back on them as my stomach collapsed.

Nick beamed at the kids and wheeled around, hands in his pockets. Bikers lounged near the trees surrounding the lively park.

He loped beside me. "Give me your hand."

When I refused to uncross my arms, he seized my wrist and ripped the ring from my knuckle. A flash sparkled through the air as he tossed it toward the playground, where Mariette and Matteo stood.

A silent howl went through me.

When would be the next time I'd see them?

Never.

THIRTY
MICHAEL

UNKNOWN

I'm ready to give up Tony Costa.

THE NUMBER MATCHED the one I'd called weeks before. The text was from Crash, who'd sent a proof of life photo. We'd pored over the grainy picture of Anthony, who still wore his jogging pants and T-shirt. His beard was overgrown. Chains wrapped his arms and legs. His clothes were dirty, but they weren't splattered with blood. His vacant expression troubled me. I'd seen it before in Vinn, after he'd returned from his service in the military. It was as though he'd given up.

Additional messages said to prepare for a call at eleven this morning, which brought us to Vinn's monochrome penthouse. We stood in his living room, streaked with black, grays, and white. Light streamed in from the wall-to-wall windows facing downtown.

Was Anthony somewhere in that maze spread below?

"I don't like this."

Vinn's colossal frame straightened over the concrete table. His eyes flicked from my phone's silent screen. "You've mentioned."

"A guy who sends notes attached to dead hookers won't hand over Anthony."

"We're fresh out of options."

"I don't think we should humor him."

"I won't ignore Anthony's kidnapper." Vinn swigged the energy drink and crammed a handful of almonds into his mouth. "You're just worried he'll ask for your wife."

"He will, which makes this a waste of time. We could be searching for him. *I have your prince*," I huffed, repeating the words on the note. "This is a game to him."

Vinn waved me off. His wrinkled shirt hung like a battered flag over his pants. He paced his monochromatic apartment, rubbing his unshaven cheek. He was fucking exhausted—we all were. Since Crash took Anthony, we'd been working around the clock to find him.

Several days ago, a shell-shocked Alessio returned from a trip to New York to visit Nico in prison. Uncle Nico was *furious*. The news about his son's disappearance went over so poorly that he'd attacked Alessio. Guards had to pull him off. He blamed *us* for Anthony's kidnapping. Nobody was off the hook. If his son died, we were all fucked.

I needed Anthony to be all right. I'd made promises to Carmela, promises whispered in the dark as I lay there, spent and wrapped in her arms.

I love you.

I will never leave you.

What good was my sentiment if I died?

"It's eleven." Vinn stood. His broad frame cast a winged shadow on the cold floor. "Maybe I should do the talking."

"He texted *me*."

"You can't fly off the handle with this guy. If he hurts Anthony—"

"He already has. Did you look at the photo?" I shook my head as Vinn shrugged. "Sadism is Crash's thing, and Anthony's an easy target."

Vinn grabbed my shoulder and pinched hard. "Don't lose your temper. No matter what he says about Carmela. Do not give him a reason to hurt Anthony."

I pushed him off. "Fine."

The phone rang.

I breathed deep and accepted the call.

Crash's loathsome face popped into the screen. He sat in a booth of what appeared to be a diner. A glass of water sat in front of him.

A smug grin curled his lip. "Costa, thanks for joining."

"Where's Anthony?"

He sipped his drink. "I'll get to him in a minute. I want to chat first."

"Are we getting to the point sometime this century?

Vinn gestured violently, mouthing, *Stay calm.*

"You're not who I thought you were. I assumed you were my total opposite. Boring. Safe. Spineless. Then I did some digging. About you. You and Beauty. Nobody could tell me when you started dating. And I mean *nobody*. They all gave me the same story. Those I persuaded to talk, anyway. They claimed *you forced Carmela into marriage.*"

The judgment ringing in his tone was precious. "If I owe an apology to anyone, it's her. Not the piece of shit looking at me."

"I'm the asshole? You dragged her down the aisle. Put a gun to her father's head." Another soft laugh shook through the speaker. "You think you're better than me? Look in the fucking *mirror,* you filthy dago."

"*Where is Anthony?*"

"Oh, fuck him. He's such a whiny bitch. I don't understand why you care about that limp dick."

"Because he's Nico's only son, and he's never been involved in the family business—"

"You Italians and your legacies. What good is that if it's attached to a man like him? *Whatever.* I'll keep him alive if you do one thing."

"I'm not giving you Carmela."

"Beauty is mine."

"Her name is Mrs. Costa," I hissed into the phone. "And I'm not handing over my wife, you sick fuck."

He rolled his eyes, grinning. "I don't need your permission. This is already a done deal."

"What are you talking about?"

"I have your wife."

"Fuck you." A horrible thrill shot into my heart. Then my phone vibrated with a notification flashing with Carmela. "She's calling me right now, Dipshit."

"That's your daughter."

"Don't talk about my kids."

"When you pick them up, I want you to ask for the present I gave them." He winked, and then he smiled at something off-screen. "Say hello, baby."

The camera panned, revealing a woman's arm and the anchor-patterned white dress she'd worn this morning, and my wife's terrified face. Carmela sat in the booth, pinned to Crash's side.

No, this couldn't be real.

"I stole her back. How's it feel, Costa?"

A wounded howl tore from my throat as he caressed her shoulder and played with her bra. It felt like being stabbed. The agony twisted my insides with fire. Carmela ripped away from him, her mouth twisting. Her pain doubled my anguish.

"Take a good look. You'll never see her again."

"Let her go!"

"Never."

"Carmela, where are you?"

"I can't tell you. Sorry." My wife shrieked from the speaker, "Get the kids! They're at Salmon Creek Park!"

No.

"Where are you?"

"She's with me," Crash boomed, shifting the view to him. "And that's where she's staying. If I catch one whiff of a Costa, I will crush Anthony's skull. Capiche?"

"You better sleep with both eyes open! Because I won't rest until I bring her home."

"She is home."

The call ended, but my phone still vibrated.

A wild hope seized me as *Carmela* flashed across the screen. I squashed the cell against my ear, but the voice that answered wasn't Carmela's husky sigh.

It was my daughter's.

"Daddy, she left us!"

THIRTY-ONE

CARMELA

I WOULD FUCKING KILL HIM.

Son of a bitch put a bullet in Matteo's pocket. He'd taunted a seven-year-old girl, terrorized her father, and kidnapped Anthony. His list of crimes kept growing, and I could've stabbed him in the neck with a fork, but that wouldn't help me win. Nick's revolting hands would never touch a child, ever again.

Nick pulled out his Zippo and lit a clove cigarette, the perfumed smoke curling around his silhouette. "Get a grip, Carmela."

"You didn't have to hurt them!"

"I didn't."

"You scared those innocent children, and now they'll think I abandoned them."

"I don't know why you give a shit about his kids." Nick's disgust seemed to grow when I slumped against the wall. "The fuck is your problem?"

"*You.*" I grabbed his leather jacket, tears shaking down my cheeks. "You're what's wrong with me. You destroy everything good. You're a cancer. You should've *never* touched them."

Nick glanced at my fists beating his chest and balled them. He squeezed hard. "You're out of your mind."

"I love them."

Nick slapped me, the sting deepening my rage. He gave me a look as though worried for my sanity. "Snap out of it."

"I'm not crazy."

"Are you that desperate for kids? You'd lower yourself to take care of another man's brats?"

"I spent weeks caring for them." My gaze wandered across the parking lot to the highway. "You ripped me away from what made me happy."

Nick glared at me through his veil of smoke. "I'll give you a baby."

Hell no.

I wouldn't want your spawn if you were the last man on Earth.

If I blurted that out loud, he'd make *me* eat a bullet. Sparring with Nick while he was this volatile would earn me a trip to the morgue. I needed to calm down.

My nails ground into my palm. "You never wanted children."

"That was before I realized you'd run off with a guy willing to give you what I wouldn't." Nick flicked his cigarette and sighed, malice lacing his tone. "You could have *asked.*"

"I did. You said no."

Thank fucking God.

Nick's jaw jumped with an angry tic. He hated being proven wrong, and even he couldn't forget our fights. He'd broken my heart so many times by quipping that he'd rather jump off a bridge than be a dad.

"It's a bad idea." Nick swallowed hard, his pupils reduced to dots. He rarely cracked his shell, but it suddenly blazed wide open. Discomfort poured from him in sickening waves. "I'll be a shitty father."

I didn't know what to say, because it was true.

"Will you?"

"Without a doubt." Nick's pale gaze raked me as he blew smoke through his nose. "I have no clue why you want them— why *anyone* wants them."

"Don't you want to pass on your legacy?"

"What do I have to pass on, Carmela? Getting so pissed I can't see straight, and I wake up with a dead hooker in my bed?" Nick took another drag. "You knew exactly what I was, and you still begged for them. You're the only girl who's ever done that."

No shit.

"I'm not father material, Beauty." His giant hand wrapped my head, his fingers like ice. "You have to realize that."

"Then release me." *Please God, make this work.* "If you don't want them, that's fine. I get it. I do. But I need to be a mom. I deserve that experience. You can't take that from me."

His eyes gleamed with emotion.

"Nick, it's okay. You can let me go."

"*I can't.*"

He yanked me into his arms and gave me his version of a hug, which felt like a steel cage. He couldn't give anybody warmth, because he didn't possess any.

Nick pulled away. "*I'll do it.*"

He kissed my temple.

I wanted to vomit.

THIRTY-TWO
MICHAEL

I slammed the brakes and wedged open the door, leaving Vitale as I sprinted the bowl-shaped park. Pink leaves scattered the ground. A girl in a yellow T-shirt played in the sandbox. Everything was blue and green. Bright and happy. The world spun in a haze of children's laughter and the groan of swings as I screamed for my kids.

"Mariette!"

It was like shouting into wind. I couldn't hear myself. Only the rawness in my throat registered.

"Matteo!"

At the sound of my voice, Matteo always streaked from wherever and collided with my knees, but there was no pitter-patter of feet.

I tore through the playground like a tornado. My gaze swept the lawn. I'd told Mariette to hide. That was probably what she was doing, but Carmela's phone battery died one minute into the call.

They had to be safe.

A flash of gold grabbed my attention to the branch of a gigantic pine. I stared at the gap in twigs. Blonde hair peeked from the thicket of needles. I approached the group of trees and crouched. Two pairs of eyes gleamed. I parted the branches, and a body flew into my arms.

I crushed my son with a giant hug, my insides collapsing. He pressed his tear-stained face into my neck and sobbed. My daughter crawled out from the tree, tears streaming down her chin. I grabbed her and yanked her into my chest.

"Are you okay?"

She shook her head.

"Did he hurt you?" I patted her stomach, her jeans, rolling over something hard and small. "What is that?"

"The bad man gave it to me."

I pulled out a bullet.

A rock swelled in my throat. It was like barbed wire cinching my heart. I clenched it in my fist, trembling. I found another in Matteo's shirt pocket.

He'd touched my kids.

A red glaze coated my vision as I hiked Matteo to my hip.

"Crash took Carmela, Daddy." Mariette's lip trembled. "Is she coming back?"

"Yes, honey. I'll find her."

The bullets clinked. I pocketed them.

I'd save them for his skull.

Crash had seen his last sunrise.

———

I COULDN'T RUN after him.

No matter how much I wanted to look for Carmela. I had to double security around my house, wait for my sister to come over, and *then* I could leave. Vinn had already put the word out, but since Rage Machine didn't wear identifying colors and its member list was unknown, nobody knew where to search.

Matteo wouldn't be consoled. I balled him against my chest and covered his ears, hissing obscenities through the phone.

"Make the judge sign a subpoena. Throttle him if you have to. We need his license plate. I don't fucking care! Do it, or I'll get you another reason to hate me."

Once I ended the call, there was nothing but Matteo's soft crying. The full weight of Carmela's kidnapping slammed into me. She'd sacrificed herself to spare them from that psychopath, who'd played me like an idiot. He'd scheduled that meeting, knowing I'd be distracted, and then he'd waltzed into the playground. Where was the soldier supposed to be watching her? Out buying a coffee. I'd have him killed.

Crash had undone the stitching of my life and ripped my soul in *half*. The visual of his hand on her shoulder tormented me. The pain radiated to my teeth.

I had to save my wife before he murdered her.

That had to be part of his end game. A man who called himself *Crash* didn't care about anyone. His ego wouldn't be able to handle that she'd chosen me. He'd torture her, and then he'd kill the woman I loved.

No.

I had to find her.

I couldn't live without her.

A chime echoed throughout the house, and I sprinted to the entryway. Liana. Fucking finally. I put down Matteo, who clung to my slacks. Tearing him off me was the hardest thing in the world. His screaming stabbed at me.

"Matteo, what's wrong?" She stepped through, her widened gaze filled with questions as she gathered Matteo in her arms. "Is he okay?"

"Carmela was kidnapped."

"What?"

"I don't have time for this. Vitale will drive you to a hotel. You'll stay with the kids. Do not step a foot outside. *Understand?*"

"Okay, okay," she whispered. "But—"

"I have to go after her." I grabbed my keys. "Be safe."

"I'll watch them. Don't worry."

"If anything happens, take Mom and leave town. Ask Vinn for help."

Liana's eyes beaded with tears as she gripped my shoulders. "Please don't do whatever it is you're planning."

"I have to."

"Your kids need you!"

I wouldn't accept that advice.

I ripped out of her hands and headed out the door.

"Michael, I love you! Be careful!"

Outside, my cousin lounged beside the gate, phone mashed against his ear. Vinn ended his call, his stony face carved with a grim frown.

"She'll be all right."

Useless words, but I clung to them.

I started the car.

"Everybody is on this, Mike. We'll find her and Anthony. Let's head to Legion."

"We're past the point of negotiations."

"Oh, I don't plan on talking." Vinn nudged the duffel bag in the passenger side. He unzipped it and slid an H&K MP5 from the black depths. "There's a suppressor and a folding stock."

"You want to shoot up the clubhouse?"

"Crash has been a problem for years. Now he's broken off with that sock-puppet club and Legion does nothing but sit on their ass. The city is in an uproar with bombings, dead civilians, and now he's taken your wife. I'm sending them a message. If they don't put down their rabid dog, I'll be back with more guns."

"Fine by me. I'll drive."

A heavy silence blanketed the car as I drove in the clubhouse's direction. Vinn screwed on the suppressor and armed the H&K, balancing it over his thigh. Once we approached the strip mall, Vinn rolled down the window.

"We'll do a couple passes."

I flipped the turn signal. "Make sure you get their fucking bikes."

THIRTY-THREE
CARMELA

As THE WIND dried my face, I dwelled on the night we met. I'd gone to a dive to drink. Dad had just informed me that I was arranged to marry Alessio Salvatore, a gangster with a violent reputation. I had no interest in walking down the aisle with *him*.

So I'd escaped to a bar.

Two drinks in, a biker slid into my booth. His thighs barely fit under the table. He shoved a cocktail into my hands—something fruity. He'd blocked my escape, but all I remembered was the giddiness of being seen by a man like him. The diamond tattoo with the one-percent should've turned me off, but the liquor had muddled my senses and sparks flew when he anchored his arm across my shoulders. I liked that he was so forward. I *loved* that he didn't care whose daughter I was.

We had nothing in common. He listened to heavy metal. That was the only music I couldn't stand. He had no family. I was all about mine. He was a playboy. I'd never had a boyfriend.

We went together like olive oil and whiskey, but that didn't stop us from falling for each other.

A half-hour later, I hopped on his bike. He whisked me from my bodyguards and brought me to his home, where he took my virginity. I lay in his arms while he smoked. Then he told me I was his old lady, and that he'd never let me go.

Nick still looked at me with that unblinking stare that shot my heart with panic that I'd previously mistaken for excitement.

We stopped in a wooded area west of Boston. The scent of pine clung to the air. Nick cut the engine and removed his helmet.

I slid off the bike.

He escorted me to the ranch-style house. Nick's boots creaked the wooden floorboards as he opened a rusted door. His fingers brushed my ass as I walked inside, and a chill iced my spine when his body pressed into my back.

"Remember what we talked about. You will *behave.*"

Michael had made a similar comment, but there was zero playfulness behind Nick's words.

"You don't like it when I behave."

"I'm not in the mood to deal with your sass."

"I thought you liked that about me," I snapped. "Or why did you take me?"

"Because I love you, you crazy cunt. I will never let another man come between us."

"I never asked to be saved."

"That's what I like about you." Nick bumped me into the wall, his kiss like steel. "Not many girls could survive being my old lady, but you're tough."

When I left him, I sure as hell didn't feel strong.

His thick fingers smacked my cheek, and it smarted, but that was nothing new. He'd hurt me all the time. Nick's hand swallowed mine as he pushed me into a living room converted into a bar. The home was ransacked. Smoke stains crawled the walls. Glass crunched under my feet. Cigarette burns marked the carpet.

"What is this place?"

"A temporary holdout. We'll move somewhere else tomorrow."

Smashed portraits of a wholesome-looking family lined the floors. Nick took one, smiling. He tapped at the polo-wearing man.

"This was his house."

Obviously. "What happened to him?"

"He wouldn't let us camp on his land, so we shot him."

My heart throbbed in my throat. "And his wife?"

"I sold her."

"Sold? As in, *trafficked?*"

"It's better than leaving a body, and I make decent cash with the flesh market. It's a big business." He tossed the portrait in the fireplace filled with crumpled cans. The frame shattered in a cloud of ash.

My horror at Crash trafficking human beings barely registered. I couldn't process anything.

"Is that what you'll do to me?"

Nick's mouth thinned. "You're not for sale."

Was he lying?

"You don't believe me," he mused with a laugh. "Would I start a war just to let you suck another guy's cock?"

Men in leather cuts greeted Nick, who gave them a magnanimous wave. As we sat at a square table removed from the chaos, a woman slid a beer in front of Nick. She wore a Metallica tank top over cut-offs. Tattoos covered her thighs and arms. She leaned over, pawing his shoulder.

Michael's face popped into my head, and a dozen other memories of being held by him, his touch, smell, mouth, everything that comforted me, lodged in my throat and swelled.

Being stuck with this asshole reminded me of what Nick had always lacked, of what Michael possessed endlessly—warmth, loyalty, and love. Real love, not this toxic obsession.

I missed him.

I needed my husband.

In my misery, I imagined him bursting through the door. I saw Nick's skull exploding and Michael yanking me into the shelter of his arms. A world without him seemed lifeless.

I wiped my eyes as the girl slid a drink in front of me. The temptation of numbed senses was too strong. I gulped it, shaking.

A frigid hand dragged me across the table, toward the man I loathed.

"I'm sorry that I didn't put it together. You and *Costa* made no sense. I knew it wasn't right. You'd never betray me. When I found out the truth, you were unreachable." His voice dropped, husky-soft. "I had no idea you were forced."

He still thought *Michael* was the villain.

Psycho. "I wasn't forced. We had an arrangement."

"Baby, come on. You're smarter than this. The guy had complete control over you."

I balled my fists, seething. "You should have stayed away, Nick. There will be major consequences for taking me."

"We wouldn't have them if you stopped running."

The worst thing I could do was submit.

He hated easy prey.

"Which is it, asshole? Was it Michael's fault or mine?"

"Both," he snarled. "You had opportunities to call me."

I couldn't face apologizing to this piece of shit. "You're the last person I'd ask for *help*. I had to leave you. You were going to kill me."

"I'd never do that."

He was in serious denial.

"Nick, what are your plans? Now that you have me, what will you do?"

"For starters, I want to get that guy's stench off my woman."
He wrenched my hand. I flew out of the seat, and he tugged
me on his lap. His breath gusted my ear. "Then I'll find that
prick. Kill him. His family. All of them. Every *single* Costa."

"You can't."

"I'd do anything for you."

His mouth swallowed mine.

I thought of pretending he was my husband, that his touch
didn't disgust me, that the clove invading me was Michael's
fresh taste, and that his eyes swirled with amber instead of
green. I tried to imagine Michael's lips, his body, his stubble
tickling my skin.

No.

Michael was in my heart. Faking with Nick was impossible.

I couldn't do it.

I wouldn't.

He dragged me upright. He made an anguished noise as he
backed me across the room. I struck a column, pain radiating
up my spine as Nick mauled me. Then we switched positions,
and he pulled me. He broke away to kick a chair aside on his
way to the bedroom.

"No—no."

He groped at my zipper.

"No."

The door slammed. My back knocked the wall. Nick tore off
his leather cut and threw it into the corner. The sound shot

my belly with fear. Then he yanked off the plaid shirt, pressing his naked chest into me.

"Nick, no!"

I slapped him.

His palm slammed into my cheek, throwing me onto the bed. A hammer-like ache pounded my skull as he sank into the mattress.

Fingers rolled in my hair as he ripped my head backward. "*Don't do that again.*"

"You wouldn't stop."

"You are a pain in the ass, Carmela. What is wrong with you? Did Costa slap you around? Did he hurt you?" Nick's voice lowered into a hush. "He did, didn't he? That's why you're so fucked up."

How delusional was this guy?

"*Never.*" I met his furrowed gaze, my fists clenched. "He never hit me. He's good to me."

"*Good.*" He smiled, caging me with his arms. "The man who threatened your father and forced you into marriage is *good*?"

"Yes."

"You are batshit crazy."

"That's rich, coming from you."

"Hey, I'm not the one in love with her kidnapper."

Me? *In love* with Michael?

The thought stabbed me, the white-hot blade of those words slicing open my denial. I couldn't deny it.

I loved Michael.

God, I loved him. I really did.

I couldn't live without our lazy afternoons, the corny jokes, his quirks and his back hugs. I loved him so much that I wanted my ashes spread with his so we could always be together. He'd brought light into my darkness. He'd breathed air into my lungs.

Another thought that gut-punched me.

Michael loved me, too.

And I hadn't said it back.

It was like a fist clenching my throat. Tears rolled down my cheeks. I sobbed. I clutched my face, but I'd never been able to hide a single thing from Nick, and now he knew. He'd kill me.

"Seeing you like this wrecks me. He fucked you up." Nick cradled my jaw, his calluses rubbing my skin. "I'll fix you."

"What?"

"Don't worry. I'll get you through this."

My throat tightened as he unzipped me.

"I'll help you forget him."

Even if I lived in Nick's dungeon for the rest of my days, the warmth of my husband's love would never leave me.

Nick descended over me. His pulse bumped my chest, an unfortunate reminder that he had a heart. He pulled down my dress. His appreciative groan made my stomach churn.

The moan deepened into an angry grunt. Nick hung over me, glaring. He pressed a thumb into a red mark. He hissed, straightening.

"What the fuck did he do to you?"

"They're hickeys," I snarled. "Not bruises."

His hand swept over my mouth. He pinched my lips shut. "Not another word about Costa."

"He didn't threaten me into bed," I snapped, seized with a need to defend Michael. "I went *willingly*."

"Hon, you only think you did. I can't stand that he touched you."

"Then why did you take me back?"

"Because you belong to me."

He said it with zero passion, as though the hickeys had stolen his desire. A wave of relief hit me until Nick's finger hooked my underwear. He started kissing my thigh.

Panic swelled behind my ribs. I was barely holding it together, my thoughts wild with prayers and begging.

"I don't want to do this."

"After months of riding his cock, you're done with mine? *I don't think so.*"

He yanked the thong off me.

"Nick, this is too intense! I'm not ready—I'm *really* not ready."

He unzipped his jeans and pinned my arms. Then he wedged open my knees, lowering himself.

"No!"

He grasped my neck and squeezed. "You once told me that being deeply loved by someone gives you strength. You can handle me."

No, I can't. "Nick, stop!"

Nick paused, his grin widening. He drank in my fear like an aphrodisiac. He kept his touch light. It staked up and down my forearm, across my collar.

"Why, you enjoy it more with him?"

Of course. "I—you're both good."

"I want the truth." He darkened like a storm cloud. "I asked you a question. Who's the better lover?"

Michael. "I won't answer that."

"You will. And I'll know if you're lying. I always do."

"No."

"Tell me." He shoved a finger in my mouth. "Or I'll stop being so nice."

I bit him until he retreated.

A blow crashed into my head. Agony radiated into my teeth. He would hit me no matter what I said, so I faced him, grinning.

"*Michael.* He can make me come with his voice."

"Because you do what he wants." He snorted, the amusement clashing with his malevolent gaze. "Otherwise you'd have way more *hickeys.*"

"He doesn't hurt women."

"Oh, baby. You're such a naive little thing. I've been to his club. I've talked to his whores. Paid one to spill her guts," he broke off with a smirk. "She told me all sorts of shit. The man gets off on punishing his women. *Just like me.*"

The comparison made me fume.

"I guess you have a type, Carmela."

"Shut up. You don't understand him."

"*Understand?* Honey, I am him."

No.

"I'll show you." Nick's fingers curled around my throat and squeezed, then his lips molded into mine, the soft pressure filling me with bile. He pulled back, whispering. "He does this when he comes, right?"

"Shut the fuck up."

"He likes it when you're tied up. Loves it when you kneel. When you struggle. Just. Like. Me."

I turned away. "Stop!"

"I don't have to fuck you. I'm inside you, Carmela." He peeled off me, his chest unsticking from me. "Always."

"*I want my husband.*"

"We'll see how long that lasts."

Vɪɴɴ ᴡᴀꜱ ꜱʜᴏᴛ in the drive-by.

The bullet sliced into the gap of his vest and slammed into his shoulder. I hauled his ass to Alessio's hospital, where the staff wouldn't report the gunshot wound to authorities.

We killed six bikers. One of them was the president.

Their faces flashed over the evening news—two members and four prospects. We'd thrown Legion into chaos, which was not our intention, but I didn't give a fuck about public safety or broken alliances. All I cared about was my wife.

Was she all right?

Was he hurting her?

I missed her with a hollow in my lungs, an all-encompassing ache that consumed me. My stomach didn't unclench in the twenty-four hours she'd been gone, because my mind ran with violent images. I had no idea what he was doing, but if he hurt her I'd run Boston's streets red with biker blood. My life's mission would be to kill as many of them as possible. They wouldn't be able to shit without watching out for me. I'd make my name known and take my vengeance.

They'd all suffer.

"Michael."

I glanced up from the gleaming floor as a palm glided through my hair. Liana stood in flannel pajamas, her chestnut waves gathered in a high ponytail.

"Are you kidding me? You were supposed to stay with my kids."

"Mom's with them. They're safe." Liana slumped into the seat beside mine. "What happened?"

I sipped my lukewarm coffee, the only sustenance I'd allowed myself. "I can't tell you anything."

"Is he okay?"

I was in no shape to comfort anyone. "No clue."

"What about Carmela?"

"I-I don't know."

She rubbed my back. "Maybe you should sleep."

"I have to find her."

"You've done everything you can."

"Not until I've strung up every fucking biker in this city."

"Are you Michael Costa?" An Asian woman in pink scrubs stepped forward. "I'm Doctor Yang. I was the surgeon assisting for Vinn's procedure. He was wounded in the brachial plexus, which is the large nerve bundle that controls arm function."

"Will he be able to use it?"

"We won't know that for a few weeks. Most likely, he'll need follow-up surgery. I can take you to see him now."

She brought us where Vinn lay, wrapped in gauze. He stared at the ceiling in a drugged haze, his mouth half-open. His expression remained blank as Liana pulled up a chair.

"*Vinny.* I came as soon as I heard."

She folded her palm over his hand. Vinn's gaze flicked to their linked fingers. His lip twitched.

"'M fine."

Liana smoothed his hair, her voice thick with tears. "I'm glad you're okay."

A knock at the door dragged our attention to a nurse. "I'm sorry, but visiting hours are over. You'll have to leave."

I squeezed Vinn's ankle. Liana bent over Vinn and kissed his cheek. His eyes flickered as she untangled from him. He brushed the spot where her lips touched him.

We left. Liana huddled in the waiting room, dragging a blanket from her big purse and draping it around her shoulders.

"Li, go home. Sleep."

"I'm staying with Vinny."

I almost said something, but a memory of Carmela's disapproval cut into my impulse. Liana curled on a plastic seat as I headed toward the staircase, so tired I could've collapsed down the steps. I descended a flight of stairs before I realized someone called my name.

"Michael!" Alessio's rugged features swam into recognition as he straightened his jacket. "I've been calling you."

"I didn't hear you." A sickening amount of hope lodged in my throat. "Did you find her?"

"No, I haven't. I'm sorry."

Of course. He'd already failed her once.

Disgust churned in my stomach. "Then get out of my sight before I cave your head in."

"I want to help."

"Make a time machine, you miserable prick. Kill Crash when you were supposed to because there's nothing you can do now." I seized his collar, a corrosive hatred steaming the air between us. "I can't stand you."

"Stop blaming me for things out of my control."

"You could've stopped him years ago!"

"He was her goddamned boyfriend," he bellowed, shoving me. "She wanted to stay. She begged me. What was I supposed to do?"

"Save her from the psychopath."

"Yeah, I should've used my magical crystal ball and predicted him turning into this, just like you should've seen what Serena was doing to your kids—"

My fist smashed into his face. He threw me down the stairs. I tackled him into the wall, and then we were tearing at each other. Pain spider-webbed across my jaw, and then he pushed me off, his eyes blazing.

"How does this help Carmela?"

My anger dissolved. I continued my descent, my misery like a jagged knife sawing my heart. It hurt so bad. "I fucking love her. He doesn't. I can't do this without her. I can't pick up the pieces and move on."

He squeezed my shoulder.

I shook off my grief. "Search for their clubhouse. Wherever he's holed up, that's where Carmela and Anthony are."

"Everybody's looking for Rage Machine members, but they don't wear patches. Nobody knows who these bastards are. The cops have no idea they even exist, but they must be paying off everyone. We need someone in our pocket who's talked to him recently. Otherwise this will take forever."

I stopped at the ground floor, pacing the stairwell. "I don't know any of his associates besides Legion."

"Can you think of somewhere he might've visited?"

I flipped through my phone, hunting for ideas until my thumb slid over the picture of Elena.

Sanctum.

FUCK THIS PLACE.

I'd dropped so much cash in here I could've opened a substance abuse clinic. Back when Alessio was Nico's protégé and Anthony's best friend, we partied here every weekend. I thought I was living the high life, but all this club had done was distract me from what mattered.

The dreampop music pulsed in semi-lit corridors as we strolled over the black marble. Alessio scowled at the brunette cozying to his side. He stepped away, flashing his wedding ring.

"That's not a problem for *me*," she purred.

"I'm not here to play."

Alessio shouted Elena's name over the noise as I scanned the sea of naked women. A glimmer of blonde caught my eye. Brooke's winged eyes flashed terror as she ducked into another room. I followed and spotted her crouching between two sofas.

"Why are you hiding from me?"

She ran for the door.

I seized her arm. "*Brooke*."

"I'm working, and you're in the way."

"Were you here when Elena was murdered?"

Brooke's pink mouth trembled as she ripped from my grasp. "Why?"

"My wife's fucking missing. She was taken by Elena's murderer, and I need details about that night."

"Lost her, have you? That sucks."

I grabbed her throat. "I'm not playing. I'll crush the life out of you."

"I don't know anything!"

"My patience is gone." I squeezed hard enough to make her breathing ragged. "Talk."

"The man whose photo you put up came here, asking all kinds of questions about you."

"About me?" I relieved the pressure on her neck, my pulse racing. "Like what?"

"Who you fuck. How you like to fuck. That kind of thing."

"And you *talked*?"

"Not me," she gasped, digging into my fingers. "It was Elena. He was dropping a ton of cash, buying everyone's silence. It must've been at least thirty grand. He asked Elena to go home with him. She said yes."

"Then he dumped her in the parking lot." I wiped my face. "This is why you're not supposed to leave the club with *anyone*. What else happened?"

"That's all I know. I *swear*."

I stepped back from her and wrenched my hair, agonized by images of Elena's lifeless body. "Who was working that day?"

"Who am I, the manager? *Look at the schedule*."

The manager.

A dark suspicion shot into my heart.

Julian.

THIRTY-FIVE
CARMELA

I'd never see Michael again.

He'd never give me tulips, draw hearts on Post-it notes, or take me to my first ultrasound appointment. I'd miss Matteo's fifth birthday. I wouldn't be there when the kids grew into adulthood.

I'd be *here*.

With Nick.

He'd get me pregnant to trap me. He'd never smile at the baby or change diapers or do anything that wasn't self-centered. Our child would grow up in a violent home. Nick's heartless infidelity would grind my spirit into dust. He'd suffocate me.

From here on out, it was pitch-black darkness. No more light. Just the soul-crushing despair of being stuck with this man.

Nick had locked me in his ramshackle bedroom. He'd settled into a restless sleep in the queen bed, his body like a block of ice. When sunlight peeked through the Roman blinds, he peeled from the mattress and disappeared on some an errand.

I dressed quickly, my gaze sweeping over Nick's belongings—clove cigarettes, Zippo, motorcycle restoration magazines. The person who'd lived here before Nick had hung a calendar on the wall and gash marks punctured where Nick had thrown knives. Cigarette butts scattered the floor. Nick was careless with his guns, but with the place surrounded with one-percenters, I'd never make it out the door.

My old leather jacket draped the chair pushed into the desk. I swallowed hard at the words stamped on the back.

PROPERTY OF CRASH.

I fingered the worn fabric that'd once covered my shoulders. Wearing it would feel wrong, like slipping into ill-fitting skin. I wouldn't wear it—couldn't stand another second of this.

Heavy boots scraped the wood as the doorknob turned. Nick bowed his head under the frame and strolled in with a plastic bag. Lines gouged the skin under his eyes as he shoved a pink box into my hands.

"Do it."

My thumb brushed the text. A pregnancy test.

A lump lodged in my throat. "Why?"

He grabbed my arm and steered me into the white-tiled bathroom, his pale gaze narrowed but resolute. "Take the goddamned test."

"Could I get some privacy?"

"*No.*"

Nick folded his thick arms. I opened the box and removed the test. It trembled as I sat on the toilet and peed on the stick.

Nick plucked it from my hand and returned to his spot, tapping the counter. He glared at the tiny window.

"How long does this take?"

"A couple of minutes."

I backed against the shower. I didn't think I was pregnant, but what if I was?

What would he do to me?

Nick left, guarding the results to himself. He raked his blond hair. He popped open the first buttons of his plaid shirt, more agitated than I'd ever seen him. My insides boiled.

His fingers whitened, and then he picked up the packaging. Whatever he read on the cardboard made him rub his forehead.

"*Shit.*"

The plastic clattered to the floor. Two lines etched the window.

I *was* pregnant.

My heart swelled and constricted, the relief chilled by the block of ice sliding against my side. Nick slumped beside me. He stared ahead, pale and lifeless. He looked like he'd been shot.

It was the best news, but my eyes flooded with the sweet misery that Michael wasn't here to share it with me. We would have a baby. It was everything I'd wanted. My vision glazed over.

He grasped my jaw. "Is it mine?"

It *definitely* wasn't his.

Nick seemed to interpret my emotion for confirmation. His palm smoothed over my belly and stroked me. "We never used a condom."

I gaped at him.

"This happened so fast. One time, and *boom*, you're pregnant. Jesus."

He believed I was four months along?

Did he know anything about pregnancy?

"You've gained like fifteen pounds since then." Nick slid from the bed, running his hands through his hair. "How'd I not see this coming?"

The idiot didn't consider that when we were together I'd starved myself from stress, and being with Michael had healed me. Allowing Nick to believe this absurd fantasy turned my stomach, but it might ease my escape.

I had to save us.

"What did you think would happen when you came inside me?"

"I wasn't thinking." Nick opened a black box, ripping out a cigarette. "Is there a test to make sure I'm the dad?"

"You can't smoke around me."

He threw it on the floor. "*Is there a fucking test?*"

"Yes, but it's not available over the counter."

Shaking, he undid the holster at his waist and dumped the gun on his nightstand.

I could grab it.

"I'll raise our baby alone."

"Hell no."

"Nick, you won't be able to handle the late-night feedings, the screaming, dirty diapers, and you'll take off when the kid's sick and needs to go to the doctor."

Nick's eyes shot lightning bolts at me. "We'll have help. Just like *Costa*."

"You're not the fucking same. He wants this with me."

He had no idea what he was talking about. All the nannies in the world couldn't replace a parent like Michael.

"He told you what you wanted to hear. He knows you'll never leave if you get pregnant. He's a good liar. That's all."

No. "You're wrong."

"Easy on the attitude, Carmela. My patience has limits."

They weren't the same.

It was getting to me, the constant comparisons with my husband. Nick was determined to tarnish my beautiful life with Michael, but it could never resemble what Nick had done—the torture, beatings, and rapes.

"I saved you from a man who used you like a slave, and you believe he's better than me. Call me broken. *Fine.* You're the one with the damaged brain. You begged me for a baby, and when I said no, you latched onto an inferior version of me."

He had it all backward.

"I don't love him because he's similar to you. He's an amazing dad and a wonderful partner, and I feel safe when I'm with him. He listens to me. He wants the best for me. You never gave me that. You're a cheat. An abuser. You are *nothing* like him."

"He killed six people last night. Legion guys. Drive-by shooting."

"I don't care!" Maybe it was sick that I didn't, but it was the truth. Michael would have to do a lot worse than kill a bunch of gangsters to turn me against him.

"You would if you were yourself." He paced the room, color returning to his cheeks. "We have to leave. I've got to find Costa. I need to put an end to this, especially now."

No. "Nick—"

"Enough!" he roared, whirling on me with raised fists. "We're having a goddamn kid together. Stop pining for a man who won't live out the weekend. Once he's dead, you'll be free. And then we'll marry."

"*No.*"

"Yes."

He pushed me toward the door, but I dug in my heels.

"Michael's not dying, and I'll never marry you!"

"Then I'll sue you for full custody and bribe the judge. I'll make him give me the brat. You'll never see our baby again."

It's not yours!

"Wear your jacket. Let's go."

Nick's steel-like presence vanished, and then he thrust the leather into my arms.

I flung it to the floor.

Nick's eyes followed. His hand whirled, smashing into my face. The blow slammed me into his nightstand. My skull cracked the wood. Something heavy wobbled on it.

His gun.

I grabbed it and fired.

A picture frame exploded beside Nick's head. He flinched as I aimed at his chest. Boots stomped in the hall. Voices outside shouted. They smashed through distant doors.

Nick stared at me, wide-eyed. "*What the hell?*"

"Hands up! I'll kill you."

"You wouldn't murder the father of your child."

You're not. "I have to get away from you."

"Kill me," he sneered. "They'll rape you. Every one of them."

"Shut the fuck up!"

"*All right.* Calm down." Nick's tone was soft, beseeching. "Take a deep breath and look at where you are."

"I have to leave."

"You'll hurt the baby."

The door burst to a man with a shotgun.

"Axel, no. Back the fuck off!" Nick gripped the barrel, shoving himself in the line of fire. "Carmela, put the fucking Sig down."

"*No.*"

Nick roared at the biker. "Back off!"

The man retreated. Nick wheeled at me, his lips thinning. Shock flickered across his gaze. "Are you kidding me with this gunslinger shit? Is this because I'm the dad?"

"I told you not to hit me."

"You whip out a gun because I *slapped* you?"

"Yes."

Nick swallowed hard. "Carmela, this isn't a game. You'll die. Lower the piece."

"At least I'll be free." I gestured toward the hall. "Move."

He backed into the darkness, laughing. "What is your plan? You'll attack the whole clubhouse?"

"I'm leaving."

A high, cold laugh boomed down the corridors. He stepped forward, eyes filled with mirth.

"I swear to God, Nick."

"Beauty, you're surrounded. There is no way you're getting out of here." Nick glowered at the men inching closer. "Any-body shoots at my *pregnant* old lady will have their balls blow-torched. Leave us the fuck alone!"

They lowered their weapons, and I walked Nick to the door as he grinned at me. He looked like I'd grabbed his dick. He enjoyed torture, but there was one thing he loved more.

The chase.

We strolled the porch, heading to the row of motorcycles.

"Want these?" Nick pulled the keys from his shirt pocket, dangling them. "Put down the gun."

"*No.*"

"You'll have to kill me to steal my Harley."

"Are you willing to test me?"

"Maybe I'll let you have a ten-minute lead."

"Follow me, and I won't hesitate to murder you."

He laughed, the air misting with his breath. "I missed this side of you, Beauty."

"Keys."

He stopped near the Dyna Super Glide. "You don't know how to ride."

"Give them, or I'll shoot you."

He tossed the ring. It landed a foot away. "Bend over, and they're yours."

I squatted and groped until my fingers latched onto metal. My hands shook as I opened the disk and slid the key inside.

"You'll never be able to move it from the driveway," Nick scoffed, his smile widening. "You can't even shift gears."

"Yes, I fucking can. It's a simple concept. I'll figure it out."

The panel lit up. I hopped on and grabbed the clutch, mashing the buttons. My control over the situation slipped into doubt as it failed to start.

Nick watched, arms folded. "Want me to show you how it's done?"

I fired. The dirt beside his boot exploded. "That was your last warning."

"How many rounds are in that clip?"

"Enough to kill you."

"Yeah, but what about them?" Nick gestured to the ranch house. "You fuck me. They fuck you."

"I'm leaving!"

"Baby, you won't make it five miles. Put it down. I won't hurt you."

I twisted the left handle and pressed a button on the right. The seat vibrated as his Harley rumbled.

Yes.

"Carmela, don't be an idiot. You'll end up a stain on the road!" Nick stepped forward, the barrel sinking into his stomach. "You're putting the baby's life at risk."

My chest tightened as that hit home.

I could've blown out his heart.

Nick slowly glided to my wrists. He pulled until the nozzle aimed at the ground. Nick clasped my hand and shook the weapon from my limp fingers, and then he buried the gun in my hair.

"Crazy bitch. You'll regret this stupid stunt." The light in his eyes died as he climbed onto the bike. "We're going home."

"I have a home. It's not with you."

THIRTY-SIX

MICHAEL

I KICKED IN THE DOOR.

It smashed the wall. I strode inside the bachelor pad filled with black patent leather. The scent of pussy and cigarettes filled the air. I followed the stench into a bedroom, where a naked Julian had fallen out of bed. Beer bottles littered the carpet. I ripped the satin sheets off. Whoever he'd slept with was already gone.

Good. No witnesses.

Julian struggled to his feet, dragging a baseball bat from under his desk. Deep lines carved his dimples. His pupils were blown with that drugged-out haze I recognized from all my dealings with Serena.

He laughed. It was half grief and rage.

"Serena was your whore. She was your fucking *slut!*" Spittle flew from his mouth as he readied his bat, oblivious to the pistol I pointed at his chest. "You knew I'd find out. You're sick. You're *deranged.*"

"Not as crazy as I'll be if my wife dies. Where is Carmela?"

"Fuck you."

I pulled the trigger.

Blood splattered the floor as a hole blew through his right knee. He collapsed, howling. The bat rolled toward me as Julian flailed, sobbing.

"Where is she?"

"It hurts. Oh my God. Help—"

"Take another hit, you junkie." I seized his hair and dragged him off the mattress, heat slicing my nerves as rubber tubing fell off his nightstand. "Is this what you've been doing with my money? Shooting up and selling out my wife! I'll kill you!"

"Please, don't! I have a daughter."

"*She's better off without you.*" I shoved the Glock to his temple, and he shrieked. "My wife! You gave that psychopath Carmela!"

"An eye for an eye," he snarled. "We know what you did to Serena."

"That's what this is about? *Serena?*"

He lunged at me with a beer bottle.

I yanked it from his clumsy grip and clocked him. He spilled over the dark floor as I lodged my foot in his upper back. As soon as I twisted his arm, Julian sagged. I'd fucked women who put up a stronger fight.

"You're inhuman. Pure evil." His voice was a low, guttural

moan. "She showed me her bruises. You beat her. You killed her."

My late wife had bitch-slapped me from the grave. She'd made her brother think the worst of me, and our children had almost paid the price. She'd tortured me with threats to take the kids. She'd done so many horrible things, and now, she'd cost me the love of my life.

I wanted her gone.

My gun ripped across Julian's jaw. He slammed into the bed as crimson poured from his nose, his eyes wide and beseeching. I hammered him until my knuckles split, his soft body breaking under my blows.

"Do you know what he did to my children?" I screamed. "You fucking degenerate! Tell me where he is."

His panic saturated the air like the unwashed, sharp scent of a man. "You'll kill me anyway."

"Your life could still get a lot worse."

"You stole from him. He just wanted her back, so—so I told him Carmela's routine. He must've snatched her. His address is on my phone. He said to bring her there if—if I got the chance."

I lunged at his cell, swiped it open, and found the information hidden in a note. I pulled it up on a map.

Fifteen minutes away.

"Please." Julian held up his hands. "I have a kid."

I had two, and he'd handed them to Crash.

I aimed at his face.

"I didn't murder Serena, but I *am* killing you."

Three holes zipped into Julian's head, blowing out his skull. Blood seeped under his hair as he stared at the ceiling. I grasped his arm and yanked, catching most of the mess on the bed. Then I walked into the hall, beckoning at the tall silhouette.

"Clean this up."

The soldier did my bidding, rolling Julian in the sheets. His sightless gaze disappeared under black.

Good fucking riddance.

There was no triumph from his death.

Only rage.

THIRTY-SEVEN

CARMELA

He kicked me downstairs.

My hip crashed into the steps. I fell, sliding off the staircase. A scream ripped from my throat as I lost my balance. I slammed into hard-packed ground. I spat out dirt and flipped to my back, groaning.

Lights flared, revealing an unfinished basement. My gaze swept across concrete walls and a low, wooden ceiling. Nick hurtled after me, gun in hand. He raised his arm.

I covered my face.

Giant bangs erupted as he fired, the clumps exploding around me. My ears rang with gunshots.

"How do you fucking like it?" His knee crushed my ribs as he leaned over me, white-faced with fury. "Crazy bitch!"

"Nick, stop!"

"No, I won't. You pointed a gun to my head, you psycho. I

don't have enough to worry about without my old lady trying to kill me? *How dare you?"*

"Let her go!"

A hoarse voice bellowed from the corner. The sound seemed to snap Nick from his rage as he faced a shirtless man who hunkered under the beams, his legs and feet bound.

Familiar big eyes peered at me, a scowl darkening his pleasant features. A thick beard masked his jaw, but it was Anthony. Dirt streaked his jogging pants. Bruises and welts painted his chest red and purple. Ligature marks circled his wrists, and his teeth chattered.

"Did you hear me, you Aryan-nation piece of shit?" Anthony strained against his bindings. "Leave her the fuck alone."

"He finally grows some balls." Nick shot Anthony a grin and turned his attention to me. "Don't tell me you sucked his cock, too. I don't think I could handle that."

His hand wrapped my throat. He cut off my oxygen with a hard pinch. I raked his arms, unable to dislodge even a finger. Everything burned. My body screamed agony, and my ears filled with Anthony's desperate scream. A chime interrupted the chaos.

Air rushed into my lungs as Nick pulled away.

He answered his phone. Then he climbed the stairs, disappearing into the house.

I gasped, crawling toward Anthony. Blood ran down his hands from his restraints, but he didn't seem to notice. He stared at me.

"Are you okay?"

"I'm fine. What did he do to you?"

"He just wants a punching bag." A tremor went through him as he glanced upstairs. "Prejudiced asshole. I've wasted my whole goddamned life, and *this* is where it ends. In a fucking crawlspace."

"Your life isn't ending. He's not getting rid of us that easily."

Anthony slumped forward, as though he'd spent all his energy shouting. I grabbed a bottle and pressed it to his mouth. He drank small sips, and then greedily, grabbing it from me as he guzzled the water. He wiped his face with the drops that spilled and tossed it aside.

Anthony was only here because of me.

I had to free him.

I ripped at his bindings and bit the plastic, but it was unyielding. Hard as a rock. Rope tied him to a pipe. I undid the knot—

"Stop," Anthony hissed. "*He's coming.*"

Nick descended the steps, looking undisturbed that Anthony was untied. "Up. Now."

Anthony glowered as Nick yanked the rope, tugging him upstairs. I followed them as he led Anthony into a sparse living room and shoved him onto a couch.

"I just got off the phone with your new owners." Nick ignored me as I joined them, focused on Anthony. "They'll get more use out of you. You're pathetic. My old lady could beat you in a wrestling match."

"Why don't you remove these zip ties." Anthony grinned. "Then we'll see who's the real tough guy."

"I'll tear your liver out with my teeth."

"Then take them off, pussy."

I gaped at Nick.

He wouldn't seize the bait. He wasn't that stupid, but something inside him had unraveled since the clubhouse. Fear. It pulsed like a diseased heart, turning his rage black. He was that fucking scared of being a father.

Nick unsnapped the knife from his waist and knelt, sawing through Anthony's bound ankles.

Anthony leaned forward, his muscles taut. He caught my eye and jerked his head at the door.

I barely reacted when Anthony launched with his feet, bashing Nick's stomach before he'd untied his wrists. Nick hit the wall, laughing. He pushed Anthony with one palm.

Nick waved the blade. "Do that again, and I'll stab you."

"Carmela, *run!*"

Anthony seized a chair and shoved Nick, who batted it aside. Anthony grimaced through Nick's blows and tackled his legs, punching the backs of his knees.

I ran, but the door was locked with dozens of latches. So I grabbed a window and threw it open—impeded by iron bars. Everything was blocked.

Fuck.

Anthony's sacrifice would be for nothing.

Their fight crashed into the foyer. Blood ran down Nick's forehead as he dragged Anthony by his hair while he pummeled Nick's abdomen.

Anthony tried. He did, but he was beaten, starved, and restrained. Even the desperation to live wasn't enough to over-power Nick.

Nick stabbed Anthony's shoulder.

Anthony screamed.

I sprinted toward him, and Nick sank his fist into my belly. I collapsed to a breathless heap as pain radiated inward. *God, the baby*.

Anthony slumped, moaning.

Nick unlocked the door and opened it, facing outside. "Take Costa off my hands before I kill him."

The guy slid into the room, but the only part I saw were his leather boots. "He was supposed to be unspoiled."

"Yeah, well. He's also a pain-in-the-ass." Nick stooped to Anthony and ripped out the knife, causing a fresh wave of screams. "I'll knock off a thousand dollars for the damage."

"Done."

They exchanged money, and several men picked Anthony up. I scrambled to my feet, glimpsing Anthony's tortured face before the door slammed, shutting them out. Seconds later, the crunch of gravel under the departing car's tires filled me with dread. I rushed to the window as headlights swept across the darkness.

He was gone.

A howl went through me.

Nick's bloody hand rolled over my neck. He dug into my skin, turning me around. Red patches burned on his cheeks, and he still gripped the knife. His lips were white and shaking.

"You fucked him, too? You did, didn't you?" Anguish rippled through his words as he cut through my denial. "You had sex with him, and God knows how many other dagos."

The slur sent a ripple of anger through me. "*I'm* Italian."

"Don't remind me."

I would die tonight.

Nick twisted the dagger, the mad gleam in his eyes sharpening. Obviously, the idea was growing on him. At this point, I was more of a nuisance than a lover. If I raised my hands, he'd beat me. If I submitted, he'd torture me. If I breathed, he'd choke me.

"I'm just being honest, Nick."

"You're never *just* doing anything," he exploded, throwing me into a wall. "You know how to fuck me up."

"All right. Take it easy."

"No, you take it easy." He grabbed my throat and shoved the dagger under my chin. "You fucking take it easy, Carmela. I will fuck all the women until you feel a fraction of what you've inflicted on me."

It was always about him.

His suffering. His orgasms.

Nick stepped back. He fisted his hair. "Loving you is constant pain. It is a never-ending agony. I want it to stop."

"Me too."

"Ever since I met you, it's like I've been dying a slow death." Nick's hand trembled, and something wet rolled down my skin. "It has to stop."

He would do it.

"Nick, if you kill me, we can't make plans for the future, raise a family, or give us another shot." Sweat beaded my upper lip as I groped for a weapon.

"No. This has to *end*."

"We'll start over—a clean slate." My fingers brushed something solid, and I gripped it. "I want to be with you."

"You're lying."

"I have to live for the baby. The baby's done nothing to you. There's a piece of you living inside me. Don't you care?"

His eyes swam with tears.

The door burst open, and Nick's head turned. He lifted the blade. I swung hard, smashing him with a fireplace poker. A red gash split his cheek. Michael grabbed him from behind, and they ripped at each other like beasts. Michael grasped the poker I'd dropped and cinched it against Nick's throat.

Alessio crashed his foot into Nick's jaw, and then Michael shoved him down. My brother-in-law rolled his sleeves before he joined Michael in pummeling Nick's ribs and stomach. Savage blows knocked Nick down, again and again. They were like wolves, tearing into struggling prey. They beat him until they'd exhausted themselves, panting.

Nick's broken hands waded in blood as he picked himself up.

Alessio seized his hair. "Where is Anthony?"

"Kill me, and you'll never find him."

"What did you do with him?"

"Sold to the highest bidder." Nick spat a mouthful of crimson. "I'll give you the information if you leave us alone."

"There is no *us*." I wiped the warmth tickling my collar and reveled in his helpless position. "You and I were nothing but a disaster. And the baby is Michael's, not yours."

"*Wait*."

I stepped around him and headed outside.

"Beauty, I lov—"

Three deafening booms cut off Nick's voice.

I flinched at the sound and settled onto the wet lawn, grateful for the tickle of blades hitting my palms and the dew clinging to them. It was like being hurled into a brand new world. Nick's death was supposed to make me ecstatic, but horror balled up inside me at how it'd ended.

Then Michael held me.

He balled me against his chest. The citrus scent triggered a bomb that exploded my every reserve of calm. I dove into his heat and buried my face in his neck. I cried like I never had before. My nails sank into his back. I ran my fingers along his stubble, the gentle cleft in his chin, his mouth. Then I smashed my lips into his.

He returned the pressure with a softness that slicked me with heat. Angling his head, he claimed me. It was like we'd been separated for weeks. His big hands stroked my hair as I choked on my tears, desperate to get it out of me.

"I love you. I missed you so much."

Michael's forehead pressed into mine. "I love you, too."

"Are the kids okay?"

"Yes, they're fine. You did good." Michael's kiss stung my cheek, and then he hovered. "Are you really pregnant?"

I smiled. "He made me take a test. Michael, we're having a baby."

Shock rippled through his bourbon eyes.

"Are you—are you happy?" I asked him.

He cupped my cheeks, beaming. "Beyond happy."

THIRTY-EIGHT

MICHAEL

I HAD MY WIFE BACK.

That was all I cared about.

The weeks since Crash's death saw a flurry of activity. Everyone worried about a still missing Anthony. All we had to go on was Carmela's vague description of an Eastern European accent and his leather shoes. My poor wife agonized over Anthony, but I compartmentalized it all. It was hard to ignore what gave me so much joy.

Carmela loved me.

She'd bounced from the incident with Crash a lot faster than I had, shelving that part of her past behind us so quickly it made my head spin. The house echoed with her singing, and she glowed whenever I walked into the room. I woke up to blowjobs. She couldn't keep her hands off me, and I loved it.

Nothing could get me down.

Not Anthony's disappearance. Not even dinner with the in-laws.

Carmela's hand stiffened around my wrist, preventing me from opening the door. She shot me a smoldering look, and then her eyes slid to the backseat.

I grinned, catching on. "You're kidding."

"Too shy?"

"Baby, it's broad daylight. You want me arrested?" I glanced up and down the suburban street. "Or does the danger of that turn you on?"

She leaned in close and nipped my ear. "I want you."

My slacks tightened as she climbed into the back. I followed, dropping in the seat beside her. She'd already ripped off her panties and straddled me before I'd settled in. She smashed her lips against mine. Her kiss got as hard as a diamond. It was all tongue—pure lust.

"The backseat of an Audi," I teased. "What are we, teenagers?"

I stopped asking questions when she unzipped me and grabbed my cock. I spent more days laying pipe than working because the second trimester had turned Carmela into a raving sex addict. Ten minutes later, her hands slapped the fogged window as I moaned into her hair. She came soon after, and then we dissolved into the leather seats. Carmela's phone beeped with text messages as we tidied ourselves.

Then I staggered out of the car. Sweat dotted my shirt, which I tucked into my slacks. Carmela chuckled as she wiped my face free of lipstick.

"Now we're *really* late."

Not that I minded. I had no desire to be here.

My father-in-law's house was still the place where my brother had died, no matter how complicated our relationship had been. Hanging out here didn't feel right, and neither did rubbing elbows with Ignacio, but I wanted to tell him the news.

Carmela slipped her hand into mine, her cheeks flushed. "Am I decent?"

"The just-fucked look suits you."

Carmela sighed, letting that roll off her shoulders. We headed to the mansion, and I knocked on the door.

Maria answered. "We're already eating!"

"Yeah, I know. So sorry." I stepped in, waving at everyone in the dining room. "Fucking traffic."

Alessio looked up from his chicken cacciatore and smirked. He laughed, drawing questioning looks from his clueless wife and our mother-in-law. Ignacio stood, his voice blistering.

"At my house, you show up on time, or you don't eat *at all*."

Fine by me.

I lurched toward the door until Carmela shot me a plea, which worked too well.

Maria manhandled us into seats. Baby Lexy sat in a highchair, mashing spaghetti into her face. I buried a stab of annoyance at Alessio's presence. As far as I was concerned, his inaction had set forth a devastating chain of consequences that resulted in Anthony being sold into slavery and Carmela's horrific trauma. Helping me take care of that asshole didn't undo the damage.

Mia and Carmela were always trying to get us talking. They invited us to the same events. Alessio and I ignored each other. Occasionally, we bickered. Sometimes it made Carmela burst into tears.

And I couldn't have that.

So I told her I wasn't doing it anymore.

Unfortunately, Carmela could rope me into anything.

I refused a seat. "Ignacio, we should talk."

"Can it wait until after dinner?"

"It won't be long."

Ignacio sighed, wiping his mouth. He ruffled Lexy's glossy hair as he passed, grabbing his wine. He drank deeply as he strolled into his study. I followed, closing the door.

"What is it?"

I unlocked my phone and showed him the photo. "Here's the first."

"*Holy shit.*" Ignacio grasped my hand, yanking the cell toward him. "That's him. Crash."

"Yeah, what's left of the prick."

I'd instructed my men to desecrate his body, and I had wheeled his bike into the Bay. Watching his beloved Harley sink into the water was cathartic. Carmela and I kept the details about her kidnapping quiet. She didn't want her parents to worry and had no desire to relive those twenty-four-hours.

"When did this happen?"

"A few weeks ago. I've been busy." Plus, I didn't exactly relish more time with Ignacio.

"You did it," he said, sounding bewildered. "You fucking did it."

"Say that I'm useless."

"You're not. I'm sorry. Thank you, Michael. You have no idea what a load off my mind this is—"

"Stop begging Carmela to have us over. I don't want to be in your life. You still murdered my brother."

Ignacio wiped his face, and I looked away.

"I never wanted to hurt him."

My throat tightened. I couldn't do this.

He grabbed my wrist before I headed out.

I shoved him into the bookshelf. "Don't fucking touch me."

"I'll tell you what happened. It might cost me, but I owe you." He gestured at the seat. "Sit."

"I'll stand."

Ignacio backed onto his desk, suddenly tired. "I didn't want to murder your brother. Nico asked me to do it. One of his associates approached me. Said to keep my mouth shut because you couldn't find out that Daniel was a snitch. They claimed he was a CI."

What the hell?

My head jerked up. "Are you fucking with me?"

He shook his head. "I had nothing against Daniel."

I believed him. He had the same tells as Carmela.

My brother was a snitch.

My insides collapsed, and I sagged on the chair. It was a blow to all I'd known about my brother. The pieces fell like dominos—Uncle Nico using the guy under my brother's protection to assassinate him, and Ignacio's bullheadedness.

"Why didn't you tell me the truth?"

"Your uncle's instructions were very clear." Ignacio's eyes glazed over as he stared beyond me. "I think he was trying to spare you."

As though being in the dark made it any better.

"Does my cousin know?"

I doubted it. Uncle Nico knew we were close. Vinn would've shared that information in an instant.

"No idea. I'm sorry, kid." Ignacio patted my shoulder.

He tried to drag me into a hug, but I pushed him aside and burst from the office, following my wife's bubbly voice into the dining room, where she tucked into chicken cacciatore. Her eyes sparkled with happiness. I didn't want to ruin it, so I left the house.

I slumped on the porch steps and buried my head in my hands.

Seconds later, the door opened. She sat next to me.

"Go back inside. Finish your dinner," I said.

"What about you?"

"I'll walk around the neighborhood."

My face heated, her disappointment leadening my guts. I'd already upset Carmela by refusing to bring the kids to Ignacio's place. After Crash and Julian, I needed to wait until I was certain they'd be secure.

Carmela leaned on me. "What about Alessio?"

Too bad I didn't have kinder words for my brother-in-law. "We don't get along."

"You know I love the way you defend me, but I wish you'd forgive Alessio. *Please.*"

"I just can't."

"I've forgiven him. I want you to do the same."

"I can't, babe." I pressed my mouth into her frown until her lips softened. "He needs to earn my forgiveness."

"Hasn't he?"

I shrugged. "He helped me take out the trash. That's not good enough."

Carmela kissed me hard, her eyes blazing. "I love you."

Warmth bloomed in my chest.

God, that never got old.

EPILOGUE

SIX MONTHS LATER

"It's my turn! I wanna play—"

"No, it's my Nintendo. Carmela got it for me." Mariette flashed her younger brother a superior grin. "Carmela, tell him it's *mine*."

Carmela sipped her virgin cocktail. "Let him play. You've had it all morning."

"Told you so," Matteo gloated.

Mariette sulked as he took the video game controller and bounced on the couch, mashing its buttons. Carmela prepared a salami board as I rolled prosciutto di parma with goat cheese. The moment she told me she'd bought a half-pound of this shit, I knew who it was for.

"Alessio's coming over?"

"Yeah." Carmela returned to her task, swallowing hard. "It's the six-month anniversary of his disappearance."

Anthony was still missing.

When she'd revealed everything that happened in that twenty-four hours, I didn't sleep for weeks.

Poor bastard.

He'd taken a knife for Carmela. Now *that* was bravery. If he hadn't been there to stall Crash...who knows?

I owed him. I wanted to get him back, but leads were thin on the ground. We'd tracked down Crash's trafficking ring on the dark web. It was how he was able to pay off so many people. He had a network of buyers who'd deleted their accounts when he died.

Carmela cried when she discovered what I'd done to Julian. She insisted on checking in on Julian's kid, who seemed like she was doing well with her mom. Once Carmela realized the kid was fine, she relaxed.

I washed my hands at the sink and wandered down the hall.

Pictures of Carmela and the children covered the walls. A photo of Serena hung in each of the kids' rooms. Carmela encouraged me to release my anger, and I was trying. But there was one thing left to do.

I found my daughter in the library, where she'd stalked after handing over the Nintendo. She smiled as I sat next to her, which was a significant improvement from "Go away."

"Hey, honey. I need to talk to you."

Mariette paused, setting down the pencil. "About what?"

I grabbed Serena's wedding ring from my pocket. "This was your mother's."

Mariette plucked it from my hand, her blue eyes widening with awe. She slipped it on her finger.

"It's too big for you but I'll give it to you when you're older." I stroked her beautiful hair, admiring how the light made it shine. "Your mother and I didn't get along, but that doesn't mean I never cared about her. One day, I hope you'll understand. Just know that I love you. Always."

"I love you, too."

I took the jewelry and ruffled her head. A glow of pride balled in my chest as she gave up on coloring within the lines and scribbled over the page. Then I headed out.

Carmela leaned on the threshold, beaming at me. "That was nice of you."

"You and that word." I hooked her waist and dragged her into an empty room. "I'm not nice."

"You are, though. You didn't scowl when I mentioned Alessio."

"He is my brother-in-law—"

"And you let me name our baby after Anthony."

"Luke Anthony Costa. It's his *middle* name, and I only agreed because he will find the whole thing so hilarious."

"*Bullshit.* You said yes because you love me. You don't complain when Alessio comes over. You do everything to make me happy, all the time, and you never ask for anything."

"You're all I'll ever need, Carmela."

I didn't want to forgive Alessio, but I would anyway because I would always bend over backward for her.

I wasn't a good man.

No doubt about that.

My impulses were just as dark as they were when we first married, but she'd softened me to people in our lives. She showed me that marriage wasn't supposed to be a constant battle of wills. That it was okay to disagree without disrespecting each other. Giving her the world seemed like a fair trade because I'd found peace.

I'd found her.

ACKNOWLEDGMENTS

Once upon a time, when I was young and naive, I fell for a man *similar* to Crash. He was a bad boy who smoked clove cigarettes and wore steel-toed boots with his heavy-metal band shirts. He took me to pool halls because I couldn't go to bars.

He was my first everything. He could be extremely passionate, sweet, and romantic. And at the drop of a hat—jealous, violent, enraged.

I don't regret dating him, but I'm very glad I got out of that relationship. I think most of us have experienced someone like my ex, which made writing this so uncomfortable. It has made me confront his disturbing behavior.

For that reason, this has been the most challenging book I've ever written. But I'm relieved I saw this through. It took many drafts until I settled on this version. Finding the right voice for Michael took forever.

Thank you, Winter and Sosie, for listening to my many messages about this book. You helped tremendously. Kelley Harvey, as always, your editing is top-notch. Thank you, Christine LaPorte, Kevin McGrath, and my wonderful readers in the Bad Boy Addicts group.

I love you! Thank you for being so supportive. I couldn't do this without you.

ABOUT THE AUTHOR

Vanessa Waltz loves to write steamy romances. She lives in the Bay Area with two crazy cats. To be the first to know about her new releases, please join her newsletter (no spam, ever).

Vanessa's Newsletter

For more information, follow her here:
www.vanessawaltzbooks.com
info@vanessawaltzbooks.com
Bad Boy Addicts - Facebook Group

69519034R00208